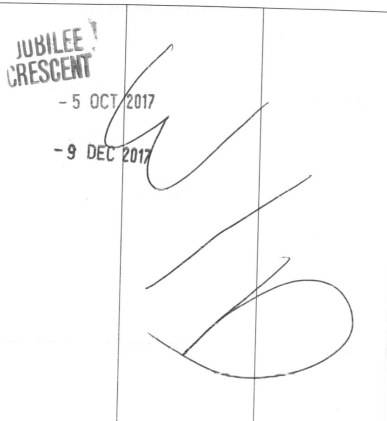

Emily Hendrickson lives in Reno, Nevada, with her husband. She has also written *The Gallant Lord Ives*, *Hidden Inheritance* and *Lady Sara's Scheme*.

DOUBLE DECEIT

Miss Caroline Beauchamp had accepted a very tricky task. She must seduce Hugh, Lord Stanhope, the handsome husband of her dearest friend, Mary. This was in order to break the hold that an infamous beauty had on the vulnerable viscount. But she also faced an even greater challenge — she had to bedazzle the most renowned rake in the realm, Lord Rutledge, to keep him from making Mary his latest conquest! Caroline knew as she began her juggling act of deception that letting down her guard would mean disaster. And falling in love would be even worse . . .

Books by Emily Hendrickson
Published by The House of Ulverscroft:

A PERILOUS ENGAGEMENT
HIDDEN INHERITANCE
LADY SARA'S SCHEME
THE GALLANT LORD IVES
QUEEN OF THE MAY

EMILY HENDRICKSON

DOUBLE DECEIT

Complete and Unabridged

ULVERSCROFT
Leicester

First published in Great Britain in 2007 by
Robert Hale Limited
London

First Large Print Edition
published 2008
by arrangement with
Robert Hale Limited
London

The moral right of the author has been asserted

British Library CIP Data

Hendrickson, Emily
    Double deceit.—Large print ed.—
    Ulverscroft large print series: historical romance
    1. Love stories
    2. Large type books
    I. Title
    813.6 [F]

    ISBN 978–1–84782–327–4

Published by
F. A. Thorpe (Publishing)
Anstey, Leicestershire

Set by Words & Graphics Ltd.
Anstey, Leicestershire
Printed and bound in Great Britain by
T. J. International Ltd., Padstow, Cornwall

This book is printed on acid-free paper

1

'I want you to seduce my husband,' declared the petite blond dressed in palest blue silk jaconet. She nervously fiddled with the lace trim of her gown while she waited anxiously for a reply to her outrageous request.

The only sound in the lovely white-and-gold drawing room was the automatic clink of a silver spoon as it was stirred around and around in a Wedgwood teacup. Shocked silence reigned as Caroline Beauchamp stared, utterly aghast, at her dearest friend.

The Viscountess Stanhope did not appear in the least put out by Caroline's reaction to the highly improper proposal placed before her. Indeed, she seemed timidly frightened, Caroline thought, as she gave Mary a considering look. The teaspoon was carefully placed on the saucer, then the delicate cup, the tea untasted, was set on the Pembroke table close to where Caroline perched on the gold-and-white striped cushion of a Sheraton chair. She said with the greatest of care, 'Did I hear you correctly, Mary?'

'You did,' replied the viscountess with a

charming smile slipping across her pleasant face.

'I cannot credit what you just asked me to do,' answered Caroline, her brunette curls bouncing as she shook her head and gave a sigh. The emerald eyes that usually danced with mischief or happiness now appeared warily thoughtful.

'You do recall that you owe me a favor,' reminded Mary, her voice a gentle reprimand.

'I have not forgotten. Having your husband investigate my aunt's affairs was a very great favor. I saw to it that her thieving steward was promptly fired. Indeed, I am forever in your Hugh's debt. Now, if only I can prevent my sweet aunt from embarking on another gambling spree, all will be well.' Caroline gave a reflective sigh, then turned once again to the matter at hand. 'But this? I am not at all certain I ought to do such a thing.' The stubborn expression that settled over Caroline's pretty countenance was all too well known by her friend.

The smile left Mary's face as she gave Caroline a worried look, then — accompanied by a frown and a brave sniff — a single tear traced its way down her pale cheek, followed by another. 'You cannot know what it has been like these past weeks, seeing my

Hugh with that ... that woman. Diana Ingleby cannot possibly care for him as I do. Yet he hovers around her like a bee about its hive. Oh, Caroline, I simply do not know what else to do if you will not help me. You know how I love that wretched man.'

At this last wail Mary burst into earnest tears, groping for an already crumpled handkerchief beside her on the gold damask sofa. Her face buried in the soft linen folds, she could not see, only sense, the hoped-for response.

Distressed to find her friend so strongly affected, Caroline jumped up and rushed to Mary's side. 'Pray do not cry. Of course I will do what you ask. Somehow. I have never tried such a thing before. But I venture to wager I will find a way if only you will cease your tears.' She gave Mary a comforting pat on her arm, then watched anxiously for the tears to subside. Caroline had never been able to resist a soft and gentle creature, and Mary seemed so helpless and fragile.

Blotting her eyes with dainty little dabs, Mary gave Caroline a truly grateful smile. 'You will not regret this, I promise. Only think how you will be saving my marriage. After all, being my only attendant when I married that man, you have a sort of responsibility, if you follow me.'

Caroline gave her a wry look. 'Fancy that. I had not realized I was assuming such vast duties when I walked down that aisle before you. Well, this task ought to serve to keep me from being bored to flinders. But how do you propose I accomplish this deed?'

'It should not be so very difficult. After all, I have seen you flirt with any number of men. You do it most charmingly.' Mary peeped at Caroline, as though to judge the success of her coaxing.

'They were not my best friend's husband,' said Caroline repressively, studying her now recovered friend.

'Yes, well, that is true, to be sure,' murmured Mary, unflinchingly meeting that direct gaze. 'But you will try, will you not? Tonight? At Lady Bentley's ball? Please, Caroline?'

'Very well, I shall try my best. Do you realize, dearest, how difficult it will be for a mere green girl like myself to lure that handsome husband of yours away from such a noted beauty as Mrs Ingleby?' Caroline momentarily forgot she was to cheer, not depress, her friend.

'The widow is certainly that, although from what I have heard and seen, she is rather proud, and certainly contemptuous of others, especially young girls just coming out in society. She can laugh very prettily, though,' said Mary with a wistful air, 'and has a fine pair of eyes.'

Caroline shook her head in puzzlement. 'I simply do not understand marriage. You are his wife, he ought to be attending you, not that woman.'

'Caroline! It would not do to have us living in each other's pockets. You know that! How the ton would laugh and scorn. Besides,' she added in a low, confiding voice, 'he does not know I have fallen so madly in love with him. I would be so embarrassed if he were to find that out. Ours was a contracted marriage, and I am so very plain, you see. It is not to be wondered at if he is attracted to a lovely face and form.'

'There is nothing wrong with your figure, and your face is very sweet,' declared Caroline stoutly. 'And,' she added in significant tones, 'you have the loveliest manners and such a delightful laugh. He is a fool and totally in the wrong.'

'Mama always said the only time a man was right was when he admitted he was wrong,' said Mary, her delightful smile creeping back into place on her nice face.

At that remark Caroline chuckled, then settled more comfortably on the sofa. 'Do you have any suggestions as to how I am to snare your husband? Dear me, but that does sound strange.' Her grin contained more than a hint of deviltry, promising Hugh a spirited time.

'Well, he has remarked on your lively expression any number of times, not to forget those speaking eyes you possess. How I envy them. My ordinary blue eyes seem so drab by comparison.' Mary made this statement without a sign of resentment. It was merely a wishful sort of remark.

'Silly, do you never look in a mirror? You are so dainty you make me feel a giantess with my five feet and six inches. And I think your eyes are lovely.'

'Thank you,' said May in her gentle voice. After a moment she said, 'I think it will be best if you merely act your normal self. With those sparkling eyes and your ability to dance and flirt, you shouldn't find the task difficult in the least.'

'Do you know, I am not at all certain I like the image you present me. Perhaps I ought to mend my ways,' replied Caroline in an odd little voice.

'If you intend to change that delightful manner of yours, do so *after* his seduction is finished,' declared Mary with a firm tone.

Startled, Caroline said thoughtfully, 'I am merely to lure him away from the Ingleby.

6

Correct? Nothing beyond that, surely.' Her hesitance was emphasized by a diffident tapping of her gloves against her knee.

Now it was Mary's turn to be shocked. 'Most certainly not! I am resigned to harmless flirts, and that is what you are to be. After all, Hugh is very handsome and attractive to women. But I do not think the widow Ingleby is in the least harmless.'

'I believe you have the right of it there. My aunt declares her a wicked woman. Expensive, too. Mind you, I do not know for a certainty, but I suspect gentlemen are quite happy to pay for her favors,' said a pensive Caroline, recalling conversations she had overheard in her aunt's drawing room.

Caroline rose in a graceful, fluid motion and began to walk toward the door, pulling on her gloves as she went. Patting her bonnet as she paused by a tall looking glass, she saw reflected the hopeful expression on Mary's face. Turning, she sought to reassure her friend. 'I shall do my best for you. What society will say, I cannot imagine. Shall we pretend to be on the outs for a week or however long it takes?'

'Oh dear, I had not considered that in my plans. I refuse to give you the cut direct, for it would look too, too shabby of me. I shall have to find a flirt of my own. Perhaps I shall attach that nice Earl of Rutledge. Giles has always been a favorite of mine, and I believe he confines his attentions to married ladies. Indeed, I once held hopes my papa would select him as my husband. I am sure he is all that is amiable.'

'Only you would see him in that light, my dear,' said Caroline dryly, thinking of the tall, black haired man with stormy dark gray eyes that had caught her notice more than once. Nice was hardly the correct appellation. Intimidating, perhaps? Irresistibly devastating, assuredly. He was prodigiously handsome with a fortune to match — hardly the sort of man a girl with only modest prospects and from a large family might look to as a suitor. Yet her heart had sighed over him.

Mary fluttered after Caroline into the hall, then walked with her down the stairs to the front entry. 'Now, do not forget your promise,' she urged. 'And pray, do not reveal my plans to Hugh, come what may!'

'I shan't,' replied Caroline with a deal of patience. 'How could I forget something so utterly outrageous?' Then, mindful of the listening ears of the nearby servants, she gave Mary a significant look before her departure.

Pennyfeather, the elderly and impressive butler of the Stanhope residence, opened the door for Caroline, assisting her to the waiting hackney her aunt preferred. Living with a lady who hated horses was a new experience for Caroline.

Daisy, Caroline's maid, scrambled onto her seat before the carriage set off on its short journey.

On her drive to where she resided with her Aunt Fanny, Caroline considered the dreadful vow she had just made. Had she actually pledged to lure Mary's husband away from that beautiful Mrs Ingleby? If Mary had not been so tearfully in earnest, Caroline would have laughed. But she knew the truth of it, that her dear, quiet little friend adored her handsome husband far more than she ought, given the standards of the day. He was free to flirt where he wished and Mary could do nothing, for, especially in an arranged marriage such as hers, affairs seemed the rule rather than the exception.

Then Caroline considered a vexing little point of her own. Secretly she had hoped she might attract the interest of the Earl of Rutledge. Giles, Mary had called him. Lovely name, Caroline mused dreamily.

And, she abruptly realized, he would be far beyond her when he observed her flirting with her dearest friend's husband. 'Oh, blast and drat,' she fumed to no one in particular.

Daisy, sitting on the far side of the carriage,

glanced at her mistress with mild curiosity, but as the exclamation was not all that unusual, she directed her gaze out the window once again.

The vehicle turned from South Audley to the quiet sedateness of South Street. They passed the chapel and stopped a few doors beyond before number 7, the neat house her aunt owned. Fanny, Lady Winnington, had been widowed donkey's years ago, and now lived in placid contentment, barring her infrequent lapses into gambling. She had expressed delight at the chance to present her beloved sister's daughter to London society. Somehow, Caroline was never quite sure, she had even managed vouchers for Almack's.

And now Caroline risked a great deal to help her friend, Mary. Then, just as Caroline was having dire thoughts about backing off her promise, she remembered the widow, Mrs Diana Ingleby. Beautiful — if you fancied a woman a bit overblown — and witty — if you did not mind a slightly loud laugh that went with her sallies — she presented a potential death blow to Mary's future happiness.

A footman appeared to assist her from the carriage, then pay the jarvey. Marching up the steps to the front door, Caroline nodded to Simpkins, inquiring as she divested herself of her pelisse, 'Where is my aunt, please?'

Bowing faintly in the direction of the room that Lady Winnington preferred to use during the day, he intoned in his lofty manner, 'Her ladyship is in her morning room, miss.'

Hurrying down the hall and around the corner, Caroline bustled into the room, giving scant attention to the scene before her. 'I must seek your advice, dear aunt. I fear I have got myself into a horrid predicament.' Then what was before her really sank into her brain. 'Good heavens!'

'Hullo to you, too,' said her brother Edmund, grinning to see his elder sister so taken aback.

'The same from me,' added his twin Adrian, who bowed with nearly the stiff punctiliousness of Simpkins. This was followed by a sly look that told he suspected the source of his sister's dismay.

'What's the to-do, sister dear? Into a bit of a pickle, are you? Seems we have arrived at just the right moment, Adrian. Told Papa you might have need of us. Convinced him to permit us a few weeks on the town,' stated Edmund with the assurance of a very young man most definitely not about town.

'Oh,' groaned Caroline at the mental image of her brothers attending any of the rather elegant entertainments that were her milieu at present. 'How . . . kind of you. Isn't it kind,

Aunt Fanny? A few weeks, did you say?' They could scarcely get into terribly much trouble in that short a time. Then she remembered the past and shook her head. Oh, yes, they most certainly might take a notion to get up to every rig and row from one end of London to the other. At least Edmund might. Adrian was different, but as likely in his own strange way to cause problems as his twin.

Caroline plumped herself onto a chair and absently began to fan her face with her handkerchief. This was a fine kettle of fish. Simply frightful!

'I daresay you boys would like to get settled in your room,' said Lady Winnington with placid practicality. 'Your papa has sent a generous arrangement for finances, and you will assuredly want to seek out a good London tailor immediately.

'That is true,' hastily inserted Caroline with relief. If they had no proper clothes, they would be out of the eye of the *ton* for a merciful few days. Then she could begin to worry.

'I say, that's a jolly good idea. We'll be off to Bond Street in no time,' said Edmund enthusiastically, with Adrian nodding his head in his usual vague way.

When the two young men had been safely seen off in the direction of their room,

12

Caroline blew out a sigh frustration. 'I suspect all young men of nineteen ought to be kept somewhere safe until they have reached the point where their common sense outweighs their desire for mischief.'

Lady Winnington gave her dearest niece a commiserating look, then replied, 'Surely they are not that bad?'

'Oh, Adrian is quiet enough, only he will join Edmund in his follies. Edmund finds a great deal of follies. Papa may well have shipped them into town out of sheer desperation. Odd that I am but a year older and have never had the urge to get myself into such briars as they do.'

'And what was it you wished to seek my advice about, child?' murmured Lady Winnington.

'Oh, dear,' moaned Caroline, 'I fear that after this you will think me no better than that harum-scarum pair now upstairs.'

'Out with it, and not in half-crown words, if you please.' Lady Winnington studied the manner in which her niece shifted about on her chair with increasing interest. Really, London was becoming livelier by the moment.

Taking in a deep breath, Caroline bravely met the faintly amused eyes of her Aunt Fanny, then blurted out, 'I have just promised to seduce Mary's husband.'

'My, my,' softly declared her aunt. The lace at her wrist fluttered delicately as Lady Winnington placed one hand against her cheek in consternation. 'I trust she has good reason for such a request?'

'Diana Ingleby' was the most adequate reply.

'I see. And she feels you can compete with the widow Ingleby? My, my,' she said once again, then fell into a musing silence.

'It is to save her marriage. What a pity she cannot simply tell her Hugh how much she loves him and be done with all this silly nonsense.' Caroline twitched her skirts into place with an annoyed hand. Had she really allowed herself to be placed in such a situation as this? Defending Mary now was a bit different from their schooldays, when Caroline had taken the fragile girl beneath her wing, so to speak.

'It isn't done, my dear, at least not in many marriages,' said Lady Winnington, nodding her head earnestly.

'I was going to say no, yet when I thought of that scheming Ingleby woman, I could not deny what help I can give Mary. Would you have had me refuse my assistance?'

Her aunt reflected a few moments before shaking her head. 'No, I believe good women must aid one another. There is the sanctity of marriage to consider as well. I shall understand and try to deflect gossip, for it is bound to crop up, you know. I am glad you informed me of this, for I would have been utterly at sea had you not said something of the plan. How shall you proceed?'

Caroline thought her aunt might have protested a bit more, yet she knew in her heart that she would do all she could to oblige Mary. Anyone as kind and good as Mary deserved better than to have her husband ensnared by the shapely widow Ingleby.

'I shall wear that new pale green silk lutestring this evening. You know, the one you thought a bit daring? If I am to attract his attention, I can hardly do so in an insipid white muslin gown.' Caroline fingered the white muslin of the gown she wore, most appropriate for a young lady of twenty summers.

'Hmpf! Well, I expect you have the right of it. Perhaps if you tuck a silk rose in the dip of that neckline, it will not seem quite so scandalous. I vow that if the necklines get any lower or the waistlines any higher, there will be nothing left of the top of a gown at all!' declared her aunt, shaking her head in dismay. 'In my day, there was a good deal more to a dress.'

'At least it has a bit of sleeve. And it is vastly becoming, I believe,' replied Caroline with all due modesty. Actually, the gown in question was of softest silk and clung most prettily to her excellent figure. Long ivory satin ribands hung from the center of the high waist, and an ivory rose would add the perfect touch. The miniscule sleeves had dainty fluting around the hem. She was quite pleased with the gown, all in all.

Since Caroline had attained the blessing of the patronesses of Almack's, she looked forward to discreet flirting with Lord Stanhope during a waltz. If only she could maintain a perfect balance between a light flirtation and anything unseemly. A good reputation was utterly necessary to attain what she had come to London for — a marriage, the higher, the better.

The sound of her brothers on the stairway brought a frown to her usually serene brow. They were a complication she had not anticipated. If only they behaved themselves with reasonable decorum.

It was to be expected that they would purchase an outrageous walking stick with which to make an impression, not to mention those odious spurs the young men adored.

Fortunately Adrian possessed an excellent notion of how to dress, so she might be spared the humiliation of brothers rigged out in the more ridiculous of the male fashions — collars so high they couldn't move their heads and waistcoats fit to rival Joseph's coat of many colors.

Then she wondered if her father had an ulterior motive for sending the boys to London at this time. Was there perhaps a need for Edmund to find a bride? As the eldest, he might be expected to assist the family coffers; was there a hope of his wedding an heiress? As far as she knew her family was comfortably well-off. But there were four other children at home, and it would take a good deal of money to bring them all out in proper manner.

'You still here?' queried Edmund from the doorway. 'I'd have thought you would be off to your room to rest. Your butler informed us that you have a social engagement this evening. Bentley, I believe? Wonder if that's good old Tom Bentley's family. Think we will give him a call-in.'

Without waiting for any comment from his sister or aunt, the twins bid a hasty farewell and took themselves off for their first day in London. It was a heady prospect, to have the ordering of a proper wardrobe totally on their own, without anyone else offering his opinion. So, naturally, they promptly sought

17

the company of one they knew to be aware of the very latest dictates on modish attire, good old Tom. A man had to be in style, don't y'know.

As it turned out, Simpkins had been quite correct. Not only were the Bentleys giving the ball that evening, they were also good old Tom's parents. Edmund and Adrian caught him just as he was about to leave his home.

'Oh, I say, this is quite famous,' bubbled Edmund irrepressibly.

Whereupon Tom, in the manner reminiscent of the elegant Beau Brummell, replied in a distant air, 'Manners, my dear Edmund. Manners.' At Edmund's astounded expression Tom could not help but grin in his more familiar way.

Relieved that his old friend was only putting him on, Edmund explained their intent. Tom wisely decided he had best see to their proper attire. After all, there were a good many pitfalls to avoid to attain the dress of a true London beau.

Brummell had not only introduced the popularity of bathing, much to the grumbling of the older set, who considered it a lot of demmed nonsense and bound to give one the megrims or worse, he had also affected a revolution of sorts in gentlemen's dress. The peacock hues of years past were now forsaken by the inner circle. Today's man dressed more soberly, with a nicety of style and a superb cut to the coat. It had been Tom's highest delight when the Beau had once commented kindly on the arrangement of his neckcloth.

So it was that in a remarkably short time Edmund and Adrian were outfitted in modish coats of blue Bath cloth and pantaloons of dove gray, being of a size easily accommodated by a clever tailor. Quiet perfection was to be the aim, the twins were informed. Other items were ordered. A pair of black pantaloons were obtained for the evening.

Edmund, who thought that cutting a dash would be far more colorful, protested. 'This ain't at all what I figured we would be wearing. I still say that puce waistcoat embroidered with gold lions would go nicely with this coat.'

Tom shuddered at the very thought of the puce satin with the elegant blue coat. 'Trust me' was all he could manage to say on the subject, then pointed out the elegance of cut in the snowy white waistcoat at hand.

Thus Caroline was spared the sight of her brothers rigged out in the latest dandy fashion, collars to the ears and a cravat with a waterfall to rival the highest in the land with a dozen fobs and seals dangling at the waist.

Once new boots had been ordered and

evening shoes bespoke, they turned their attention to hats and young ladies, both equally important to a gentleman.

'M'mother's having a ball tonight. Don't see why you couldn't come, with careful attention to what you wear, mind you.' Tom patiently advised on the purchase of linen, how to tie one's neckcloth, then other necessities, while offering other tips on how to get along in society.

When the twins left their friend and headed toward their aunt's house, they were both deep in thought, mulling over all they had heard and learned from their old friend.

Adrian summed it up for the both. 'Dashed if I thought we would be trying to be the quietest, plainest, and most unpretentiously dressed men in town!'

★   ★   ★

After her brothers had departed, Caroline trailed up the stairs in absentminded confusion. In her room, she issued a request for the pale green lutestring to be readied for the evening, then settled on her bed for a brief nap. She must look her very best tonight, for her competition was indeed formidable.

Later, refreshed, she quickly dressed, then

examined her reflection in the looking glass. Her hair was impossible, she decided, and was that not a spot emerging on her forehead? Perish the very thought of such. She frantically dabbed soothing lotion on the offending area while searching for other imperfections. Perhaps if she found enough of them she could cry off and stay in her room?

No, not for her the path of a coward. Time was slipping toward the hour she must leave for the Bentleys' ball. Caroline braced herself for the evening ahead.

Her maid stood patiently to one side. 'You look a treat, miss, and that's the truth!' At Caroline's startled glance of thanks, Daisy finished her ministrations, then saw her down the stairs.

At dinner, Lady Winnington and Caroline were treated to the sight of Edmund and Adrian in their temporary attire. While not perfection, it did remarkably well, thanks to two figures that were easy to fit with the stock coats kept for such emergencies. Both wore the plain blue Bath cloth coats and black pantaloons with cravats tied almost as well as Tom had taught them. The promised valet would undoubtedly provide practiced assistance in this matter.

Caroline took one look at the restrained elegance and sent up a prayer of thanks.

'What do you plan this evening? You look prodigiously fine in such short order.'

'Tom invited us to the ball,' replied Edmund in all innocence. 'He said this rig would do us.'

Caroline had to be thumped on the back by Adrian when she choked on a piece of turbot. 'You shall be there tonight? I trust you will behave with all propriety and not disgrace our papa by getting foxed.'

Adrian gave her an affronted glare. 'Tom said one must be able to hold one's wine.'

'I believe it is something that is not learned in one evening, however,' commented Lady Winnington in an aside that was heard quite distinctly by both young men.

'There is nothing that will turn away the interest of any young woman of refinement faster than the sight of a man in his cups,' asserted Caroline earnestly, wondering again if Papa had sent the boys to town in search of a wife.

'Not to worry, sister dear. We shall behave,' said Edmund, the twinkle in his eyes not reassuring in the least.

'Edmund, did Papa give you any instructions, any special instructions, before you left?' Caroline toyed with her fork while peeking at her brother to see his reaction to her question.

'Nothing out of the usual, like he did with you.'

'I was told to find myself a good husband,' she retorted.

'Well, if we were to find a filly that captured our hearts, we might consider it,' Edmund replied with a grin.

'I suspect the only filly that will capture your heart is one to be found at Tattersall's auction yard,' said Caroline with good grace.

'There is surely no rush for you boys, is there?' said Lady Winnington, giving them each considering looks.

'None in the least,' assured Adrian in reply.

Caroline was still puzzled when she later descended the stairs to receive the enthusiastic praise of the twins.

'Nice,' commented Edmund, his look approving.

'Better than I've seen you look before,' added Adrian with rare consideration for his sister's feelings.

'However did I manage to leave the house in the past without such fulsome praise, I wonder?' Caroline laughed at their combined expressions. She gave a reassuring pat to the ivory silk rose tucked into the front of her gown, then permitted Simpkins to slip her cape over her shoulders.

At last they were off in the hackney

Simpkins usually arranged for them. Hating horses as she did, Lady Winnington did not keep a carriage. It had been most fortunate that the butler had been able to find a jarvey who had recently bought a vehicle from a under-the-hatches peer.

The crush of carriages approaching the Bentley home promised a goodly sized crowd, Caroline informed her brothers. Once close to the house, they left the carriage and walked up the short flight of steps to the door, then on up to where Lord and Lady Bentley were receiving their guests.

From the pleased look adorning Lady Bentley's face, the party was a huge success. The addition of two agreeable young men only added to her joy.

Caroline wanted to tell the twins to behave, but knew better. She watched them disappear with feelings of misgiving. Yet she could not fail to note the heads that turned to watch their progress. Among them were several pretty heiresses.

'The boys must learn sometime, my dear,' said Lady Winnington gently.

'But why tonight?' whispered Caroline as she espied the handsome figure of Lord Stanhope. Beside him was the laughing widow, Diana Ingleby.

Not far away stood the aloof and disdainful

figure of the Earl of Rutledge, surrounded as usual by seductive ladies — all married. He looked bored to Caroline's surprised eyes. But, oh, he was handsome, dressed all in black save for his white linen and an exquisite white satin waistcoat. Such noble restraint, elegant simplicity. He bowed his head for a moment, and the candlelight caught sparkling lights in his raven hair.

Caroline took a fortifying breath, ordered her heart to behave, and stepped forward.

2

Caroline's plans were thwarted when another gentleman approached her with a request for a dance. He was quickly followed by another and soon Caroline began to despair of achieving her goal.

Seeing her niece's dilemma, her Aunt Fanny neatly solved the problem by nodding to Lord Stanhope, conveying in a most subtle manner that she wished to speak with him.

He immediately excused himself from the side of Mrs Ingleby and strolled over to where Caroline stood close to her aunt. The widow Ingleby, garbed in ravishing red jaconet ornamented with blond lace, shot a dark look in Caroline's direction before assuming a faintly bored air, turning to chat with a man who had rushed to take Hugh's place.

'Lady Winnington, Miss Beauchamp, how lovely to see you this evening.' He bowed over Lady Winnington's hand, then turned to Caroline, his eyes questioning.

She thought of how much his gentle wife adored him and longed to punch him on that handsome nose. Instead she lowered her lashes in what she prayed was an alluring manner, then laughed up at him, her green eyes sparkling with what she hoped would accomplish her task.

'Since when have you been so formal? I am Caroline to you, I should trust. I have not seen you in an age, Hugh. You are still Hugh to me, are you not? Or have you grown so lofty that I must address you as Lord Stanhope? And here I was, longing for a waltz with you. I suppose I dare not so much as hint for one, you wretched man.' She playfully tapped his arm with her fan and relaxed, finding flirting with Hugh to be more great fun than a challenge.

'Minx. How could I deny such a delightful suggestion? As I recall, you are rather good at that outrageous dance.' Hugh gave her a slightly puzzled look, but apparently decided she had her reasons for the flirtation. Like most men, he was not averse to casual dalliance.

She did not remind him that she had taken waltzing lessons with his wife; rather, she smiled and indicated her card, where she had carefully saved a waltz in hopes her plan might come to fruition. He signed his name in the space, then cast a glance in the direction where her brothers were included in a gathering of young men.

'I see young Edmund and Adrian are come to Town. You will have your hands full, Lady Winnington. Though I must say, they have received good advice as to their dress so far.'

'We have Tom Bentley to thank for that, I understand.' Caroline tried very hard to concentrate on Hugh. 'Edmund is trying to find a first-rate valet, for he says a truly good one will be the making of them. I believe he was nattering on about a cravat being dashed hard to do at the time.' She was aware of several assessing stares, most notably from the Earl of Rutledge. What attracted his curiosity to her was beyond Caroline at the moment.

Lord Stanhope rubbed his chin, smiling slightly as he recalled his first Season in London, and the urgent need to acquire Town bronze. 'I can understand their desire. I trust they will enjoy their stay and not cut up your peace too greatly, ma'am,' he said, bowing to Lady Winnington.

The conversation continued for several minutes before Lord Stanhope excused himself to return to his party. Caroline felt very vulnerable and slightly uneasy when he left. She turned to her aunt. 'Well? I was not too bold, was I?' she whispered.

'La, child, I have seen far worse than that innocent exchange. You performed your part with creditable ease. Just manage to continue in that vein this evening and you shall have made an excellent beginning. Remember, you will not accomplish this business in one night.' Lady Winnington retired to a chair beside one of her friends along with the other dowagers, mothers, and chaperons.

As was proper, Caroline danced with the first young man who had signed her card. Relaxing now that the first hurdle of her assignment was past, she was shaken when Lord Rutledge presented himself at the end of the country dance. She glanced about for her next partner and gave a relieved sigh when he drew nigh to where she stood near her aunt.

Unfortunately, he took one look at the stormy eyes of the man who stood so close to Caroline and bowed his concession.

Caroline gave a helpless glance to her aunt, who merely nodded, then turned again to the intimidating earl.

'That was not well done, Lord Rutledge. I fear you frightened away my next partner.' Caroline met those gray eyes with a wild fluttering in her heart. Why did this man have such a strong effect on her?

'Good. For I was unable to get near you earlier so I might sign your card. Had I been able to wend my way through the crush, this might have been my dance anyway,' he said with irrefutable logic. He smiled and Caroline noted with a sinking heart that he had an irresistible little dimple on his right cheek. Faint, but discernible if one watched carefully. It simply was not fair, she thought. No man ought to have such a weapon at his disposal. She could only carry on as though she had not noticed that delight.

Caroline laughed at his errant bit of nonsense. It was highly unlikely he would ever have difficulty doing anything he wished. She cast a half smile up at him, almost as she had at Hugh, and said in mock severity, 'What a lot of silliness. However, I am yours . . . for the moment.' With that, she swept her lashes down, then peeped up at him with a curious glance. He had never sought her side before. Why tonight?

It must be her new gown, she decided as they performed the first figure of the contredanse. She glided through the measure, smoothly advancing, then retreating as the pattern required. He was a very good dancer, she realized. For a man, he was extremely graceful.

He also was giving her new gown quite a thorough assessmeat. Was the neckline beyond what was acceptable? She wondered if the silk rose was sufficient. He took her arm and she could feel his gaze sliding over her. When she glanced up at him, she sensed that gaze had come to rest on her bosom. She was well endowed, and for that she had always been grateful. Now she wondered if it might be a liability.

'Lovely silk rose, my dear Miss Beauchamp. It matches your ribands perfectly. And how clever of you to place a few roses among those ebony curls of yours.' He paused, then added in a barely audible voice, 'Although I must confess that the one at your, ah, neckline is more riveting.'

Caroline stifled a gasp, and would have left his side had it been possible. She gathered her poise and merely bowed her head a moment, then replied, 'How kind of you, Lord Rutledge. I am very fond of roses. Although I do regret they have thorns on them. Thorns can be so daunting. Do you not think so?' Her gaze was level; she studied his face with no hint of flirtation. Then she turned her head and the eye contact that had shaken her was broken.

What a wicked man, to so improperly comment on the neckline of her gown. When she again turned to accept his hand in the third movement of the dance, she dared to meet his gaze, only to discover he appeared to be trying not to laugh. At least it seemed so to her after years of observing her brothers.

He was a strange man, she decided. Perhaps it was just as well that she could never attract the interest of such if that was what he was like upon closer acquaintance.

Caroline could only breathe a sigh of relief when the dance came to an end and she was dutifully returned to her aunt's side. Rutledge bowed over her hand, then held it a moment. 'No thorns, please, Miss Beauchamp. I rather envy my good friend Stanhope that he can command such sparkling smiles from so lovely a miss. You are a friend of his wife, are you not?'

Wishing she might tug her hand from his clasp, which while it appeared light, was one of iron, Caroline said, 'Yes. I know Lady Stanhope well.'

'I thought so.' He cast a glance to where Hugh stood chatting with Mrs Ingleby and another gentleman.

Her hand suddenly released, Caroline turned with more than a little relief to accept her next partner, who had promptly presented himself to her aunt come the proper time.

The evening progressed, not quite as quickly as she might have wished, but well enough. The hostess declared the twins to be pretty-behaved lads. Caroline danced every dance, and most agreeably snagged Hugh as a partner for supper. Yet she was conscious of someone's gaze following her quite often. Lord Rutledge, she suspected, although why, she couldn't imagine. She tried to avoid looking at him, not wishing to become entangled in that dark stare. Somehow she sensed it would not be kind or even flirtatious.

And then came the moment she had waited for all evening. Hugh presented himself for their waltz.

'You are quite a success this evening. I must say that gown is becoming, green is certainly your color.' He swirled her out and around with a deftness she could enjoy. No wonder Mary loved him so, he had many excellent qualities. Which was probably why the widow sought to get her hands on him, come to think on it. Handsome men who were wealthy and possessed lovely manners and could dance like a dream did not grow on trees.

'How kind of you, Hugh. I have begun to feel more at home in the city and in society. It was all so strange at first. I do wish my aunt had a carriage, though. It is a bit wearying to always be walking in the afternoon.'

He rose to her words with gallant speed. 'Then I shall take you for a drive in mine.

Should you like to see my new pair of bays?'

'Oh, I would adore it. What a dear, thoughtful man you are.' She beamed up at him with heartfelt appreciation. He was being most helpful, really. She hadn't expected seduction to be so easy. Not that she really knew that much about the subject, mind you.

This plan was going much better than she had hoped it would. Did he think it odd that she hadn't mentioned his wife? He was well aware that she was close to Mary. He twirled her about in one last, marvelous swing, then walked with her to where Aunt Fanny sat on one of those uncomfortable-looking chairs that often line the walls of ballrooms.

'Are your brothers going to present any problem for you? I would be happy to assist you in any way I can,' Lord Stanhope offered in a very fraternal manner.

'No, er, that is, they may possibly get into some sort of difficulty, I suppose.' She had been about to deny any potential for trouble when she had caught sight of the widow in her flaming dress positively glaring at her. If need be, Caroline might use the excuse of advice on how to cope with the twins to get Hugh's company. 'One never knows what they will think of next, you know.'

'I overheard Edmund mentioning some-thing about Tatt's to the group he is with. I expect he will be inspecting horses come morning.' Amusement lurked in Stanhope's voice as he recalled the importance of a truly excellent mount for a young fellow just come to London.

'Oh, dear. If he can just manage to stay within the allowance Papa sent for them.' Caroline forgot about the widow Ingleby, indeed, forgot she was supposed to be seducing Hugh, and turned to give her cherished brothers an anguished look.

'What is Adrian's interest? I don't believe I have ever heard it mentioned.' Stanhope devoted his whole attention to her, standing as close to her as was seemly. His smoldering good looks and that insouciant grin undoubtedly contributed to Mary's admiration of him.

Caroline gave him an appreciative glance. He certainly knew how to cooperate with his seduction. 'Adrian is totally absorbed in all things Roman.' She sighed a bit wistfully. 'I do believe he would dig up any area where he thinks they may have lived, just to see what he might uncover.'

'I wonder if he knows that London was once a Roman encampment, indeed the capital of the Roman settlement in what we now so happily call England.' He gave her a lazy smile and Caroline began to wish, just a little, that she had met Hugh before he wed Mary.

'Good heavens! Do not, whatever you do, say that within his hearing. He may know of it, but I can only hope he does not, for he will contrive to dig up the entire city!' She gave him a horrified look, then shook her head and laughed ruefully. 'You are naughty, my Lord Stanhope. I can only pray that you drive a team better than you tease.' Her concern for her brother was relegated to the back of her mind, for this business of flirting was becoming rather fun, and she desired to pay it her full heed. It seemed to her that to speak of one's younger brothers was not quite the path to take when seducing. And, she reminded herself, it was necessary to accomplish this work with all speed.

'I shall collect you shortly before five tomorrow afternoon, and we shall enjoy a leisurely drive through the park.' He grinned down at her in the same way Edmund was wont to do. Would Mrs Ingleby know the difference between a brotherly grin and a flirtation at this distance?

Caroline frowned slightly. 'I expect there is no other way to manage it than at that pace, given how crowded Hyde Park can be at that hour. I shall look forward to my treat, you can be sure,' she said. Catching sight of Rutledge looking in their direction, Caroline fluttered her lashes at Hugh in what she hoped to be a seductive manner.

Diana Ingleby sauntered toward them with the Earl of Rutledge at her side. 'Did I hear you mention a drive in the park? How lovely.' She gave Lord Stanhope an expectant look, but Hugh merely glanced at Caroline.

'Would you do me the honor of driving out with me tomorrow, Diana?' said the earl in that rich voice that made Caroline think of fine coffee laced with cream.

Diana turned her bewitching smile on him and purred, 'Why, what a divine notion, to be sure. We shall most likely see one another at one point or another.'

Caroline was delighted at the frosty look the Ingleby bestowed upon Hugh. When that frigid glare was turned on herself, it was not quite so pleasant Suddenly she realized she had made a formidable enemy, not one a girl during her comeout year was wise to cross. She stifled a shiver and did her best to look as though she were totally unaware of any undercurrents.

'How is it that you waited so long to make your bow to society, Miss Beauchamp? You come from a rather large family, so I have heard.' The implication seemed to be that Caroline's father could not manage a come-out with so many mouths to feed.

Smiling sweetly, Caroline dipped a respectful curtsy, such as one does to one's elders, then said, 'My mother presented us with another member for our happy family two years ago. She wished me to come to London, but I could not leave her. She had a very difficult time and I preferred to help her rather than be in Town. Otherwise, there is no reason why I should not have been here then. I daresay I shall enjoy myself as much now. Especially when a good friend is willing to help me,' she added most daringly, casting a fond look at Mary's Hugh.

It hadn't hurt her cause to treat the other woman as her elder, Caroline saw. It had clearly vexed Diana to be reminded of her age. Nor had she been best pleased to see Lord Stanhope accorded such familiar treatment.

Lady Winnington appeared at this moment, touching Caroline gently on the arm. 'We must leave now, my dear.' She nodded her head an inch or so to the widow, bestowed a friendly look on Lord Stanhope, and cordially offered her hand to the Earl of Rutledge.

Caroline dared a glance at him, and thought he seemed to be amused again. At Aunt Fanny's cool snub of the widow? La, the woman ought to be accustomed to such by now.

Her brothers were left to find their own way to the house, understandably preferring Tom's company to that of their sister and aunt. Caroline hoped they would avoid the horrid gaming dens which she knew abounded in the city, and get home in one piece.

'Well, dear aunt? What think you of the evening?' asked Caroline with studied casualness as they entered the waiting carriage.

Lady Winnington tapped her fan against her hand while she considered what had transpired. 'I believe you are doing well. The drive in the park will be a step, for certain. Did I correctly overhear that the widow Ingleby will drive with Rutledge?'

'Yes. I confess I am a trifle confused about his behavior. Why did he seek my hand for a dance this evening when he has paid not the least attention to me in the past?' Caroline's voice revealed what the dim light in the carriage could not. She was more than confused, she was concerned. Lord Rutledge normally *never* looked at a young miss in her come-out year, even if it was a delayed one as had been the case with Caroline.

'Puzzling indeed,' murmured Lady Winnington.

Simpkins held the door for them as they entered, then hustled out to pay the jarvey, Baxhall. Caroline bestowed an appreciative nod and a pleasant smile when the butler returned to assist them. Her gracious ways had endeared her to the staff at her aunt's house.

★　★　★

In the morning Caroline woke late. She welcomed the tray with her chocolate and toast. The maid bustled in shortly after that with a large bouquet of lovely ivory roses.

'These be pretty, miss, but mighty diff'rent, and that's the truth,' muttered Daisy as she placed the vase on the stand not far from Caroline's bed.

'They appear to be ordinary roses to me,' murmured Caroline. Her morning chocolate finished, she handed the tray to her maid, then slipped from her bed to take a closer look at the roses Daisy thought so unusual.

'My goodness!' Caroline exclaimed as she examined the roses more carefully. 'All the thorns have been clipped off. Not one remains.' Curious as to the sender of such a bouquet, for she had already noted the color was identical to her silk roses worn last evening, she extracted the folded note that was tucked in the depths of the leaves.

Daisy lingered close by, straining to see what was written, for she was able to read just a little if the handwriting was clear.

'Rutledge!' The note in her hand seemed to burn as Caroline read the inscription: 'No thorns for such a lovely lady. Would that I could pluck a complete garden.' Cryptic words, yet she had an uneasy feeling what he implied by those two short sentences, green girl though she might be. How highly improper! Her cheeks flushed with color at the images that flashed through her mind as she considered the matter.

Her hand ruffled her curls as she considered the best way to handle this, should it prove necessary. When she went driving with Stanhope this afternoon, they were bound to meet Rutledge and the widow. The park was not all that large. She crossed to the writing desk and dashed off a brief note.

Handing the little piece of folded and sealed paper to her maid, she requested, 'Please see that this is delivered to Lady Stanhope immediately.'

After Daisy had left the room, Caroline sank down on the edge of her bed and stared at the beautiful roses. They were perfectly formed buds just on the verge of opening, a rich, satiny ivory, and her room was now filled with their exotic scent. She breathed deeply, savoring the fragrance.

Could there possibly be a further message? In the language of flowers a thornless rose meant early attachment. Ha! She might be a green girl, but she was not so foolish as to think the Earl of Rutledge was enamored of her.

So what did they mean?

A rap at the door was followed by her aunt's entry. 'My, you are late this morning.' Then, espying the roses, she exclaimed, 'How lovely. Who sent them?'

Wordlessly, Caroline handed her the note.

'My, my,' murmured Lady Winnington in a quiet voice. 'What a strange man. Handsome, rich, and titled, though.'

'And most definitely not for me, dear aunt. I have the oddest notion Rutledge would like to collect me as his doxy! I very much doubt if he has the least idea of getting wed. I want a loving husband, if possible,' stated Caroline in firm tones.

'Caroline! You ought not even think of such things as doxies. And what do you know of them, pray tell?'

'Aunt Fanny, you forget I am from a large and rather outspoken family, and have helped my mother a great deal these past years. I

42

would have to be totally deaf not to hear some of what is said around me.'

'What can your mother be thinking of, to sully your tender ears with such tales?' exclaimed a dismayed Lady Winnington.

'I expect she feels that if I know something of life in London, I'll be less apt to make serious mistakes.'

'And now you are embroiled in seduction, no less.' Lady Winnington smiled wryly at her niece, chuckling softly at Caroline's frustrated expression.

'I sent a note to Mary, asking her to come over as soon as she could. I decided it would be best if I didn't go there for the time being.'

'Wise girl,' declared Lady Winnington. 'Best get yourself dressed, in that case.' She glanced at the green silk dress that still hung out, then at the ivory roses in the vase by the bed. 'Life is certainly more interesting now. I am so glad you came to me for your come-out, dear child.' With that remark she left Caroline to her toilette.

When Mary arrived, breathless and rosy, she was ushered into the morning room with all speed. Caroline greeted her with affection, then motioned to a chair.

'You had best sit down.' Quickly she explained what had occurred, then about the afternoon drive.

'Famous!' cried a delighted Mary. 'I shall ride my pretty new mare this afternoon. Perhaps I can glimpse what is going on, if you do not think it will complicate matters?' She deferred to Caroline as the expert, which made her very amused.

'Why not? Who knows, it might provide an added twist.'

Caroline discreetly made no mention of the note that had come with the roses.

So, at shortly before five in the afternoon, Caroline, carefully dressed in a pomona green gown with a chip bonnet trimmed in matching riband, drove off with Lord Stanhope toward Hyde Park at the hour calculated to be seen by everyone and anyone who counted in society. Especially the widow Diana Ingleby.

'You are looking very well this afternoon, Caroline,' said Lord Stanhope as he tooled his shiny blue carriage along the drive into the park.

'How very kind you are, Hugh. And I must say, those bays of yours are superb. I can only hope my brother does half as well in choosing his mount.'

'Has he said anything as to what he bought?' Amusement lingered in Stanhope's voice.

'Only that I shall be treated to the sight of

him shortly,' replied Caroline, the concern for her brother clearly heard.

The crush of carriages slowed their progress considerably, much to Caroline's satisfaction . . . and dismay. While she was luring Lord Stanhope away from that awful Mrs Ingleby, she was also on display in his carriage. She could only pray that society would remember the close friendship between her and Hugh's wife and treat her kindly.

And then she caught sight of the one carriage she had hoped to see — Rutledge's. He was dressed all in gray, and drove a team of beautiful grays to match. At his side Mrs Ingleby wore a peculiar shade of red, which while odd, went well with her chestnut hair. Those pale blue eyes narrowed at the vision of pomona green in the Stanhope carriage.

Rutledge reined in his team and tipped his elegant gray hat. 'Miss Beauchamp, Stanhope. I trust you are enjoying the day. The weather is unusually nice for this time of spring.'

Edging just a tiny bit closer to Hugh, Caroline nodded graciously and agreed. 'How true.' Then something prompted her to add, 'I must thank you for the lovely roses. So unusual, too. I have not seen thornless ones before.' She bestowed a bland smile on

Rutledge, then noticed the stiffening of the figure at his side.

Diana Ingleby apparently knew the significance attached to flowers as well as Caroline did, although such meanings were a bit old-fashioned. Diana drew in a breath and glared, daggers drawn, at Caroline, for a moment only. Her face then smoothed and she stifled a yawn, as though her evening had been long and tiring.

The two carriages were about to part when a diversion occurred. Viscountess Stanhope approached on a pretty chestnut mare. She was dressed in a pale blue habit, one that Caroline thought did little for her.

'Hello, Hugh, Caroline. Good day, Lord Rutledge.' Her gaze went to the widow.

Lord Rutledge sighed with apparent resignation. 'Lady Stanhope, may I present Mrs Ingleby.'

The ladies nodded slightly, but said nothing other than vague murmurs.

Lord Stanhope had assumed a grim visage at the arrival of his wife. Caroline had the wildest desire to laugh. A chance glance at Lord Rutledge caught a similar expression on his face, fleeting but nevertheless there. He schooled his features even as Caroline kept her neutral. Could they share the same feelings about this absurd scene?

There was a strange, tense silence hovering over the carriages. Caroline observed others nearby gazing with curiosity and nudged Hugh. He seemed about to urge his team forward when another rider came toward them at a rather fast pace.

'I do believe it is Edmund,' whispered Caroline, not knowing whether she dared look or should shut her eyes, lest she see some horror.

'Do not worry, Caroline,' said Hugh quietly. 'I believe your brother has done very well for himself, from what I can see.'

Edmund came to a stop before the two carriages and gave Caroline a triumphant grin. 'I found just the horse I want. I think he will be a grand beginning.'

Edmund was astride a very fine bay, sleek like a greyhound. 'He looks like a racehorse,' was Caroline's first comment.

'Reminds me faintly of Stubb's painting of the great Eclipse,' offered Lord Rutledge. His gaze strayed to where Mary sat quietly, virtually ignored by the others.

Edmund preened himself while Caroline wondered what he had paid for such a magnificent horse.

'It seems your brother needs no instruction on what kind of horse to purchase, given a desire for a racehorse,' said the man at her side.

'I intend to race him, Lord Stanhope,' inserted Edmund proudly. 'If I can win, I shall have myself a stud.'

Mary glanced about them to see the road becoming clogged with traffic, carriages unable to make their way around the group. 'Let's ride a bit, Edmund. I shall see you later, Hugh. Good day, all.' She gave a gentle farewell to the others and turned her horse away.

In remarkably few minutes, they had all gone their separate directions. Caroline hoped that any gossip that might have ensued over the incident would have been dissipated with the arrival of Edmund and his superb racer.

Hugh was oddly silent on the drive back to South Street. Caroline did not disturb him, for she was also deep in thought. What manner of game was Lord Rutledge playing with her? One might think that he was angry over her flirtation with Hugh, not that it was any business of his!

Both subdued, Hugh bid her good afternoon, politely noting her comment about seeing him at the Ellisons' rout this evening.

Simpkins directed Caroline to the stillroom when she inquired as to the whereabouts of her aunt.

'Washing day so soon, dear aunt?' Caroline

entered the room to the sound of coins being swished about in a basin of water.

'Filthy things,' sniffed her aunt disdainfully. She peered at the clean coins turned out onto the soft towel. The now polished coins won whilst playing cards were collected by Lady Winnington, dumped unceremoniously into a soft bag, then carried along to the morning room.

'A report! I can see you are bursting with news,' Lady Winnington said. She placed her bag of clean coins into the wall safe behind a portrait of her late husband, then rang for tea.

'We all met as I had planned. Hugh seemed a bit uncomfortable when Mary came along on her new little mare. Fortunately, he was with a friend rather than that scheming widow. Not too surprisingly, the Ingleby woman looked happy enough to be with Lord Rutledge.'

'And?' demanded Lady Winnington, plumping herself on the sofa.

'Edmund has bought a fine, and I fear, very expensive horse.' Caroline spared a thought for the size of the purse Edmund had to draw from and began to worry.

'And?' the old lady persisted.

Caroline rubbed her forehead. 'I had the oddest notion that Rutledge was sorry for

Mary.' Her brow cleared. 'If that is true, she ought to be able to persuade him to be her flirt with no problem at all.'

Lady Winnington agreed, and the two settled down for a cup of tea and short gossip. The precise shade of red worn by the widow had to be discussed. Her expressions, smiles, annoyance, all must be debated.

When Caroline walked up to her room later on to dress for the Ellisons' rout, her thoughts returned to the scene in the park. Rather than Lord Stanhope's expression — which had been strained last she saw him — Caroline found herself wondering about the enigmatic Lord Rutledge. His amusement had puzzled her. Did his sense of humor match her own?

What went on in his mind? Suddenly she very much wished she knew.

3

The rout was a sad crush, much to Mrs Ellison's delight. Caroline found herself feeling trapped by the sheer number of people making their way up the stairs, people who paused to gossip, thus blocking her way, not to mention the slow process of greeting the host and hostess, who wished to say a few words to each person who came.

'Do you see anyone?' said Aunt Fanny close to Caroline's ear, lest she be overheard and thought strange, for they were surrounded by people. They had greeted the Ellisons and now were in the blue salon.

Knowing precisely what the older woman meant, Caroline stood on her tiptoes, peered about the room, then motioned that they should proceed to the next room, the green drawing room. As they passed through a relatively quiet area, Caroline said as softly as she could, 'Not a sign of Mary, Stanhope, or the widow Ingleby. Rutledge either, for that matter.'

'Well, we shall simply have to make the best of it, my dear.' Lady Winnington bowed slightly to someone she knew, then stopped to chat with a close friend, leaving Caroline on her own for the moment.

Looking about her, Caroline absorbed the lovely colors and fabrics worn by the women attending, not to mention the bright hues of some of the older gentlemen who refused to bow to the dictates of that upstart, Brummell. Rumor had it that his days were numbered. What with his insults and all, he was walking a fine line. Caroline wondered how he managed his finances, given his propensity for gaming.

If only she could keep a close watch on her brothers. But it was likely that they would get in the suds, then come to her when she was helpless to extract them. She nervously fingered her reticule as she considered what might be the most likely frolic they could find to plunge into in the next week or two. Her frown deepened as several occurred to her.

She engaged several friends in the sort of conversation one does at these kinds of events, the bland, meaningless stuff, lest one be overheard gossiping and judged to be a tattler. She drifted away from them when the topic changed to horses. It brought Edmund to mind again.

'Good evening, Miss Beauchamp. Alone?' The rich male voice came from behind to her right and very close to her ear.

She whirled about, nearly colliding with Lord Rutledge. The proximity took her breath away. 'No, sir,' she said in ruffled dismay. 'My aunt is with me. She was nearby, but you know how these affairs can be. I trust I shall find her before it is time to depart.' The frown on her brow had flown at the sight of his face, and she could only pray he did not think she felt deserted.

That hope was lost when he smiled down at her and said, 'You seem troubled. Could it be that someone you expected to meet here has failed to arrive?' There was a suave smoothness in his voice that irritated her.

Not willing he should believe any such thing, she denied it emphatically. 'No, I confess it is my brothers who occupied my thoughts. Can you not recall how it was when you first came up to Town? If so, I need say no more on that score. Except to add that I am the one most likely to have to rescue them from their foolishness, should it come to that.' She was gratified at the sympathetic expression that crossed his face, even if it was short-lived.

'Lady Stanhope is with me this evening,' he murmured, looking about him. 'I hope I have not lost her. She is such a tiny, defenseless thing.' He gave Caroline a measured look, then turned to discover Mary not far from his side, distracted for the nonce by a matron arrayed in puce velvet, with pink plumes nodding wildly above her elaborate hairstyle as she conversed with a good deal of animation.

Caroline was about to reply that Mary could well care for herself, when she espied Lord Stanhope wending his way through the crowd. She gave him a relieved smile. 'Hugh, how lovely to see you.'

'There is never so welcome a sight as the face of a good friend in a crush like this.' He took her hand, kissed it lightly, then glanced at Rutledge with less than pleased eyes.

'I see you are beforehand this evening, Rutledge.' Lord Stanhope once might have smiled with warmth at his old companion. This evening his greeting bordered on the frigidly polite.

'I have found it pays at times,' replied Rutledge somewhat obscurely. 'I miss the charming Mrs Ingleby this evening. Is she not well?' At that moment he observed Diana Ingleby on the arm of an aging but very wealthy peer. He raised his brows at the sight. 'I see I need not have worried. She appears in fine fettle.' He turned to rescue Lady Stanhope from the puce velvet and pink plumes, then disappeared into the crowd with her at his side. The attentions Rutledge bestowed on Mary were not missed by Hugh.

Stanhope stared after them for a moment before glancing down to the quizzical face at his side. 'Odd fellow, if you know what I mean.'

'Oh, don't I just,' murmured Caroline. She had the distinct impression Hugh was about to say something far stronger, but as she was overly conscious of Mrs Ingleby's approach, she put the subject from her mind. 'I believe we are about to be joined.'

'So I see.' He moved slightly closer to her, as though to protect her from attack, thought Caroline with rising hope. Could it be that Hugh was having second thoughts about the beautiful widow? Or did he find that possessive attitude of hers a trifle beyond what was acceptable to him?

'Stanhope, good to see you,' said Lord Mortland, his white hair neatly arranged and his garb quite immaculate, contrary to many an elderly gentleman Caroline had observed in society. Lord Mortland seemed smugly pleased to be escorting the beautiful widow this evening.

'Mortland,' replied Hugh civilly.

He performed the introductions, to which Caroline absently but nicely replied. She was covertly studying the beauty at Lord Mortland's side. Again dressed in what apparently was her favorite shade of vibrant red, she seemed to survey the scene about her with languid ease. Yet Caroline was struck by the idea that not one thing transpired that was missed by those limpid blue eyes. When her gaze settled upon Caroline, little doubt remained. The widow was alert and very displeased about something, and Caroline suspected she knew precisely what that might be.

For a few minutes the conversation was rather general and quite benign. Caroline had just begun to believe she might escape unscathed when the widow gave her a raking glance, then spoke, leaning toward Lord Stanhope in such a manner that her voluptuous bosom was magnificently displayed.

'How kind of you to take a young girl under your wing, Lord Stanhope,' said Mrs Ingleby in an attractively husky voice. 'Usually men find it such a tedious task, green girls being what they are and all.' Her dark lashes swept down, then up in a fetching way before she gave him a bewitching smile. Caroline felt sure that were she to remain close to the widow, she would receive a complete tuition in the art of flirting and seduction.

Caroline smiled sweetly. 'Hugh has been

most kind, I assure you. Green girls appreciate a gentleman's gracious attentions. You must have done so when you were my age, am I not correct? You do recall?' It was a hit direct, as far as Caroline could tell. Mrs Ingleby looked a good deal taken aback. She apparently had not anticipated Caroline would dare to counter in her own behalf.

Lord Mortland shifted from one foot to the other, obviously wishing himself elsewhere.

'Miss Beauchamp and I must leave early, as we plan to ride in the park tomorrow morning. I trust you will excuse us?' Hugh did not give any of them a chance to comment, but bundled Caroline off to where he could see her aunt still chatting with friends. He murmured a soft apology as they strolled the length of the room. The widow's waspish dig had not helped in her pursuit of Hugh.

Lady Winnington took one shrewd glance at Hugh's face, then Caroline's. 'I declare, I am quite overcome with the heat in all this crowd. Most fatiguing. Would you be so kind as to escort us to our carriage, Lord Stanhope?' Although it was warm, it was not that warm. Caroline greatly appreciated her aunt's perceptive nature.

'It will be my pleasure, Lady Winnington.' Hugh carefully made a path for the two ladies through the rooms and down the stairs, where a line of carriages waited along the street.

The crush of people had thinned only slightly, as there was no other really interesting party on tonight. Often the *ton* found its way to two or three in an evening.

'Thank you, Hugh. You *are* very kind to this green girl.' Caroline chuckled at the expression of chagrin that crossed his face.

'You will allow me to atone for that remark by riding in the park tomorrow?' He held her hand firmly as he assisted her into Baxhall's above-average hackney after seeing Lady Winnington safely inside.

'Nine in the morning?' Caroline paused on the step to the carriage and gazed at Hugh with pleasure that he was coming along with his wife's plan so nicely. What a shame that dearest Mary could not meet him in the park in Caroline's place. But perhaps it was too soon. She would watch and wait for the chance to bring these two together. However, in the meantime she must go along with the scheme and hope that odious Lord Rutledge would be elsewhere. She had not crossed his path so many times since coming to London as she had in the past few days since commencing her planned seduction of Hugh.

'Tomorrow at nine.' Lord Stanhope saw the

door of the carriage closed before strolling off in the direction of his house. He had no desire to find Diana Ingleby and explain his behavior. That beautiful demirep had wasted no time in attaching herself to old Mortland. Although Stanhope had entertained certain ambitions as far as Mrs Ingleby was concerned, he did not mind in the least transferring his attentions to Caroline Beauchamp. As a matter of fact, in view of what he had seen this evening, it might serve his purpose even better.

In the dim light provided by the carriage lamp, Lady Winnington surveyed the pensive girl at her side. 'Well, I trust you were successful this evening, if our leave-taking is any indication. Mary ought to be pleased.'

'I hope so. I admit to a little concern. Mrs Ingleby does not strike me as the sort of woman who very easily lets go of what she wants. I suspect I must be on the alert around her. Although Hugh does not respond overmuch to my flirting, he has taken steps from the widow. He certainly reacted to the sight of Lord Rutledge hovering over Mary.'

'I saw Diana's face when she swept from the room,' Lady Winnington agreed. 'Mortland was following her as best he could. She looked like one of the Furies, my dear. You will do well to guard your back, as the saying goes. As for Hugh, he needs to suffer a little.'

With that scarcely comforting thought Caroline subsided into a considering silence that lasted until she was in her room, broken only to wish her aunt a good night's sleep.

So Diana Ingleby was furious with her, was she? However, it seemed the Ingleby was not the only one who had taken umbrage with Caroline this evening. If she was not mistaken, Lord Rutledge had seemed displeased with her when Hugh joined them. She had caught the expression of tightly leashed anger on his face when Hugh had so lightly kissed her hand. Rutledge had appeared to want to do some manner of violence to dear Hugh.

Deciding that the entire situation was too much to bother her head with that night, Caroline tumbled into her bed and fell into the soundest of sleeps. Sleep of the just, her aunt called it the next morning when Caroline chatted briefly with her before leaving the house following a substantial breakfast.

She walked briskly to the mews where her horse was stabled. Lady Winnington did not ride, indeed, avoided horses as much as possible. 'Nasty things,' she had confided to Caroline one day. 'Hard in the middle and dangerous on both ends. Can't abide the animals. But if you wish to risk your life, I shall arrange the stabling for you.'

And so Caroline, taking care with her new emerald green riding habit, walked to where her horse was kept in the grand stable of the equally grand home located behind her aunt's more modest but very nice abode.

She had never queried as to who might be the owner of the magnificent home she could see from her window on the second floor of her aunt's house. Once she had caught sight of the beautiful building, she'd meant to, to be sure. She had seen the tall edifice through the trees that surrounded the gardens of the place, and been most attracted to it. But there had been so much to be done in such a short time that the matter had been quite forgotten in her rush.

Going to the stables herself rather than ordering the mare brought to her gave her an opportunity to see her brother's new purchase once again. He was a marvelous animal. She recognized him immediately and commented on him to an admiring groom. Upon further questioning, Caroline discovered both of her brothers had gone out. Edmund was off to a race somewhere with friends. But it seemed Adrian had tied a valise to his saddle and informed the groom he was off to Bath. Bath? Caroline was bemused as she mounted her horse with a bit of help from the groom.

When Hugh met Caroline at the entrance to the mews, his questions about her direction were stilled by the confused look on her face.

'Nothing wrong, is there?' He glanced back along the deserted mews, seeing no sign of anyone who might have bothered her.

She smoothed her riding skirt across her knees, then tried a reassuring smile. She decided not to complicate this seduction business by entangling Hugh in her personal affairs. 'Nothing of importance.'

Hugh had intended to quiz her about the stabling of her horse, but she was having trouble with her restive mount, so instead they rode in silence toward the park.

Fortunately, her aunt lived close to the entrance, and within minutes they were cantering along Rotten Row, exercising the fidgets from the pretty mare whose dark coat exactly matched the color of Caroline's hair.

When the mare had enjoyed a lengthy run, Caroline reined her in to a more dignified pace, turning in the direction of home. One could scarcely converse if they were tearing along the Row at a canter, now could one?

'Did I tell you how charming you look this morning? That is a very good color on you,

Caroline.' Hugh's eyes were warm with affection for this pretty young miss who was a good friend of his wife's.

Caroline wondered if he had ever told his sweet wife how lovely she looked in blue or what a dear girl she was. How many of the men of the *ton* were like this? Caroline knew full well that she would not tolerate such a marriage. Any man who would treat her thus risked being murdered in his bed — if he ever slept at home, that is.

'You appear to have slept well.' She nodded graciously in a roundabout reply to his compliment.

'After I saw you and your aunt off, I enjoyed a brisk walk home. I think one always sleeps better following a bit of exercise.'

She wondered a little at the dryness of his voice, but made no answer to this remark other than to raise her brows. 'Is that not rather dangerous at such a late hour? Footpads and the like are at their worst in the evening, so I have heard.'

'I carry a small gun as well as a rather special cane with a concealed blade. Since I do not walk when foxed, 'tis not likely they will come after me,' he assured her.

Caroline thought of her younger brothers and resolved to admonish them to always take a hackney late at night rather than run such risks.

In the distance, a woman dressed in a deep red riding habit trimmed with black braid came riding toward them seated on a black mare. The gentleman at her side was becoming more and more familiar to Caroline as the days passed. She recognized Rutledge immediately and guessed the woman in red might be Mrs Ingleby. So, Mary had not managed to snare him as her flirt yet. Pity. A confrontation during the morning ride would have suited Caroline admirably. Besides, time mattered to her.

The control exerted by Diana Ingleby was superb, Caroline acknowledged. Not by the flicker of an eyelash did she reveal that she was extremely angry at the desertion of her most favored escort.

'Good morning, Stanhope, Miss Beauchamp. Out to catch a bit of air before the rain arrives, I see,' Rutledge said in that superbly rich voice Caroline reluctantly admired.

She looked up at the sky, observing for the first time that it was that pervasive, dense gray that settles over the land before a steady drizzle begins.

'How nice to see you both again,' Caroline lied through her teeth. Being polite was obviously not the path to heaven, given the admonitions to be truthful at all times. She wondered if Rutledge had also walked home last night, or if he had ridden in a carriage. Had he even made it to his own door? She did not miss the sidelong glances or the possessive touch of Mrs Ingleby's hand on Rutledge's arm as she sought his attention whenever Hugh looked her way.

Caroline might be a naif, but she was fast learning that men had vastly different standards of behavior than women. Wives were allowed more freedom than a young miss, but even they were required to toe some manner of line. Widows seemed to garner the greatest freedom of all women. As a bachelor and man about town, Rutledge was entitled to do just as he pleased. Caroline entertained the happy thought of doing him some sort of violence, then realized she was becoming rather bloodthirsty in her musings. This would never do.

She smiled at Hugh, pretending a need to control her restive mare, hoping they could move on rather than remain in conversation with less-than-wanted company.

Before Mrs Ingleby could attack, Caroline was saved by the weather. A mist began to fall, the kind Caroline well knew would turn into a drizzle before long. She touched her smart new hat with a tentative hand before turning to Hugh.

Mrs Ingleby apparently was of the same mind, for she nodded abruptly to Caroline and Hugh, then wheeled about, rather crudely, Caroline thought. She spoke tersely to Rutledge, then rode off, not waiting for him to ride with her.

The three, who were apparently the only hardy souls left in the park, also rode briskly toward the entrance while the mist turned to rain. At the end of the mews, Caroline said farewell to a concerned but thwarted Hugh, then hurried toward the stables. She was followed.

Once in the stables, she confronted Rutledge with a baleful stare. And then she made a most unwelcome discovery.

'Nasty turn to the weather, milord,' said the groom with more than a touch of deference in his voice and manner.

'Right, Davy. Rub them down well.' Rutledge handed over his horse to the groom, then watched as Caroline's pretty mare was led away. Beyond the stable door the rain pounded on the cobblestones.

From the behavior of everyone in sight as well as Rutledge's own air of possession, Caroline knew, with an increasingly sinking heart, that the stables belonged to him.

'You'd best come in with me. If you try to run for home now, you'll ruin that lovely habit of yours and it looks quite new. If you slipped and fell on the cobbles, you might well break an ankle or arm.' His gaze was not only assessing but also warm. That elusive dimple peeped out at her with fatal results.

'Come in with you?' Those were the only words that had registered. *He* was the one who owned the magnificent house seen from her window. She glanced out the open door of the stables to see the drizzle had turned to a steady rain, more than enough to indeed ruin her new and most cherished habit. And yet . . . His grin was infuriating, Caroline decided as she stood there, still undecided as to what she must do.

'There is a covered walkway to the house from the stables. You shall be quite safe . . . from the rain.'

Caroline glanced at him to find his gaze slowly roving over her in what she considered a rather rude way. Those gray eyes danced with amusement when he realized she had caught him looking at her bosom again. She straightened her spine, refusing to be in the least intimidated.

'Perhaps your housekeeper could give me some hot tea. I feel quite chilled.'

As a rejoinder it was barely passable, but

she thought she had made herself clear on one count, she wanted female company and she offered none of the warmth that radiated from him. She knew full well that going into his house unchaperoned was unacceptable behavior. But she was terribly curious, and besides, she could not afford to ruin her new habit!

'Your wish shall most certainly be granted.' He paused to give instructions that a message be delivered to Lady Winnington as to the safety of her niece.

Had he chuckled at her reply? she wondered while they made their way from the stable to a covered walk. Shrubbery screened both sides, making a snug passageway in spite of the rain.

'How fortunate I do not have to worry about being compromised — found in your company. With the rain, no one shall be out and about,' she said with a strained smile as they entered a side door to the stately house.

'And you can slip from here the same way you entered once the rain stops. If it stops. Soon, that is.'

She suspected he was vastly amused, and with chilly condescension she swept her eyes up and down his form before turning away to walk at his side. He probably had a plan all worked out that had proved useful before.

She would have run ahead of him if such a thing were possible and if she knew where to go. The place seemed deserted. He left her in a small room, returning promptly. At a discreet knock on the door, Rutledge accepted a tray from an unseen (to Caroline, deep in her chair) person. The tray was placed close to where she sat and tea poured for her into an exquisite china cup.

Once seated by a pleasant fire and warmed by a cup of hot tea, she felt more the thing. Rutledge leaned against the fireplace mantel, holding a glass of brandy in one hand. 'Your brothers are stabling their horses with me as well, but I suppose you know that.'

She frowned at the very notion of being obliged to him in any way. 'Aunt Fanny made the arrangements for all of us, I suspect.'

'With such large accommodations I am able to take the animals for several of my neighbors. It pleases me to do so.' He bent down to stir the fire with a highly polished brass poker, then looked at her again. 'I understand one of your brothers went to a race today. He should be able to seek shelter. Your other brother rode to Bath?'

'Yes,' she agreed, forgetting momentarily that this man was her enemy. 'I cannot fathom why. He said nothing to our aunt, which is more than a little vexing.'

'He has an interest in antiquity, you said?'

She could not recall what she had uttered precisely. 'Roman ruins. At least he has not attempted to dig up London. But Bath?'

'He will be making slow progress, for this rain came from the west. I imagine he is holed up in some snug inn until this weather passes.' Rutledge's voice was smooth and bland, quite innocent of anything outrageous.

'I hope he has not met with an accident.' Caroline set her empty teacup on its saucer, then placed them on the convenient table. She wanted to get up and pace about the room, but somehow she suspected that was not the wisest course. It might place her in proximity to that man, unfortunate proximity.

'A game of cards perhaps? We need a diversion to pass the time, and since the most delightful one is probably out of the question, cards it should be.' He crossed to a table, opened its narrow drawer to extract a deck of cards, then turned to find Caroline struggling to keep her face straight.

'You are a complete hand, sir. I believe you rather enjoy trying to shock this green girl. I fear I don't shock all *that* easily.' She gave him a reluctant smile before joining him at the card table he had pulled close to the fire, drawing up a companion chair before he could do so for her. She thought it best he remain on his side of the table.

He dealt out the cards and they began to play. Minutes ticked by as cards were set down, won, lost.

'You were a very dutiful daughter to remain with your mother so long after her last child was born,' he commented idly. 'I should think most young women would have managed to get to London, given a willing aunt and the means.' He glanced at her and she felt a sudden need to unbutton the neck of her jacket. The room was becoming increasingly warm.

'I am fortunate to have a delightful mother, but one who is, unfortunately, not as strong as she might be. I trust this will be her last confinement, as I do not see how she can bear another child in her state of health. As usual, Papa has gone off to visit several relatives.' Caroline's thoughts winged to her devoted and considerate parents as she played the next card in her hand.

In the quiet intimacy of the room, with only the sound of a crackling fire and the occasional spate of raindrops on the windows, she was lulled into a feeling of closeness, almost companionship.

'As usual?' Those dark brows drew together; he was truly perplexed. His soft, low voice invited confidences.

'For a month or so after the birth of a child, Papa usually goes away on a journey, often a long one. I believe it gives Mama time to be restored to health.' Caroline stopped abruptly as she realized where this conversation was leading her. It was not seemly for a young woman to be conversant with the problems of family planning. That she had learned far more from the midwife who had attended the births of the four youngest of her brothers and sisters than even her own mother guessed was best kept a secret. 'But,' she said, changing the direction of their talk, 'the children are delightful. I enjoyed spending the time with them, especially when they were infants. Babies do not know enough to be naughty, you see.'

That elusive dimple peeped out at her when he smiled. Caroline was so entranced by the sight of it, she quite forgot she was supposed to beware of this dangerous man.

'Your friend, Mary, has never had any children. Does she not enjoy them?'

As a question it was utterly beyond the acceptable. It probed into the most private part of life. Caroline merely looked at

Rutledge and replied somewhat austerely, 'Her husband is often from home. It is difficult to have a family when one is alone.' She thought of the luscious body offered by Diana Ingleby in such a blatant manner, and her resolve to lure Stanhope from his mistress increased.

Rutledge's eyes narrowed and that dimple disappeared, probably forever. 'You are very outspoken.'

'For a young miss, no doubt. My hasty tongue often leads me into trouble.' She rose from the table, placing the cards from her hand into a neat stack. 'I had best return to my aunt's house, Lord Rutledge. I do not know why I did not think of an umbrella before. I trust you have such a thing? If I return to the stables, I ought to be able to make the distance from here to our back gate with little difficulty. The rain appears to have lightened somewhat.'

She hurried to the door, intent on leaving as quickly as possible. Their conversation had ranged from the general to the unacceptable, and she could only wish she was miles away, or at least safe within the walls of her aunt's house.

'You will stay at home this evening, I trust? The rain will most likely be with us another day or two. I shouldn't like to think of you ill.'

He motioned her to remain, then stepped out, returning moments later with a large black umbrella, the kind a footman uses when assisting guests to a carriage.

Caroline could not fathom why he should care in the least what her plans might be. 'I do not recall what my aunt intends,' Caroline said stiffly. Then, more politely, 'I thank you for the tea and shelter. It would have been better had I not come here, however,' she said frankly. 'Fortunately, I have not been observed by any of your staff. There is always the worry of stray gossip. You are very discreet, no doubt from years of practice.'

'My, you do have a hasty little tongue.' He studied her from where he now stood in front of the door. 'Those green eyes of yours tell me more than you think. I hadn't realized how intriguing a green girl would be . . . in more ways than one. I must find out one additional thing, however.'

Caroline was perplexed as to what he meant. She glanced warily at his hand when it reached to touch her curls, then her soft cheek. She took two steps away from him, fearing the warmth that now crept through her veins.

He handed her the umbrella, then before she knew what he was about, pulled her close and kissed her quite thoroughly.

Astounded at such behavior, even from one she didn't trust, Caroline yielded for a few deliciously terrifying moments, then used the umbrella to good effect.

'Green girl, indeed,' murmured the Earl of Rutledge, grinning his amusement and not hurt in the least by the battering he had taken from the long black umbrella.

Her eyes blazing with a frosty dislike, Caroline snapped, 'You are an unprincipled man to behave in such a manner. Good day, sir.' She fled the room, part of her still longing to sit at ease before that welcoming fire and chat with the handsomest man she had ever met.

She raced through the green tunnel of the walkway, past a startled groom, and down the cobbled mews, taking care lest she fall. The back gate was unlatched, and in seconds she was through it and up the steps to the house. Once inside she placed the umbrella when it could be returned later and marched up to her room.

'You have come to no harm, I trust?' inquired her aunt, taking note of the rosy cheeks and blazing green eyes. 'It was civil of Rutledge to be so concerned.'

'Do not ever mention that abominable man in my presence again!' declared Caroline and rushed off toward her room. 'Civil! He does not know the meaning of the word.'

Lady Winnington stared after her with a considering look. Interesting, this come-out season. One never knew what might turn up next.

4

The miserable rain continued until well into the next day. Lady Winnington puttered about the house while Caroline made frequent trips to the windows, hoping to see some sign of her brothers.

At long last a note from Edmund was delivered. 'He has won a tidy purse and now visits a friend in the country,' Caroline reported to her aunt after she finished the brief letter. 'But we hear nothing from Adrian. How provoking of him. 'Tis as bad as being a mother. But at least ours can be spared this worry. What she does not know cannot worry her.' Caroline omitted the distressing news of a shooting that had occurred along the Bath road. She had torn the article from the paper, tucking it down in her bosom before her aunt could be frightened by it.

Lady Winnington gave Caroline a concerned look. 'You refine too much upon Adrian, my dear. After all, he is no longer a lad in skirts.'

Shaking her head, Caroline replied, 'True, but with Adrian I have greater fears. He can get into the most awful hubble-bubble without half trying.' Like being accidentally shot. Her restless steps took her across the room again before she paused. 'I must do something. Perhaps I shall take my horse and ride along the Bath road. I may be able to find word of him somewhere.' Pray he is alive! 'The rain has eased sufficiently for me to go.'

Lady Winnington was about to admonish her niece that her plan was foolish in the extreme, then thought better of such action. Caroline was a bit stubborn, and needed a wiser head and a firm hand that was also stronger. Stanhope would scarcely do, he couldn't even sort out his marriage properly. No, it must be someone else.

While Caroline rushed up the stairs to change into her oldest riding habit, Lady Winnington picked up a pen, dipped it into her standish, and scratched out a note. It might not be the most polished writing, but she thought she conveyed the essentials. Handing it to her footman, she admonished him to deliver it as quickly as possible.

When Caroline returned to bid her aunt good-bye, she found Lady Winnington busily working at a piece of tapestry. Had Caroline given the scene much thought, she would have considered it odd, for her aunt loathed such occupation.

'You must have a cup of tea and a scone or two,' insisted Lady Winnington, setting aside her tapestry in a most casual matter, as though not too concerned about her niece. 'I have ordered a small repast so you will not leave here unfortified. I still believe you are foolish to hare off like this, my dear.'

Lady Winnington greeted the tea tray with barely disguised relief. A plate was heaped with buttery scones, and a pot of Fortnum and Mason's finest strawberry jam sat beside it. She quickly poured a cup of tea, then urged Caroline to sit down and rest. 'You must be sensible, my dear. Your stomach will protest at the most unlikely time, and then where will you be?'

'Hungry, I expect,' replied Caroline with good humor. Seeing the eminent sense of her aunt's suggestion, she perched on the edge of a chair while sipping her steaming tea and nibbling a fragrantly warm scone. 'How fortunate I am to have you to look after me. I can only hope Adrian will be pleased when I come to his rescue.'

'You feel it is so serious, then?' Lady Winnington succumbed to the attraction of the scones, and bit into one with evident pleasure.

'I have this feeling, you see,' explained Caroline, not wishing to mention the shooting. 'I have always been able to sense when the boys are in trouble. And I feel it now. Edmund is, I hope, safe. So it has to be Adrian who is in a pickle. I must try to help him, Aunt Fanny.' Why she felt so strongly that her brother was in trouble was difficult to explain to another. If not shot, it was something dire.

Lady Winnington glanced at the dainty little dock that sat on the drawing room mantel. It was a pretty thing with a cupid who swung back and forth beneath a glass done, and it kept excellent time. Her eyes flickered with relief as she noted the passage of minutes since Caroline had first dashed upstairs and the note had been sent off.

Turning to her niece, she said, 'I wish you success. The roads are not the thing for a young girl by herself. You must take a groom from the Rutledge stables along with you, for you may find him helpful.' Not to mention the propriety of the matter.

'That is an excellent idea, Aunt.' Caroline rose after taking a final sip of tea, brushed the crumbs from her habit skirt, then dropped a kiss on her aunt's cheek. 'Thank you, dearest. And do not worry about me. I shall be fine. I have sufficient money with me for any emergency.' She held up a neat reticule, one normally not taken when riding.

Her aunt walked to the top of the stairs to watch her niece run lightly down the steps, then returned to the drawing room. She subsided on her chair for a moment, then rang for the footman once again. She issued instructions, then added, 'Report back to me as soon as you can.' Satisfied she had done all that was possible, Lady Winnington began to reflect on the day ahead.

Caroline walked quickly to the Rutledge stables, the heels of her riding boots clicking sharply on the cobbles. She was in the process of arranging to hire one of the grooms when there was a stir behind her. The head groom nodded deferentially. Caroline's heart sank.

'Lord Rutledge. Good morning.' Caroline gave him a demure nod, hoping he would mount his horse and be off so she might continue her discussion. The stolen kiss still lingered in her mind. It had haunted her hours, quite unforgettable. She couldn't bring herself to look into his eyes. Surely he would see, know, all that was in her mind. As the silence lengthened she dared to glance upward.

'Out for a ride in this inclement weather, Miss Beauchamp? I had not realized green girls were so hardy. The ones I see in the ballrooms usually look as though they would melt at the first drop of rain.' Those stormy gray eyes now danced with amusement at her obvious annoyance.

He was dressed to the nines, she reflected. Wretched man. He had no right to be so utterly bright-eyed and handsome at this hour of the day with that audacious dimple peeping at her when he smiled. He ought to be looking haggard and worn from a night of dissipation. Only his cravat was less than perfect, appearing to have been very simply tied in a great hurry.

'Pray, do not let me keep you,' said Caroline with a deference Edmund would have declared suspect in a moment. 'I am certain you are eager to leave, perhaps to meet someone?'

'No, no,' he replied with a slow drawl and a wave of his hand. 'I believe I would keep you company this morning.' He strolled over to lean against the stable wall quite close to where she stood. He appeared ready to stand there all day if need be.

'She's asked for a groom to go with her along the Bath road, milord,' inserted the most disapproving head groom, meeting his lordship's gaze with man-to-man understanding.

'You will permit me to hire one of your men for a few hours while I search for my brother?' Caroline sensed she had a better chance of achieving her intent if she were truthful. 'I sense he has need of me. There was a shooting along the Bath road mentioned in this morning's paper and . . . '

'I think a carriage would be best for this purpose, considering the weather.' He nodded to his man, who disappeared for a few moments, then returned leading a pair of bays pulling an elegant phaeton.

'I thought you intended to ride?' said a suddenly suspicious Caroline. It was odd the carriage would be ready and waiting, was it not?

'You assumed it, my dear Miss Beauchamp. Come, let us be off with no more roundaboutation. My tiger will be with us,' he added as though it erased all objections. He motioned the groom forward.

Before she could complain about this high-handed treatment, Caroline found herself being helped up the steps into the elegant carriage. She sank down on the morocco cushions, leaning her head against the squabs in confusion.

She felt rather nonplussed at this turn of events. Had he actually ordered the carriage in advance? And why, more interestingly. Daring a look at him, she could see he was not in a mood to communicate. He nodded to his tiger, who jumped up behind, and they were off.

She remained quiet as he tooled their way out of the city. Being so close to the Hyde Park corner tollgate, it did not take long before they were trotting along the Great Road to Bath. The road was in good repair as far as Turnham Green. The scenery had a fresh, rain-washed look about it. Indeed, a fine mist continued to fall, but not enough to be hampering. 'I actually preferred to go by myself,' she ventured to announce.

'There are times when an escort is helpful. I imagine you will find I have my uses, Miss Beauchamp.'

Caroline tried not to be aware of her escort, which was the silliest exercise in the world, given the circumstances and who he was. It was like trying to ignore the warmth of the sun on a chilly morn when the heat was desperately desired. And she had not forgotten the kiss, even if he had.

It was as they began the stretch across Houndslow that Caroline began to perceive trouble might lie ahead. Even a superb driver such as Lord Rutledge was having difficulty.

'Nasty road, is it not?' said Caroline, taking care to speak during a moment when the road seemed not too horrid. Ruts and badly drained areas made progress slow and difficult. She heroically refrained from reminding him she would have had an easier time of it on her mare.

'That it is,' Rutledge replied. He glanced back to where his tiger clung to his seat, grimly determined he would not fall off while going over the bumps. 'Why do you think your brother decided to go to Bath?'

'His valet handed me some notes Adrian had left behind regarding the Roman ruins in and south of Bath. Apparently he wants to see the head of the goddess Minerva that was excavated some years ago. If only he could find someone who might provide guidance, rather than tearing off on his own,' she mused aloud. She dug into the neat, small reticule she had carried along and fished out some sheets of paper. 'He notes here that some farmer has discovered a hoard of coins thought to be very, very old. I suspect Adrian believes them to be Roman. I imagine he hopes to see them.'

'Your brother seems a determined person. I gather it runs in the family?' This last was said lightly, but Caroline knew full well it was a heartfelt comment.

'I did not ask you to come with me on this journey. You might have sent your groom,' she declared with asperity, at long last yielding to her earlier desire.

'Lady Wilmington would have been most distressed.'

Suspicion reared once again. 'Did she request you to assist me?'

Seeing he might have a spot of trouble with an irate young woman if he told the truth, Rutledge merely replied, 'Well, I can scarce believe your dear aunt would appreciate your haring cross-country with naught but a groom in attendance.'

Acknowledging the truth of this statement didn't totally alleviate her doubts. Further questioning was prevented by a nasty lurch, accompanied by the tiger being tossed to the ground.

Rutledge stopped the carriage to inspect possible injury. Relieved to find his tiger in fair condition, he resolved they must stop at the next inn.

'We shall stop to rest at an inn in Longford.'

'Yes, sir.' Listening to his curt command, Caroline could only be thankful she could shrink against the squabs and remain silent. Now was not the moment to pursue the subject of her aunt. Rutledge looked none too happy.

The carriage was brought to a standstill before the King's Head, a neat building without any pretensions. The tiger assisted

Caroline from the phaeton. Pausing to check on Lord Rutledge, she perceived he was occupied with his tiger and the carriage. She entered the inn to find the landlady, dressed in black bombazine with a white apron and mob cap, waiting to attend her.

'Have you seen a young man about nineteen, tall and thin with black hair? He was wearing a gray jacket and biscuit pantaloons as far as we know.'

The landlady observed the obvious signs of quality in this young woman with the strange green eyes, then glanced out the window to see the impressive phaeton with the two men fussing over it, and nodded. 'He was here.'

'When?' demanded Caroline, clutching her reticule to her chest in her anxiety.

'Yesterday, it be.' The woman automatically poured a cup of strong tea into a brown mug and placed it on the table where Caroline had suddenly dropped onto a chair.

She sipped gratefully. 'He is my brother and I fear a trifle absentminded. He quite neglected to let us know where he would be. I am frightfully worried about him.'

The landlady nodded. 'Aye. My boy had to run after him with his baggage, he near forgot it.'

Rutledge entered the inn at that moment. Caroline rapidly appraised him of the news.

He made a rueful face.

'Have you any word of the roads from here to the west?' he politely inquired of the plump landlady.

'Aye. You've a strong pair. You ought to make it at least to Maidenhead. Beyond there I couldn't say.' She looked out the window once again as though to check the weather. 'Pity about that shooting. One o' the drivers told me it was a fearsome sight.'

Rutledge glanced to where Caroline sipped her tea. 'Ale and a pie, I believe. The same for my man.' He drew up a chair and studied Caroline. 'You are a remarkable young woman.'

'Why, sir?' Caroline shifted uneasily in her chair under his sapient stare. The last thing she sought was the praise of this most odious man.

'Not so much as a word of complaint about that abominable road. No silly pleas to spring the horses. No swoons at the mention of the shooting. I shall most definitely have to revise my opinions regarding green girls.' He welcomed the pint of home brew and the large beef pie that was set before them. The fragrance that rose with the steam set Caroline's mouth watering. Her tea and scones had been a long time ago.

'Perhaps,' she said daringly, 'I am not so

green as you think.' She considered the pie, then added. 'I wish to pay my own way, if you please.' At his dark look, she continued. 'If a man were with you, you would not argue, but split the cost.'

'You are not a man, and dismiss the notion at once. I shall make an accounting to your aunt, if you wish.' He gave her a raking look that made her feel decidedly warm in spite of the chill she had felt upon entering the inn.

Caroline did as bidden. When it came to food, she was never behind to enjoy her meals, and the King's Head possessed an excellent cook.

Once replete, they both stood by the fire to warm themselves, preparing for the damp that pervaded the carriage in spite of being so well protected against the elements. Shortly they left the inn, again heading west.

They paused at Salt Hill, where the stagecoaches all stopped. Rutledge sent the tiger into the inn to question the innkeeper. He returned with a nod, signifying, Caroline supposed, that Adrian had been seen here, and they were off once again.

It was rough going, for the roads were being made worse by the increasing drizzle. Caroline gave the tiger a worried look, then turned to Rutledge. 'I hope we can find that dratted brother of mine soon. I have the strongest feeling he is in trouble.' The matter of the shooting was left unspoken.

Her driver barely spared her a glance, keeping his attention focused on his bays and the slithery road before them. Ruts were filling with muddy water, the surface becoming worse and worse. At Maidenhead they stopped before the Bear Inn, which, as Rutledge explained to her, was where most of the stage-coaches stopped. His relief at their safe arrival was obvious. Caroline began to wish with all her heart that she had remained in her aunt's morning room instead of hazarding this wild trip across the countryside.

She gingerly stepped down from the carriage, then hurried into the dry interior of the inn. No stagecoach was due in for an hour or more, so it was peaceful inside.

About to seek the landlord of the establishment, she espied what looked to be that gentleman involved in an argument with a tall, very familiar young man. 'You Lunun gents think you can get by with sech puny 'curses. Never, I says!'

'Adrian!' Caroline cried in exasperation as well as joy.

At her voice, the landlord turned and, seeing a woman of quality rushing toward him, retreated to stand by the side door, watching.

'Caroline! Whatever are you doing in Maidenhead? And in such rotten weather to boot?' He studied her, then added, 'Don't tell me you rode your mare all this distance, for I won't credit it in the least.'

'No, you abominable boy, I drove in a nicely covered carriage. Is all well?' she inquired cautiously, observing that the landlord was keeping a close eye on them.

'Well,' Adrian replied with reluctance, 'thing of it is, I lost my purse and can't pay my shot. So I holed up here for the nonce 'til I could think of a way to get out. I think he twigged to my being pockets-to-let. He wanted me to leave. Claimed he needed my room.'

'I knew it,' said Caroline softly. She sighed as she heard Rutledge enter the inn. Turning to face him, she nodded at her improvident brother. 'He is here,' she offered with a resigned manner. 'Alive and well.'

'And?' inquired Lord Rutledge, knowing Caroline would waste no time relaying the information he wanted.

'No money, he lost it.' She cast a baleful glance at her brother before addressing Rutledge. 'The thing of it is, the rain is getting worse. Dare we attempt the trip back to London? I'd not harm those bays for anything.'

His admiration grew for the young woman he had decided to help at Lady Winnington's behest. 'You do not mind if we remain overnight, then return in the morning?'

She did, very much. What society might say if they heard this tale was beyond thinking. Yet she had a regard for the bays. She knew full well he would not wish to leave them behind and be obliged to use a pair of job horses. Besides, her brother was present to lend respectability. 'Of course not, sir. 'Twill be getting dark before long. Best be settled by a cozy fire rather than risk the carriage and our necks.'

'Not to mention the bays,' he murmured in agreement, trying hard not to grin at this stalwart young woman. They shortly retired to a private parlor for a hearty meal and more conversation. Rutledge turned to Adrian and began to converse about a variety of things, drawing him out in regard to his plans.

Caroline felt she might just thaw out from the chilly damp that had permeated her very bones. Along about her third yawn, she decided to excuse herself and sleep. She bade the men good night, then went through to the tiny but clean bedroom with the hope she might actually find sleep.

In the morning she entered the private parlor to discover Lord Ruedge and her brother drinking steaming cups of coffee and consuming steak with eggs.

Rutledge gave her a welcoming look, but his words were reserved. With a significant glance at Adrian, he said, 'The road to Bath is in a sad state. Rain has made the road nearly impassable. Even the most experienced coach driver is reluctant to say as to when it will be easy traveling again. Unless your brother is prepared to remain here, I believe the best course is for us to return to London before we are stranded as well.'

Caroline nearly choked on a sip of hot tea. 'Stranded?' Casting a glance at Adrian, who looked as innocent as their younger brother, ten-year-old Thomas at his very best, she answered, 'Perhaps it might be as well if we return to Aunt Fanny's house. You know, Adrian,' she concluded, 'it might be a good idea if you found some expert who could be of help to you in this search. Surely there is someone?'

Adrian took one look at his sister, then Lord Rutledge, and prudently decided he had best agree.

Breakfast concluded, the trio hastily entered the carriage and turned in the direction of London. Caroline had pressed money into Adrian's palm, knowing a young man would not like to have his sister paying his bills. Neither did she wish Rutledge to pay for him.

On the drive to London, she had ample time to mull over the assorted thoughts that had occupied her for some time before sleep had claimed her. One was that she had possibly misjudged Lord Rutledge. Surely if he was such a rake, he would not have such consideration for an inexperienced girl, not to mention her screw-loose brother. Still, she could not quite forget those angry eyes of his when he had watched her with Hugh. She just hoped Mary appreciated what Caroline was doing on her behalf.

Lady Winnington was relieved when Caroline and her wayward brother slipped from the mews through the rear gate to the back entrance of the house. Their discretion meant their absence would most likely go unnoted.

'I am happy to see your faces once again. Adrian, dear boy, should you do such a thing again, you may take yourself back to the country,' she declared in firm tones. Then she turned her attention to his weary sister. 'Caroline, you had best rest, as we are to attend the Bantings' assembly this evening.' She paused, then casually added, 'I believe Lord Stanhope is to call for us.'

Once the two youngsters departed to their

rooms, Lady Winnington sat down with a silly smile on her face and made a few plans of her own.

Caroline was the last one to come down when it was time to leave. Lady Winnington was seated on the sofa in the drawing room, while Lord Stanhope stood casually near one of the windows, turning as Caroline entered the room.

'You look no worse for the wear, my dear Caroline. I understand your brother is up to his tricks again.' Hugh bowed over her hand, then turned to Lady Winnington. 'You are indeed a generous woman to so kindly entertain these three.' He slanted an understanding smile at Caroline.

Her ire at being included with her tiresome brothers lessened slightly. She turned away to face her aunt.

'Well, Caroline is a good girl. It's her brothers, you know. And the passage of time will help them, I am certain. Shall we depart?' She rose, drifting over to the doorway in her usual purposeful manner. Caroline and Hugh followed with shared amusement.

At the Bantings' assembly Caroline was able to relax at long last. She saw neither Diana Ingleby nor Lord Rutledge.

Her relief was short-lived.

'I see your nemesis has arrived,' murmured

Hugh as he partnered Caroline through the steps of a Scottish reel.

Turning her head just a little, Caroline was able to see Lord Rutledge standing near the door. She also observed that Mary was at his side. It was a very pretty, glowing Mary in a silver-and-blue tissue gown that very well became her.

Lord Stanhope missed a step when he realized Mary was with Rutledge. His brow creased with a momentary frown as he glowered at Rutledge.

Caroline gave Hugh a considering look and smiled inwardly. When it came their turn to move down the center, she said very softly, 'They make a charming couple, do they not? He is so dark and she so fair.' Caroline prudently refrained from adding that Hugh and Mary also made a lovely pair. Hugh could do a bit of thinking for himself, she hoped. Caroline had flirted madly with Hugh whenever Diana Ingleby could see them. Now Mary must do what she might, providing Lord Rutledge continued to cooperate.

'I must talk with you when you are free.' Hugh cast a worried look in the direction of his wife and Rutledge, then completed the steps of the dance.

While he walked Caroline to where her

aunt sat with the other chaperons, she chanced to remark, 'My next dance is free. Should you wish to converse now, it would be agreeable.'

'We might avail ourselves of a glass of something cool,' he replied, steering her in the direction of the refreshment room as he spoke.

Caroline waggled her fingers at her aunt to signal all was well, then turned her attention to her escort.

Her aunt was not the only person in the room who took careful note of Caroline's departure. Diana Ingleby was standing on the farthest side of the room. Her eyes quickly espied the two who wended their way through the crowd. Stanhope's magnificent blond hair above those broad shoulders was impossible to miss.

Near the door, Lord Rutledge gazed over the heads of the throng of people to observe the hasty exit and drew his own conclusions. Only Mary was unaware of the situation, carefully shielded from the sight by the thoughtful lord, which was a pity, for she would have been most cheered by the knowledge.

Sipping from the glass offered her by a somewhat absorbed Hugh, Caroline walked to where a bank of flowers was arranged at one end of the room. She plucked a drooping

hyacinth from the bouquet to sniff apprecia-
tively.

'Well, Hugh? What is it you wish to say that
must be said in relative privacy?' Caroline
had been most careful to make this
conversation fairly public. It was a room
where people came and went frequently.
Anyone who paused in the doorway would be
able to clearly see them admiring the flowers
and sipping a refreshing drink. Wine for
Hugh and lemonade for herself. Most proper.

'I don't like Rutledge squiring my wife
about.'

'Really?' Caroline wished she could tell him
he ought to perform that task himself, but she
refrained. Mary had begged her to lure him
away from the Ingleby widow. Presumably
Mary would try to capture his interest on her
own. Caroline believed Hugh needed a strong
nudge. The man had to be blind not to see
that Mary was interested in him.

'It is one thing for him to be gallant and
rescue Adrian from his improvidence. It is
quite another to poach on another man's
territory.' Hugh glanced back to the large
drawing room that had been nearly cleared of
furniture, save for the chairs that now lined
the wall for the chaperons. If he expected to
see his wife, he failed.

'I take it that widow ladies do not count?'

'What? Of course not. Although they do have their uses.' Hugh rubbed his chin with one lean hand while staring moodily at the contents of his glass.

It was not the lighthearted flirting Caroline was accustomed to from her escorts. She stifled a sigh, then set down her glass on a small table. 'I do not see how I can help you with the problem of your wife and Lord Rutledge. A single man often escorts a married lady to a party. I see nothing wrong with it.' That was an out-and-out bouncer, but Hugh needn't know it. 'Especially when that lady's husband completely ignores her. You might ask her to dance, Hugh,' prodded Caroline none too gently.

'I could, couldn't I?' mused the elegant Lord Stanhope out loud.

'I assure you that 'tis quite respectable,' replied Caroline in a dry tone.

After returning Caroline to her aunt, Hugh casually sauntered to his wife's side, where he asked her to dance. Caroline watched with pleasure as the two moved among the small group now dancing to the music.

'Deserted?' said a voice from behind her. It was that rich masculine voice that had haunted more than once.

She knew better than to look surprised, or for that matter to bother turning about. 'Lord

Rutledge. I trust you are well. You suffered no ill effects from the damp?'

'No more than you appear to have done, fair lady.'

At that near compliment Caroline turned away from where her aunt was discussing the best treatment for gout with an elderly friend to stare up at Rutledge.

'I am really obliged to engage in pity on your account, Lord Rutledge. While I am not deserted, it appears you are on your own. Ah, well. 'Tis said disappointments do not kill anybody.' She bestowed a pert look at him, then made to walk from his side.

'Allow me.' Before she knew what he was about, he had adroitly taken her hand and led her out for the next dance. From where she moved about, Caroline could see Hugh and Mary in conversation, so she said nothing to Rutledge about his high-handed manner in the hopes that those two would be permitted a few minutes to themselves.

'You would not be so cruel as to deprive me of your company.' Rutledge's smile as she grimly accepted his partnership for the country dance was wryly amused.

Giles, the Earl of Rutledge, had also observed the dance, then the conversation between Mary and Hugh. He wanted to keep Hugh from returning to the side of this uncommonly brazen miss. That she could countenance a flirtation with the husband of her best friend placed her beyond the pale. Unfortunately. He had found himself reluctantly attracted to her, most likely due to the surprise of her anxiety over her brother, he told himself.

He rather admired that side of her, he admitted, as he took her hand to lead her in a pattern of the dance. All too often family ties were neglected. Her concern the day before yesterday had seemed genuine. That she had tolerated his company when she clearly had not wanted it was estimable, he supposed. Didn't do a chap's self-esteem any good, however. His own had taken quite a battering since he first laid eyes on her. Not only had he felt obliged to defend Lady Stanhope, but also he had deemed it necessary to intrude regarding the divine widow, Mrs Ingleby.

Not that flirting with Mrs Ingleby was precisely a hardship, but heaven help him were she to take a notion to sink those delicate white pearls she called teeth into his skin. He had heard how tenacious she tended to be.

'Is your brother finding another interest?'

'Yes, at least I devoutly hope so. This afternoon he muttered something about going to the British Museum.' Caroline gave

Rutledge a limpid look, then glanced to where Diana Ingleby now conversed with Lord Mortland.

'And you, Caroline? How do you occupy your hours when not chasing after your brothers?' They had paused in the pattern of the dance, so she was at his side.

She inspected his face before answering. The beguiling dimple was not in evidence. 'I keep watch on my aunt,' she decided to reveal. What he would make of that, she really didn't care.

'Perhaps you ought to have a regard for yourself. It does not seem quite the thing for a young miss to be flirting with her dearest friend's husband, you know.'

He didn't know why he had said that to her. What was it to him if she became the latest *on-dit* of the *ton*? Her faint gasp satisfied him that she had been shocked by his remark. Perhaps she would take it to heart. He hoped so. Once she left Hugh alone and poor little Mary was no longer the object of raised brows and pitying looks, he could return to his own pursuits in clear conscience.

Caroline held her tongue until the dance concluded. Then she glared at him, saying quietly, 'You know not what you say, my lord. What you see is not always what it seems to be.' With that pithy comment, she whirled and marched off to her aunt's side. They left shortly after that.

Rutledge smiled with satisfaction as he led Mary, Viscountess Stanhope, into the next waltz. Over near the door, her husband looked fit to throttle him, then followed Caroline from the room. With a wicked raising of an eyebrow, Rutledge swung the little viscountess about with extra dash.

5

'Are you certain that we do the right thing with this plan? I think it is infamous that you must resort to such measures to gain the attention of your own husband.' Caroline was again stirring the tea in her cup while seated in the gold-and-white drawing room of the Stanhope residence. She took a dainty sip, then gave her friend a wary look. 'I fear your husband will be excessively displeased when he discovers the truth of the matter.'

Viscountess Stanhope crumpled slightly in her chair, giving Caroline a sad little look. 'It seems he merely wants a wife to say yes and amen to every word he utters — when he is home, which is seldom. I declare, it is enough to put a saint out of temper.'

'Rutledge seemed prodigiously pleased with himself last evening,' said Caroline by way of answer. She reflected a moment, then continued. 'At least you appear to have acquired a champion. He looked so fierce when he compelled me to dance with him.'

It was impossible to conceal all she had felt at his behavior during the dance. Never had she received such an extreme of civility. Was it possible to be frozen with excessive courtesy?

Mary darted a sudden, rather perceptive glance at her friend. She placed her cup on the tray, then composed her hands in her lap. Taking a deep breath, she said, 'Perhaps we *ought* to abandon this silly idea.'

'What can you mean by such a remark?' A puzzled frown creased Caroline's brow for a moment, followed immediately by determination to see this dearest of friends truly united with the man she loved so deeply. If only Rutledge retreated from his watchdog position. There were moments when he was almost likable. Or more.

Throwing up her hands in a gesture of resignation, Mary said, 'It is wrong. I had no right to ask you to assume such risks.'

At the word *risks* Caroline stiffened her spine and sniffed. 'No man is going to frighten me. Although he does not precisely frighten me, but,' she said in all honesty, 'he does affect me in some manner. 'Tis most curious.' Her thoughts jumped back to that shattering kiss.

'You feel warm and shivery, your heart beats too quickly, and you feel as though in a dream?' prompted Mary quietly.

'How did you know? 'Tis a rather peculiar thing.' Caroline studied the contents of her teacup as though she might find an answer there.

Mary gave a wise little smile, but said nothing as to her opinion of Caroline's affliction. With a shake of her head she said, 'I suppose nothing will dissuade you?'

Not missing the hope in her voice, Caroline replied quite staunchly, 'Nothing in the least. I shall do my very best to convince that odious Mrs Ingleby to look elsewhere for her *affaire d'amour*. It is possible she has already done so, for you must know I saw her with that elderly Lord Mortland again last night.'

'He is neatly dressed and his hair is not so *very* white,' reflected Mary in a soft voice.

'If he continues to eat like he did last evening, he will be as fat as a flawn in no time. Goodness, I could scarcely touch a bite and I do believe he consumed two plates of food. I suspect Diana Ingleby lost her appetite when she espied Hugh dancing with you, then gave him her plate.'

'I shouldn't wonder but what she eats very little in order to keep that fine figure of hers,' said Mary in a considering voice.

Thinking of the magnificent bosom that had been so prominently displayed, Caroline was inclined to disagree. 'Nonsense, she eats well. Only I believe she is like so many other women who eat at home, then merely nibble when dining out to give the impression that they scarce consume a bite of food. She could never keep that luscious figure did she stop eating!'

Mary's laugh rang out at the image Caroline brought to mind. 'You are good for me,' she declared. Sobering, she added, 'I only wish I could set aside the notion I am harming an interest you have.'

'If you mean the Earl of Rutledge, be assured that I stood little to no chance of gaining his attentions even before I agreed to help you.' Caroline was resigned to the loss of Rutledge as a prospect, had she entertained the hope of catching his eye in the first place. Which she had not in the least, she assured herself. She placed her cup on the tray, then rose. 'I had best return to my aunt's. Edmund came home late last night and I want to hear about his stay in the country. I am uneasy about him — both of the boys, as a matter of fact.'

'It was kind of Lord Rutledge to come to your aid in the matter of Adrian.' Mary rose to accompany Caroline.

'He did it only because my aunt requested that he help. I would like to know what she wrote in that note that brought him so promptly,' Caroline said. She walked slowly to the door, adjusting her bonnet, then drawing on her gloves. At the door she turned. 'Stay where you are. Pennyfeather will see me out.' She gave Mary a mock salute. 'To our success!'

'Our success,' echoed Mary. When her friend had gone, Mary sank slowly into her chair to sit in contemplative silence for a long time. If only she were more brave . . .

★   ★   ★

Edmund was in the breakfast room and about to make a hearty meal when his sister paused at the doorway. Glancing up from his plate, he beckoned her to the table. 'Come in, do. I have so much to tell you.'

Lady Winnington was behind Caroline, and the two joined Edmund at the table, Caroline grimacing at the size of his portion of food.

'Pray, what has you in such high spirits after the nasty weather we have sustained these past days? Mrs Wanting declared we might have need of an ark if it continues.' Lady Winnington reached out for a delicate scone and took a nibble.

Simpkins entered and, seeing the mistress at the table, slipped out to return moments later with a pot of hot tea, which he placed on the table close to where she sat. She absently poured herself a cup and sat listening to her dearest nephew. A worried look crept into her eyes as he talked.

'Well, the most famous thing, actually. When I went to that race, I won a tidy bundle, don't y'know? Then I rode down to Chubby Kenyon's home south of here. Kenyon Oaks is quite a place, I can tell you,' he added as a bit of an aside. 'They raise racehorses. I saw a prime one, a really sweet goer. I gave Lord Kenyon all I had won as a partial payment for her, but I need a good deal more blunt to close the deal on Marigold. Oh, wait 'til you see her, Caro, she is the most smashing mare I've yet clapped my eyes on. With Thunder, the horse I bought last week, this mare will be a grand beginning to my stud.' He enthusiastically waved his fork about in the air to emphasize his point.

'And how much more money do you need, pray tell?' Caroline had a sinking feeling that these few weeks in London were going to be costly for her family, especially Edmund, if he continued to buy horses.

He told them the price of the mare, how much he'd placed down on her. 'I need a bit over forty pounds, but she's worth every cent of it.' He seemed to wish he had someone to support him in the face of the dismay on his sister's face.

'Heavens,' murmured Caroline, aware her

brother's allowance didn't extend to such extravagance after purchasing the other horse for a similar sum, not to mention a new wardrobe.

A glance at Lady Winnington revealed no more favorable response. Then her brow smoothed out. She cleared her throat, saying, 'I expect a first-rate racehorse stud will be a costly matter to set up. Pity you are not in the line for marriage. A healthy dowry would assist you to no end.'

'Me? Leg-shackled?' His expression would have been laughable at any other moment.

'It is done all the time, dear brother. But I fear you are rather young for marriage. And I pity the wife who is taken solely for convenience' sake,' she added, thinking of poor, sweet Mary. 'You shall have to approach Papa.'

'Papa!' He shook his head. 'Not on your life. I ain't in Dun Territory yet, y'know. Maybe,' he mused with great optimism, 'I shall get lucky at the races again.'

'And you might lose everything,' declared Caroline with little sympathy. 'You know how Papa feels about gaming.' She glanced at her aunt, praying that dear woman would not get any harebrained ideas. Her face was bland, but that was no clue to what went on inside her head.

'I still say . . . ' Edmund insisted, stopping his flow of words at his sister's dark look.

'Promise me you will not try to get the money you need by gaming.' Caroline placed her fists on the table, meeting her brother's gaze with an intent stare of her own. Not by the blink of an eyelash did she reveal that she inwardly wished she had the money to hand him so he could buy his dreams. One had to be firm with Edmund, and she had bills of her own to pay. He must learn to plan and proceed wisely. A little waiting would be good for him. 'Promise?'

'I promise,' he muttered, downcast from his earlier enthusiasm.

'You will get the money, I feel sure of it.' Caroline relented to pat his hand, relieved to have won her argument so easily. Edmund pushed aside his empty plate, then left the room with a determined expression on his face. That he was not going to give up just yet was plain to see.

'I believe it will be a better day. The rain has ceased,' declared Lady Winnington. She had risen from the table to look out the window. She was glad Caroline didn't know what was going on in her head. She had plans to make and now she needed to get her niece out of the house for a few hours this afternoon. 'Do you intend to shop for that pretty plaid we discussed the other day?'

With the Prince Regent declaring his interest in the exiled Stuarts, planning to have Canova sculpt a monument to them, the Stuart tartan — and others as well — had become very popular. Ladies were having dresses made, cloaks and fancy bonnets as well.

'I think that red with the touch of white and green would be vastly becoming for me. I shall go to the shops this afternoon to select the fabric. Will you come with me?' Caroline paused on her way from the room to look at her aunt.

Lady Winnington made a dismissive gesture with her hand. 'No, child, I am promised to Mrs Banting this day. Take your maid and be off when you please.' Once Caroline had whisked herself around the corner, Lady Winnington breathed a sigh of relief.

Caroline and her maid left the house an hour later, Simpkins having summoned the usual Baxhall and his hackney for them to use.

The vehicle drew to a stop before the impressive front entrance to Schomberg House. Since the regent ordered so much of his furnishing fabrics from Harding, Howell and Company, a stylish occupant of this building, Caroline had assumed that this was undoubtedly the best place to search for the tartan she wanted.

She entered the fashionable shop with Daisy trailing behind, muttering in awe at the sight of the goods displayed.

Just inside the door was the area for furs and fans. Caroline eyed a fan in green lace with mother-of-pearl sticks. She passed by the elegant trifle with a sigh.

They trailed past the array of lovely jewelry, French clocks, and modish millinery to find the dress department, where the finest silks and muslin were to be found.

'Lord-a-mercy,' said the maid, 'I never saw the likes of it afore, and that's the truth.' She gazed at the floor-to-ceiling selection of fabric-bolts and bolts of it — with dazed eyes. Sheer anglo-merino wool from the merino flocks at Windsor Park competed with Spitalfields silk in charming patterns designed for the royal family.

'Quiet, Daisy,' whispered Caroline. The maid would have many tales to tell when they returned to their country home, an event not too far away. It seemed Caroline's Season was going to be an unsuccessful one, what with her foolish, but devoutly sincere, desire to assist Mary. A flirtation with a married man was no help in finding a husband.

There were a number of bolts of tartans displayed at the end of the first counter. Walking quickly to these, Caroline deliberated. She hadn't realized how many pretty patterns existed. When she had said she was going to buy the Stuart tartan, she hadn't known about the rest. The Cameron was such a lovely shade of green and the Hunting Fraser a delightful red with blue, green, and white. How could she possibly choose? The Royal Stuart was perhaps her favorite of all, and not simply because the regent had declared an interest in the exiled Stuarts. True, any loyal subject of the crown would wish to honor them as well.

What really attracted her was a book she'd read. Sir Walter Scott had made the Scots' history of days past seem so vivid. Caroline had enjoyed his tale *The Lady of the Lake* when it had come out in 1810. She had read it aloud to her mother. How they had sighed at the closing line, 'And now, 'tis silent all! — Enchantress, fare thee well!' The words still had the power to affect her.

'Shopping, Miss Beauchamp?' The beautifully lush tones of Mrs Ingleby's voice reached through the abstraction that had fallen over Caroline.

At the sound, she turned to see the elegantly dressed woman standing close to her, next to the tartans.

Hesitantly smiling at the woman she had wished would take a long trip to Belgium, she replied, 'I thought to have a dress of tartan.'

'They are lovely. Is there any particular pattern you prefer? That Stuart would be charming with your hair and coloring.' Diana Ingleby held up a length of the fabric against Caroline, examining the effect of it.

Flattered that the widow would bother to take notice of a 'green girl,' as Rutledge persisted in calling her, Caroline blushed. 'I do like it.' Even if she did not care for the woman, Caroline had to admit she was always exquisitely dressed in the very latest mode.

'Look, Giles, Miss Beauchamp has selected such lovely fabric for her dress, the Stuart tartan. I adore the effect of this red against her hair, and the touch of green is perfect with her eyes.' Diana's voice fairly purred. 'Do you not think she has chosen well?'

Caroline spun about to discover Lord Rutledge not far behind her. She clutched at the length of tartan as his icy glare seemed to envelop her, leaving her feeling as though she had been left out in a Highland blizzard.

'Lord Rutledge! How pleasant to see you,' she said most warily.

'You intend to indulge in the current fad, Miss Beauchamp?' His words were clipped, his manner barely civil.

Bewildered as to what might be the cause of his animosity, Caroline murmured, 'I had thought to buy a length of this lovely fabric, yes.'

'I had not realized you were such an avid supporter of the prince's expensive notions. Nor was I aware you embraced the Tory philosophy. But then, perhaps you have discovered a way to pay for all his follies. He certainly hasn't.' The words were bitter and manner abrupt.

Never had Caroline been more conscious of someone being a member of the peerage than at this moment. His hauteur was tangible, as was his obvious contempt.

'I thought the Canova sculpture was to be paid for by the French, from the surplus funds after returning their loot to Rome.'

Caroline almost raised the point regarding Mrs Ingleby, who had certainly pushed forward the idea of Caroline in the Stuart tartan, then belatedly realized she had been cleverly manipulated. Mrs Ingleby had wanted Caroline to be discredited in Rutledge's eyes. But what possible difference could it make to her? Surely she could not believe Caroline to be a threat to her ambitions! That was quite laughable.

Darting a wry glance at the luscious widow

in her deep red anglo-merino walking dress, Caroline returned her gaze to Rutledge. 'I confess I had not remotely considered the politics of the matter, sir. I saw what I believe to be a charming pattern and wish to purchase sufficient to make a pretty gown. Upon reflection, I shall buy the Stuart. As Mrs Ingleby says, the color well becomes me.' Looking at the widow again, Caroline added, 'That yellow and black Menzies plaid would suit you nicely, madam.'

Ignoring the fuming peer at her side — who had totally ignored the defense she had presented — Caroline turned to the hovering clerk, clearly fascinated with the conversation that had been going on before him. 'I shall have ten yards of this, please. At only two shillings a yard, it is an excellent buy and will make a lovely carriage dress.'

'Well, well,' said a familiar voice. Lord Stanhope approached the trio, a jovial smile on his face. 'Caroline, your aunt told me that you were most likely to be found here.' Taking note of the aloof Rutledge and the triumphant-looking Ingleby woman, he went on, 'Doing a bit of shopping this afternoon, Rutledge?' He bowed politely to Mrs Ingleby. Caroline noted with a great deal of satisfaction that his attitude was more than a trifle on the cool side.

'Miss Beauchamp is going to purchase a length of tartan — Stuart tartan — for a carriage dress, so all the world and his wife may view it when she goes out to the park of an afternoon,' Lord Rutledge said, bestowing an even frostier glare on poor Caroline's head.

The look she returned was defiant. No man was going to tell her what she might or might not wear, merely because he was a Whig. Politics, indeed. She had heard how angry the Whigs had been when the regent had had the effrontery to have someone announce before Parliament that he planned a monument to the exiled Stuarts. She knew it had less to do with the cost than with the memory of the family it celebrated.

Quickly sizing up the situation, Lord Stanhope gallantly rose to Caroline's aid. 'I shall deem myself most fortunate to be favored with the first sight of this creation. We shall enjoy a drive through the park once the gown is ready to wear. I trust that it shall not take long?' The warm look he bestowed on Caroline was a strong and agreeable contrast to the cool glance he had given the widow.

Happy that Mary's plan was proceeding so well, Caroline smiled with delight. 'That would be welcome, Hugh. I always find your company most pleasant.' She slanted a flirtatious look at him, the sort she would never have dared to give Lord Rutledge.

After paying her bill, preferring the discount given for such cash transactions, she accepted the arm Stanhope offered. 'Good day to you, madam, Lord Rutledge. I trust you will have success in finding just what you want, Mrs Ingleby,' she said. Tucking her hand inside the crook Hugh had made with his arm, Caroline made it quite clear that Lord Stanhope was not included in that wish.

'Quite a minor contretemps, my dear Caroline. Would you care to tell me what prompted all that?' Hugh studied the angry young woman at his side as they left the building.

'While you take me to a mantua maker so this tartan can be transformed into a carriage dress, I shall tell you what has transpired.' Daisy quietly slipped into the open carriage before they drove off.

It didn't take long for Caroline to relate what had occurred. Hugh frowned, seemed about to say something, then changed his mind. 'I have something I wish to discuss with you, perhaps tomorrow. I must think it over more carefully first. Do you have plans for this evening?'

Upon learning that Caroline and Lady Winnington intended to go to Almack's, he declared he would see her there.

Caroline worried all the way home that a patroness of the important assembly would castigate her for flirting with a married man. They might do such a thing, indeed did so, but that was different. It was a case of do as I say, not as I do.

★   ★   ★

Giles escorted Mrs Ingleby from Schomberg House, barely concealing his ire. He had been trapped into this scene, although how Diana Ingleby might have known that Caroline Beauchamp would be shopping here today, he couldn't imagine. Perhaps she had merely taken clever advantage of the situation. He had never underestimated her cleverness.

The nerve of Caroline Beauchamp, to flaunt that tartan in his face. She could scarce *not* have known the implications of her action. Buying a tartan merely because she thought it would be pretty on her? Poppy-cock. Not that it wouldn't be ravishing against her hair.

He was utterly furious with Stanhope. How could the man be so taken in by a beautiful pair of green eyes, even if they were enhanced by that exquisite dark hair? Her skin was incredible. When most young things were plagued with spots, Caroline Beauchamp possessed velvety skin touched by a blush of pale rose. Remembering what it had been like to kiss those sweetly curved lips, he considered something ought to be done about the chit. She shouldn't be allowed to go about as she pleased.

Especially when it appeared she pleased to go toward Stanhope, a happily married man. Well, perhaps not so happily, recalling the anguish he had seen flash across his wife's face during the assembly when she had observed Stanhope with another woman.

He saw Diana Ingleby off in a hackney, much to her obvious displeasure, then strolled along the street for a block. Taking a chance that Caroline would not fail to appear at Almack's that evening, he turned in the direction of the Stanhope mansion. A plan quickly formed in his mind, one that would help set Caroline in her place.

A half hour later found him exiting the Stanhope house, jauntily whistling a merry tune as he briskly walked toward his club on St James's. Vastly pleased with his astute handling of the situation, he inhaled a deep breath, grinning at the thought of confounding Caroline Beauchamp. He could not permit her to ensnare poor Stanhope. Why, the man would be caught in that beauty before he knew what he was about. No, a wiser, saner head was needed here. And, Giles decided, he was just the man to relish the job.

Ignoring his motivation, which was suspect at best, he applied himself to a glass of wine and some excellent conversation with an old school chum. Once comfortably settled in his favorite chair, surrounded by the aroma of leather, good wine, and agreeable friends, he relaxed with the knowledge that he couldn't fail in his mission. He hoped that someday Stanhope would come to thank him for the sacrifice being made on his behalf.

* * *

Across London, Lady Winnington sat absorbed in a game of deep Basset. Intent upon her cards, she gave no thought to the hour or the risk involved in her play until she had won the final hand. Mrs Basting tapped her shoulder.

'My dear, if you plan to attend Almack's this evening, you had best return home before your niece should ask uncomfortable questions.' Mrs Banting had been apprised of the situation and heartily endorsed her friend's ambitions.

Glancing at the long-case clock near the door of the establishment, which catered to ladies of breeding who cared to indulge in a bit of gaming, Lady Winnington exclaimed in horror, 'Gracious, whatever was I about!' She rose from her chair with all speed and in minutes was borne away from the place in Mrs Banting's carriage.

'I shall be there this evening, just in case you have need of my support, dear Fanny,' said Martha Banting after stopping in front of Lady Winnington's house.

'I shall welcome it, you may be sure. But I am prodigiously pleased, Martha. I have won a sizable part of what dear Edmund needs for that stud he wants so badly. Poor boy, with all those children my sister has, 'tis no wonder there are few shillings to spare for his future. Adrian's either, come to think of it. Only he doesn't seem to know what he wants in life yet and Edmund does.'

Mrs Banting nodded sagely, knowing how costly it was to set up a child in reasonable style.

In his customary starched voice Simpkins revealed that Miss Beauchamp was in her room. Giving a relieved nod, Lady Winnington slipped up the stairs and into her room with no one else the wiser. For all her niece knew, she had been prudently napping in preparation for the evening ahead. The money she'd won was carefully put away. She could see to the washing of it come morning.

Caroline had spent the past hour restlessly pacing back and forth in her bedroom. How she wished she had her confidante with her now. All she had been able to do was to send a note urging Mary to attend Almack's this evening, with Rutledge if possible.

A tap on the door brought her maid with a note in hand. An answer. Eagerly reaching for it, Caroline's face was wreathed in a smile when she finished reading.

'Good news, miss?' Daisy was fascinated with everything that went on in this town. It had been like something from the pages of one of those storybooks to watch her mistress out with the lords and ladies. She gazed hopefully at Caroline.

'Mary writes she will be at Almack's this evening. And she will be with the odious Lord Rutledge. That man! How dare he tell me what I might wear. Merely because he is opposed to anything the prince might fancy doing does not give him that right.'

'All this talk of lords and princes gives me the shivers, and that's the truth!' declared the maid in awed tones.

Caroline chuckled, then went about dressing for dinner. The gown she wore was a simple one of palest green muslin trimmed with delicate pink silk rosebuds. It reminded her of the other gown she had worn, that evening when Lord Rutledge had been so condescending to her. Only the trip out the Bath road had been free of that feeling. Then he had treated her like any other gentleman might.

Once dressed, she surveyed herself in her cheval glass. Although the gown had a low neck that went straight across the front from sleeve to sleeve, it actually was quite demure, as the sleeves went to her wrist, ending with a charming ruffle. There were tiers of ruffles at the hem with dozens of tiny rosebuds tucked in them. She was delighted with the effect. Lord Rutledge would not be able to look down that handsome nose and criticize her in any manner this evening. Of course, one did take greater care to be circumspect when attending the assemblies at Almack's than at other placcs. Reputation, you know.

Lady Winnington was enthusiastic in praise of Caroline's looks. 'You shall be the belle this evening, my dear. What a pity you must spend so much time with Stanhope. I pray that he and dear little Mary get this all sorted out before the Season comes to an end. Not that I find you remiss in your duty to your friend. It is merely that it endangers your own chance for happiness.'

Since she had been thinking much the

same, Caroline found she could not scold her aunt for her words. 'He has dropped the Ingleby woman, I feel sure of that. Today he positively turned his back on her. If only Rutledge does not ruin our entire effort.'

'He is a handsome young man, is he not?' Lady Winnington darted a glance at her niece, noted the faint blush that spread rapidly across that lovely skin, then took another bite of her delicious turbot in mushroom sauce.

'I believe I have heard you declare time out of mind that a handsome man does not necessarily have the brains to match.'

'If one can pick and choose, 'tis better to choose brains than looks. Rutledge has both, my dear, and don't you forget it. You are sailing in dangerous waters when you decide to cross him, remember that.'

Caroline gave her a wavering smile and wondered for how long she would have to endure Almack's. But what could possibly happen at such a public place?

6

When Caroline entered Almack's that evening it was with more than a few trepidations. The seventh heaven of the fashionable world was undoubtedly the place one wanted to be, but Caroline suspected that the exclusiveness of the establishment was largely due to the insistence that no young woman could hold up her head in society unless admitted to the Wednesday night assemblies of the aristocracy. That, in addition to the knowledge that all in attendance were carefully screened by those despots, the patronesses, and were highly eligible as marriage partners. For after all, Almack's had to be the cream of marriage marts.

Caroline had heard some rather tall tales of the intrigues, not to mention the diplomatic arts, used to obtain vouchers. Even, it was rumored, discreet blackmail. One presented that all-important card before being allowed to cross the threshold. Those furious nobility who were shut out gnashed their teeth in impotent frustration. There were no appeals for the excluded.

Caroline's aunt had whispered once that

the patronesses were petty tyrants. Mind you, she had never hinted anything of the sort while inside the sacred precincts of the Assembly Rooms.

Lady Cowper was the most popular, and Caroline sighed with relief to note that the lovely lady was on duty this evening. That high stickler, Mrs Drummond Burrell, was not in evidence, and for that Caroline breathed a sigh of relief.

'You look quite charming this evening, Miss Beauchamp. She does you credit, Fanny.' Lady Cowper smiled graciously at them both before passing them along to Lady Jersey.

Caroline feared this woman, for she was the uncrowned ruler of society. Were Lady Jersey to take note of Caroline's attempt to attract Stanhope, she might not find it amusing. And though Caroline had an excellent sense of humor, she did not wish to test it.

'Lovely,' commented Lady Jersey as she studied Miss Beauchamp while she sank into a graceful curtsy. Since Emily Cowper was the acknowledged authority on fashion, Caroline Beauchamp must indeed be rather special. Rumor had reached Lady Jersey's ears of a contretemps regarding a length of tartan. She had found it amusing that

Rutledge had been so cut up over the business. The girl would bear watching. Anyone who could stir the wrath of Diana Ingleby was someone of note. Also, the Earl of Rutledge usually never paid any attention to young girls. If he was taking notice of this one, she was quite out of the ordinary. Could it be that the earl was deciding at long last to settle down and begin a nursery? After all, Diana Ingleby was out of the question. Totally ineligible. Besides, she transferred her affections too often to count. Hadn't she been dangling after the handsome Lord Stanhope just days before?

Following her curtsy, Caroline walked with Lady Winnington to where the mothers and chaperons sat in agreeable conversation on the chairs ranged along the wall.

Caroline was chatting with Sarah Thurlow, a young blond of seventeen summers with whom she enjoyed visiting, when she saw her brother approaching. Beside him strolled a tall, thin young man with a nice sparkle in his eyes. Caroline found herself liking him on sight. She introduced Sarah, then waited.

'Caroline, Miss Thurlow, may I present Henry Kenyon, Lord Kenyon's eldest son.' The gentleman bowed, and the girls smiled pleasantly in return, dipping pretty curtsies.

Caroline clamped her mouth shut lest she

say something utterly ridiculous. *This* was Chubby Kenyon?

Mr Kenyon presented himself as a partner. Caroline quickly accepted, giving her aunt a merry look.

'Do I detect a hint of laughter in your lovely green eyes, Miss Beauchamp?' He deftly led her through the first measure of a country dance. He possessed a grace unusual in such a young man, and one so tall in particular. Caroline had found they tended to be terribly awkward. Not so Henry.

'How ever . . . ' Caroline began, then stopped, unsure whether she dared to inquire.

When they met once again, he grinned and continued, 'I suspect you were about to ask how ever did I acquire the nickname your brother uses. Am I not right?'

Relieved, Caroline nodded in reply.

'As a lad at Eton, I found my greatest pleasure in stuffing myself. More padding when I was felled in a fight, you know. I grew out of fighting and eating about the same time as I began to sprout upward.'

'But the label lingers on?' Caroline couldn't refrain from a giggle at the nonsense of it all. Glancing to one side, she caught the severe gaze of Lord Rutledge on her and her smile faded. She was not flirting with Hugh, so why the frown? What a pity Lord Rutledge had to be so wretchedly handsome and well-to-grass to boot!

'Nothing to be sad about. I'm well used to it, you know.' He took her hand to lead her down the center of their set.

He seemed to sense Caroline's change of mood, for he was considerate of her in the extreme. What a pity she must cling to Stanhope this evening. It would be much more agreeable, and undoubtedly profitable for her future, to flirt with Lord Kenyon's heir. Mindful of the four youngsters at home, not to mention the twins, she well knew her duty. Yet she had promised Mary and she could not desert her best friend. Perhaps once firmly secure, Mary would assist in finding Caroline an eligible *parti*? It was a thought to consider.

At the conclusion of the country dance, she withdrew to watch the formation of a quadrille. Lady Winnington had forbidden her to dance this outrageous and difficult dance.

'Most of the dancers are as gawky as country clods, tripping all over their feet,' Lady Winnington had declared, citing the example of an overweight peer who had fallen heavily to the ground when attempting an *entrechat*.

The denial hadn't bothered Caroline overmuch, as she considered the dance a bit pretentious, with all those ballet-like movements. Now, the waltz — that was something else. Princess Lieven had been the first one who dared perform the dance on such hallowed ground. It was she who had given Caroline permission to dance it as well, declaring Caroline to be exquisitely graceful. Lady Winnington had been forced to acquiesce to such a command. One did not deliberately deny a patroness.

'I am surprised, Miss Beauchamp. You are not going to dance the quadrille? Perhaps I should offer myself as a partner? I cannot imagine you would willingly forgo such delight.' Rutledge spoke from a discreet distance — close enough so he could speak softly, yet far enough so as to be most circumspect.

Caroline tilted her pretty little nose. 'It is hardly necessary, my lord. My aunt has decreed that I shall not join in the dance. She considers it rather silly.' Caroline didn't know what possessed her to say such nonsense. Lady Winnington might indeed think the dance silly, but one scarcely said so in public.

Her remark earned her a sharp look from Rutledge. 'I trust you have not expressed such sentiment near Lady Jersey. You do know she was the one to bring it here from France.'

Casting a nervous glance toward the group now performing the quadrille, of which Lady Jersey was a polished member, Caroline replied, 'Of course not, sir.'

'Rather quiet evening.' Rutledge stood with his hands clasped behind him, surveying the large room. 'I see your protector is absent?' He studied her carefully composed face as he made his outrageous comment.

'I cannot imagine who you conceive that might be,' said Caroline in a furious whisper. Her eyes flashed green fire when she glared at him, momentarily causing him to stare as he absorbed their rare beauty.

'Perhaps I chose the incorrect word, but you must confess Stanhope did come to your aid at Schomberg House.'

It was quite obvious that Rutledge had neither forgotten nor forgiven Caroline for purchasing that length of Stuart tartan. She could not wait to wear it.

Bowing her head in faint agreement, Caroline frostily replied, 'A lady appreciates the escort of a true gentleman.' Her look intended to imply that Rutledge would never qualify for such a position.

'Stanhope and I were once rather close,' mused Lord Rutledge quietly.

'I daresay you have only yourself to blame

if that has altered. I find Hugh to be all that is amiable.' With that parting shot, Caroline edged away from the disturbing man who always frustrated her. It was that kiss, she had decided. She kept recalling her tumultuous feelings.

The dratted man persisted in following her. Caroline found her arm being taken and herself steered ever so gently toward the refreshment room. Handed a glass of the lukewarm lemonade, Caroline raised her brows and sighed. 'I wonder that Brummell does not make some devastating remark about the blandness of these refreshments.'

'Yes, I can see that simple lemonade would not do for you. Champagne, most likely? Ambrosia most certainly, for such delicious lips as yours, Miss Beauchamp.' The irony in that remark was unmistakable and his expression forbidding.

'Why, Lord Rutledge!' She fluttered her lashes, then sweetly smiled. 'Good gracious, I can scarce believe you mean to set up a flirt. Or are you seeking a quarrel with this poor 'green girl'. Fie, sir, 'tis a May game you make of me and I'll not have it.'

'You cannot deny you have taken a fancy to Stanhope,' he said. Had his look been more severe she would have wilted.

'You have no right to ask such a question. You men flit from lady to lady with no one taking you to task. I know,' she sighed dramatically, 'it is different for you. You may do as you please in all things.' She withdrew slightly, then turned to see Mary walking toward them. Caroline managed a discreet wink, then extended her hand. 'How pleasant to see you, my dear.'

'Am I too late? I intended to get here earlier, but things contrived against me.' Mary looked fresh, her cheeks naturally rosy, and eyes bright with mischief as she turned to Rutledge.

'Allow me to make up for it all, Lady Stanhope. Will you partner me in this waltz?' He offered his arm. Mary glanced at Caroline, then with a sly smile accepted his escort.

'Only if you call me Mary as you have been wont to in the past.' Her small face glowed with pleasure. Caroline thought Mary looked delicious in another silver-and-blue gown. It was of a simple design and hung straight to the floor without ornamentation. It gave her a taller, more regal appearance, if one can have such at a mere five feet.

A pang of regret assailed Caroline as she observed Mary glide across the floor in Rutledge's strong arms. How she envied

Mary. Knowing well what it felt like to be in those arms, Caroline rubbed one of hers with her hand, recalling the moment quite vividly. She drifted across to where her aunt sat, thinking Rutledge ought to have escorted her.

Lord Pierrepoint sought her hand belatedly, and Caroline agreed rather than remain watching Rutledge and Mary whirl about the floor.

She was returning to her aunt's side when Lord Stanhope walked up to her. 'Hugh, how lovely to see you,' she said most politely, her eyes dancing with her delight in meeting the object of her flirtation again. How provident. Even if Mrs Ingleby could not attend, there was always someone who would pass the news along. And prattle-boxes abounded tonight. Caroline hoped the widow got an earful.

'May I have this dance, Caroline?' He didn't wait for her answer, but drew her along with him, taking for granted she would not deny him her company.

Caroline decided that handsome men tend to become a trifle spoiled.

They began the first of the patterns. 'What if I had said no?' she said with a catch in her voice. It was hard not to laugh at Hugh, for he looked quite put out. Then he chanced to catch sight of a couple across the room and he frowned.

'How long has that been going on? Every time I encounter Rutledge lately he is with Mary. My Mary!' He gave a significant look in the direction where Rutledge now stood chatting with Mary, flirting outrageously with her, from what Caroline could tell.

'Some time now, I suspect,' declared Caroline, wanting to rouse a fierce jealousy in Hugh. Not enough to make him call Rutledge out, mind you. Just enough to bring him to his senses. 'They dance rather well together.'

Hugh maintained total silence throughout the remainder of the dance, much to Caroline's amusement and growing expectations. He looked grim. Darting glances at the various patronesses in attendance, Caroline hoped they did not attribute his glum countenance to being her partner.

Once the final notes of the dance concluded and the various dancers had paraded about the floor, Hugh guided her toward the refreshment room. Caroline stifled a groan of dismay. Insipid lemonade again?

'If the cake were better, I would urge a sample.' Hugh glanced at the table, then began to stroll along the room, leading her with him. Seeing no one was near, he quietly said, 'Caroline, I have a great favor to ask you.'

'I cannot imagine what I might do for you.' An involuntary laugh escaped her. His request brought to mind the one from Mary, that Caroline seduce Mary's dearest husband. And see what that had brought her!

'Tell me, how often is she with Rutledge?' Hugh allowed the question to be dragged from him against his will, it seemed, for he appeared to be sorry once it was said.

Caroline turned her head to catch a glimpse of the two in question. Mary was smiling at something that had been said. Apparently Lord Rutledge could charm when he chose. Carefully skirting the truth, which was that Caroline did not actually know, she said, 'She seems quite taken with his wit, does she not?'

'Would that it were all.' Hugh appeared genuinely upset, although he tried to conceal it.

Bestowing an engaging smile on her friend, Caroline refrained from chuckling at his woebegone expression. 'Hugh, I almost believe you actually have a concern.'

'I do,' he said most ruefully. Then, as if a dam had burst and he now felt unrestricted, he went on, 'I know she was pressured into our marriage because it was advantageous to both families, but I have grown to care deeply for her. I have tried to give her the freedom she must long for, but it becomes more and more difficult as time passes. Look at her. She is like a wisp of moonlight in that gown. Her hair is so lovely. And she laughs and flirts with Rutledge!'

Sobering, Caroline took a serious look at Hugh and saw he indeed felt anguish at the sight of his wife with another man. She ventured to say, 'Perhaps she is but flirting with him because she sees you with someone like Diana Ingleby?'

'Do you think so?'

His eagerness was encouraging. Yet Caroline felt unsure what to tell him now. 'It is possible' was all that she permitted herself to admit. Mary had not said a word about revealing their plan to draw Hugh away from the Ingleby.

'Then do me that favor. Lure Rutledge away from her. I saw him talking to you when I entered the room earlier. He seems fascinated by you. You are the first unmarried woman I can recall him paying the least attention to in donkey's years.' Hugh studied her a moment, then added, 'It should not be that difficult, for you are an exceedingly lovely young miss.'

Caroline's pleasure in this compliment was

dimmed when she perceived that Lord Rutledge had undoubtedly overheard the last of it while fetching a drink for Mary. What meaning he placed on those innocent words she could only guess. From the corner of her eye she observed him pick up a glass of orgeat, then return to Mary's side.

From where she stood she could see her brother Edmund dancing with Sarah Thurlow, her aunt making her way to the card room, and Mary chatting happily with Rutledge.

Edmund was safe, as was her aunt, for the stakes were always small here. But Mary and Rutledge? For the first time Caroline wondered if Mary might have acquired a tendresse for Lord Rutledge. After all, he was handsome and polished. So was Hugh, but she had nearly given up on him. Did that mean she had turned her interests to Giles, as she referred to Lord Rutledge in such fond accents? Although she and Mary had not discussed whether Caroline ought to tell Hugh of their plan, Caroline figured it best to keep silent. But what to say? Perhaps Hugh needed to do more than merely pay attention to his wife. It might be he must woo and win her.

'I see what you mean about them,' said Caroline consideringly. 'And you truly care for her? Why do you not simply tell her so?' Caroline thought it would save a good deal of time if the two involved got straight to the point.

It was not uncommon for a husband and wife to be silent regarding their feelings toward one another, it seemed. Indeed, the bond forged between Mary and Hugh was likely to be more legal than romantic. Caroline resolved that her marriage, if it came about, would be based on love, no matter what she had promised Papa. So far she had not felt one throb of that feeling she cared to admit.

'Care for her?' Hugh echoed. 'I believe you know that as well as I do. How can I speak, Caroline? And have her laugh at me? I know Rutledge; he finds married women safe for dalliance. I will not have him dallying with my wife!'

Alarmed at the fierce tone in his voice, even if she had wanted it earlier, Caroline tried to soothe him. 'I shall try, dear Hugh. I cannot promise I shall succeed, for he seems to have the oddest notions about me. However, if you will remain my friend long enough to take me for that ride in the park on Friday when I wear my new tartan carriage dress, I will do what I can to help you in return.'

Hugh shook his head, sighing with relief. 'I

141

wouldn't trust anyone else to do this, you know.'

Caroline tried not to laugh. She accepted her promised partner for the next dance while thinking how wildly improbable her situation had become. Mary had asked her to seduce her husband. Now Hugh wanted Caroline to seduce Mary's flirt, one Mary had encouraged just to make her husband jealous. What great fun the playwright Sheridan would have had with such a situation.

The thing of it all was that Caroline now wondered if she dared to confide in Mary. Suppose Mary had changed her mind? Supposing she no longer wanted her tongue-tied husband, but sought the arms of her dear Giles? She could well put a spoke in Caroline's plans, whatever they might be. For Caroline had not the slightest idea how to go about luring Rutledge away from Mary. That politely civil visage seemed most off-putting.

When her eyes had met his this evening, there had been a look of censure in his. What man in his right mind would believe a flirtation from her after all that? Whatever else Rutledge might be, he was not stupid.

Henry Kenyon sought her hand once again, and she welcomed him with considerable warmth. How lovely to have such an uncomplicated partner.

'Edmund tell you his plans to start a stud?' he said abruptly.

'Yes. Dear me, we hear little else from him.' Caroline gave Henry an encouraging smile, for she could tell he had something on his mind.

'Costs a mint. Miss Thurlow, she's well set up, is she not? Has a fine dowry?' He appeared to be casual, but his glance toward Sarah was anything but.

Realizing where his talk was leading, Caroline frowned, then replied, 'I believe she is. However, Edmund seems horrified at the thought of being leg-shackled to anyone at this point in time. I do believe all he thinks about is horses. In his room are stacks of Rally's Racing Register, The Sporting Magazine, and who knows how many other publications. I should think that any man who was truly interested in Sarah Thurlow would find no opponent in Edmund.'

'She is quite pretty, you know, and with all that money, well, a fellow would be daft . . . ' He nobly sought to appear disinterested in Sarah.

'I thought she seemed quite pleased when you were introduced to her. She mentioned she enjoys riding. Perhaps you might invite her to go out with you some morning?' Caroline casually suggested.

Henry eagerly agreed to that notion and left Caroline standing as he hurried off to find Sarah.

'Deserted again, Caroline? Really, how inconsiderate of him.' The warm drawl was seductively close.

Rutledge had appeared suddenly at Caroline's side, and she began to wonder if the evening would never draw to a close. She caught sight of Hugh walking toward Mary. Turning to Rutledge she smiled back at him, a trifle grimly, she feared.

'How good it is that I am not a 'Miss Nancy' to object at your familiarity, sir.'

'You? An overly prim one? Somehow I cannot quite see such a thing, dear Caroline.' The look of censure had gone. In its place was something she could not define. Those dark gray eyes had a melting quality to them she found most disconcerting. What was he up to now?

'You were calling me Miss Beauchamp earlier, sir.'

'But I overheard my good friend using your given name and decided it suited me quite well to use it, too.'

'I gave him leave to do so. Hugh has been a friend for ages,' Caroline could not help but say in her defense.

'And I thought you were a friend to his

wife as well. Come, dance this waltz with me. I am not done with you this evening.'

Caroline resisted his compelling touch on her hand for only a moment, then she gracefully yielded. Lady Jersey was watching them. It would not do to be observed brangling at Almack's. As she moved into his arms, she caught sight of an approving look from Hugh. Good grief, he thought she was going to his aid.

'Fortitude, Caroline, my dear,' Rutledge murmured a trifle close to her. A faint grin flashed across his face as he caught sight of her expression.

'I do not trust that caressing note in your voice,' she shot back before she considered how it would sound.

'How quickly you learn. I am disappointed that your neckline is so . . . banal this evening. Not that your gown is not lovely. But . . . banal.' That warm gaze roamed across the expanse of creamy skin exposed by the square cut of her gown.

Caroline smiled sweetly while wondering how to be avenged for all these little barbs of his. 'I am so sorry to have disappointed you. Perhaps you will like the carriage dress I intend to wear on Friday better. Weather permitting, I shall enjoy a drive in the park. With Hugh, naturally.' Of course, Caroline neglected to explain she had coerced Hugh into taking her on that drive.

'Why not with me?' Rutledge found himself saying, much to his amazement. By Jove, this miss would not further separate his once best of friends from his sweet little wife. 'Would you not enjoy a drive behind my grays?'

Having longed to ride in that sumptuous carriage for all the *ton* to see and admire, Caroline gave him a considering look. 'Maybe.' She fluttered her lashes in what she hoped was a demure manner.

'Minx,' he replied in a low, appealing voice that sent shivers down her back, in fact, all the way to her toes. Did she really know what she was getting into with *this* flirtation? She had the distinct feeling she was sinking — drowning — certainly going over her head.

'I shall inform him that I shan't have need of him, if you insist.' Caroline wondered if Rutledge would credit her maneuverings. She found them hard to accept and she knew, or thought she knew, what she was about!

'I insist.'

Caroline kept her face carefully blank to hide her surprise. He actually intended to take her out for her ride. How thankful she was that the mantua maker had promised all speed with the carriage dress. Because of the tartan, the dress was to be simply cut, with few seams and little trimming. That made it easier to sew. A few tucks above the hem and a bit of decoration at the bodice would be all the extra touches required. Caroline could not wait. How lovely a way to avenge herself for those little darts.

'How is your brother, the one who wants to dig up Bath and half of London?'

'Adrian? Odd you should mention him. He has been strangely quiet of late. I do hope he hasn't conceived a plan to exhume the oldest part of the City or some such.' Caroline was glad they could find a neutral subject upon which to converse. Brangling and sniping was not in the least to her taste.

'Perhaps he has found someone who is excavating for a new building? As long as he does not get into legion with the resurrectionists,' Rutledge said absently, referring to the men often called body snatchers.

Alarmed, Caroline gave him a wide-eyed stare. 'Oh, you do not think he would resort to employing such men in his efforts? That would indeed be infamous!' Her face paled and she compressed her lips as she thought of what her dearest papa might say if he got word of such scandalous behavior. That her brother might get involved with the scurrilous men who hung about graveyards at night to dig up bodies before they had barely come to rest frightened her greatly.

Lord Rutledge had tossed out the comment without a great deal of consideration, and now he could have bitten his tongue when he saw her genuine fear. He sought to atone for his rash words:

'If you like I can do a bit of sleuthing, try to discover what he's up to. Brothers are apt to keep things to themselves rather than burden a sister with them, I suspect.'

Caroline bestowed a grateful look on him, her heartfelt gratitude shining clearly in her eyes. Rutledge had the oddest sensation of how knights of old might have felt.

'If it would not be too much trouble, I would be vastly in your debt, sir.' Her tremulous smile seemed genuine.

In his debt was precisely where he wanted her at the moment. So he smiled what Caroline thought a highly satisfied smile, saying, 'No trouble in the least, dear lady. And I shall inform Hugh that he may take someone else with him in the carriage come Friday.'

Would that it was not Diana Ingleby, hoped Caroline as she nodded her acquiescence. The waltz ended. Caroline returned to her aunt in a haze.

Lady Winnington rescued Caroline from further confusion by announcing, 'We simply must go home, my dear. The hours have sailed past all too fast.'

That might be debated, Caroline wanted to say in return, but didn't. 'Of course, Aunt Fanny.' She took leave from Rutledge with a peculiar sense of relief. He had her terribly befuddled. He had frowned at her, watched her, smiled at her — in short, disconcerted her no end. And now he was to help her with Adrian?

Caroline stopped short at the remembrance of Rutledge's words about Adrian. Fortunately, her aunt could not see the alarmed expression on her niece's face due to the dim lighting from the flambeaux outside Almack's. They entered the hackney, Caroline fussing over her aunt a trifle.

'Home, Baxhall,' declared Aunt Fanny in a carrying voice.

'Well, girl, you had quite an evening of it from what I could see.' Lady Winnington drew her wrap a bit closer around her in the chill of the wee hours.

'Yes, that I did.' Her aunt didn't know the half of it. What would she think if Caroline were to tell her that Adrian might be in trouble? It would be just the stupid sort of dumb nonsense Adrian might do.

'You are to drive in the park Friday with Stanhope?'

'That has been changed. Lord Rutledge insists I drive with him behind that superb set of grays,' she said, exchanging a look with her aunt. Even in the dim light provided by one flickering oil lamp, Lady Winnington could make out the naughty grin.

'I see.'

'La!' cried Caroline softly. 'I wonder what he will make of my new carriage dress.' At the perplexed look on her aunt's face, Caroline added, 'He detests the Stuart tartan, dear ma'am. What shall he believe when I present myself arrayed neck to ankle in Stuart?' She giggled, revealing the mischief that danced in her eyes. Satisfaction!

'You do have a problem. Cancel the drive?'

'I cannot, for I hope that Hugh will seek Mary's company while I drive with Lord Rutledge.'

The hackney pulled up before the house on South Street, and Simpkins was there to open the door, escorting the women into the house, then quickly returning to pay the driver a handsome amount. From the expression on Baxhall's face, it seemed he believed he might just stick to servicing this house alone. It certainly appeared that buying that carriage from the lord hard pressed for cash had been a wise move.

Mounting the stairs to the upper floor,

Caroline avoided her aunt's penetrating gaze. 'I shall think of something.'

'Wear a different carriage dress, then.' Lady Winnington was too pleased with the sack of coins won in tonight's play to be overly upset with her niece. Tomorrow she would have a tidy pile to polish.

'But I said I would wear my new dess, and even if he did not know which one it is, I shall, and so shall a number of others. I cannot be thought a coward, dear aunt.'

'I suppose not,' replied her aunt vaguely.

Realizing her aunt had her mind on other things, Caroline paused before her door. 'You had a good evening?'

'Indeed, yes,' declared Lady Winnington with pleasure. 'I am accumulating a lovely hoard of coins, you know. What fun to polish such a nice sum.' She drifted off to her room, her mind occupied with the game of deep basset she intended to enter on the morrow.

Caroline stared after her aunt, all the troubles of her tartan dress, Mary and Hugh, her dratted brothers, and the puzzling behavior of the handsome Lord Rutledge set aside. Whatever was Aunt Fanny about?

7

A faint breeze blew in through the window of Lady Winnington's sitting room. It was a smallish room, papered in pink roses on a cream background, with a profusion of her favorite pieces of furniture crowded about her. The day was warm and she welcomed the cool air. She busily worked away at polishing her hoard, as she gaily referred to the pile of coins neatly set out on a linen towel. Not even the butler, who did the silver and plate, handled Lady Winnington's gaming profits.

A peek around the door revealed to Caroline that her aunt possessed excellent spirits this morning. Slipping quietly into the room, Caroline peered over Aunt Fanny's shoulder. 'I believe you did rather well last evening. I had not realized Almack's permitted anything but chicken stakes.'

'Dear girl, good morning. I trust you slept well? 'Tis a lovely day to polish, is it not?' The answer to Caroline's question was neatly avoided.

Caroline picked up a square of paper to roll up a stack of ten gold coins, adding it to the pile of rouleaux placed off to one side. There were rouleaux of shillings to one side, gold to the other. The thought struck Caroline that Lady Winnington might easily have worked in a banking house. She was precise to a pin and could estimate the sum of money involved by a mere glance at a pile of coins.

'You have a wondrous amount there. Extraordinary luck at the cards, ma'am?'

'Heavens, yes. Pity, today's coinage is so disgracefully dirty. Not that it was ever clean, mind you. I so dislike tarnished, grubby coins, as you well know. 'Tis imperative I clean them, lest my hands be equally soiled, for I prefer to take off my gloves when gaming. I simply adore the glitter and color of silver and gold. And I detest dirty hands.'

She held up a shiny shilling in her cotton-gloved hand to admire the gleam of the silver. The coin was placed to one side with others, then she picked up a guinea, polishing the gold with a soft cloth until it glowed with a soft luster.

'I shall be interested to see what this new coin we are to have shall look like when it is produced,' murmured Lady Winnington. ''Tis to be called a sovereign and will depict Saint George and the dragon on one side. I shall like that, I believe.' She flashed a twinkling smile at Caroline before returning to her diversion.

'Have you been playing cards more than usual?' asked Caroline with great casualness. She did not wish her aunt to be on guard with her answer. From the pile of coins to be cleaned it would seem that either Aunt Fanny had been prodigiously lucky of late or that she had gambled often. Or both. Either way, Caroline grew concerned as she considered possible consequences. Were she and her brothers too great a drain on Lady Winnington's resources? She hoped not.

'I daresay we play much the same,' replied Lady Winnington with less than her usual truthfulness. 'Mrs Banting and I have enjoyed a bit of a flutter, true.'

'She has excellent *ton*, a charming lady,' murmured Caroline, wondering why she felt dissatisfied with the answer just given her.

'You did nicely last evening.' Lady Winnington handed Caroline a stack of crumpled bank notes, indicating the basin of water, the fresh linen, and a small charcoal iron. 'You may as well keep busy while we chat.'

Thinking this had to be the strangest way of passing time yet devised, Caroline performed the task she'd done before for her aunt. She rinsed the bank notes, patted them dry, then ironed them until they were freshly crisp.

'I fear my life is becoming something of a tangle.' Caroline stacked the ironed bank notes to one side, glancing occasionally at her aunt to see if she was attending as she recounted the details of the previous evening.

'Do not permit this business to sink your spirits, dear. As I understand it, Mary wishes you to lure Stanhope from the widow Ingleby. Mary also set up a flirtation with Lord Rutledge in hopes of making Hugh jealous. Now Stanhope desires you to entice Rutledge from Mary's side. What says Mary to this, and for that matter, what part shall Rutledge play?'

'How succinctly you put it all, dear ma'am. I fear I do not know which way Mary leans at the moment. That was a rather sly smile she gave me last evening as she went waltzing off with Rutledge. Perhaps she has changed her mind,' said Caroline with a touch of wistfulness. 'After all, Lord Rutledge is not only handsome but an entertaining man. He most assuredly had Mary enthralled. Hugh said Rutledge watched me last night, and I am sure I do not know when or why. Whenever I caught sight of him, he was dancing attendance on Mary.'

'And yet you say you are to drive out with him in the park.' Lady Winnington's ears astutely caught what wistful note in her niece's voice.

'On Friday,' agreed Caroline. 'I dare not consider what shall happen when he catches sight of me in that tartan.' She darted a roguish glance at her aunt. 'Pray, do not tax me with my foolishness on this. I am quite determined to wear my pretty new dress. If it comes on time,' she added half to herself.

'One wonders if you hope the mantua maker will be late with her delivery,' observed Lady Winnington wryly.

'Aunt! I am not the least afraid of Lord Rutledge.' That this statement appeared to directly contradict her previous remark seemed to bother Caroline not one whit.

'So you say. He is possessed of great address, I must say. Could be intimidating to a girl of lesser backbone. I wonder how the widow Ingleby shall respond to all this,' mused Lady Winnington softly, holding up a guinea to admire it before wiping it and setting it on top of a stack. 'I scarce believe she will take the removal of two gentlemen without a whimper. Mind you, I cannot say that Rutledge has been in her pocket for some time. Perhaps she intended to lure him back?'

Caroline raised her head to look out the window. Across the mews and through the trees and gardens could be seen the stately grandeur of Thornhill House. Rutledge was undoubtedly still abed, or perhaps he was having steak and ale with his morning paper. She tried to picture him in a domestic situation and failed miserably. The image of him still abed, that muscular body tangled in soft linen sheets, hair tousled, and those wicked gray eyes half closed with sleep, she dared not consider at all. Her father had a prim nightshirt he wore to bed; her brothers seemed to ignore night wear. Which group did Rutledge favor? Somehow she couldn't picture him in her father's flannel.

She turned her thoughts from such an improper subject and back to the problem at hand.

What was his motivation in all this? At first she had considered him a gadfly. His alteration into a helpful friend surprised her. He had done well with Adrian, even offering to check on the boy again. That had been gracious of one who seemed quick to criticize her.

She tried not to remember the episode in that cozy room on that rainy day not so long ago. It was difficult, especially since every time he touched her, memories flooded back of being crushed in those strong arms, kissed with a passion she hadn't dreamed existed.

Those mysterious gray eyes of his could hold her utterly spellbound with little effort. Unfortunately.

She placed the small charcoal iron on its stand and stood staring out the window. A thought struck her most forcibly. Whenever she had dared to meet those eyes, there had been a special glint in them. She now realized what it was. Laughter. He found her amusing, although heaven knew why! A small crease formed in her brow. When he viewed her in the new tartan carriage dress, those eyes would not laugh at her. But what would he do? Or could he do, more to the point. Why, he would assuredly refuse to take her for a drive!

A rather feline smile crept across her face. Caroline knew she would regret missing a drive in that fabulous equipage behind the special pair of matched grays. But the alternative — changing her dress for some-thing unobjectionable just to please him — was to subject her person to his influence again. Only her aunt, Hugh, and possibly Mary knew that Rutledge had insisted upon taking her to Hyde Park in Hugh's place. No repercussions would result if there were a change in plans.

Might he think it a deliberate, willful act? Hardly likely. Like Hugh, Rutledge had been spoiled with a surfeit of females languishing after him. He would scarce believe there was a woman alive not perishing to have his attentions, and especially a drive in his park phaeton.

Dare she continue with this outrageous plan Mary had dreamed up? That is, if Mary still desired to have Hugh in her arms and bed?

'I believe I ought to have a chat with Mary.'

Lady Winnington placed the last of the polished coins in a stack on a paper, then rolled and twisted the small square to form a rouleau. 'That might be a very wise idea, my dear. If, as you wonder, she has altered her intentions, the sooner you know, the better.'

'Precisely.'

By the time nuncheon had been consumed, Caroline was quite of the mind she would present herself at the Stanhope residence with the hope that Mary would be truthful regarding her plans. About to retire and dress for the visit, she was surprised when she met Simpkins coming down the stairs as she was going up to her room.

'Lady Stanhope is here to see you, miss. I have shown her to the drawing room. I trust that meets with your approval?' He well knew the friendship that existed between Lady Stanhope and Miss Beauchamp. It would be most unlikely that his actions would be frowned upon.

'Splendid, Simpkins. She's just the person I wished to see.' Caroline raced up the stairs as quickly as was seemly, hurrying into the drawing room with outstretched hands. Mary stood at the window, gazing out at the street.

'You cannot see Thornhill House from here, can you? I thought you might.'

'I see it from my room, which overlooks the mews as well.' Caroline dropped her hands, feeling somewhat foolish at the enthusiasm of her welcome, since it had been ignored. 'Sit down, please. Would you have a dish of tea, perhaps?'

Mary nodded and Caroline rang for tea. Simpkins had anticipated the event, for within minutes a tray was brought to the drawing room and placed on a dainty rosewood table her aunt had recently purchased.

Once safely alone, Mary sipped from her cup, then carefully placed it back on the saucer. 'Do you drive in the park with Giles tomorrow?'

'Why not?' Caroline challenged. Something was in the air — tension, an unseen gauntlet about to be flung down.

'And you wear the Stuart tartan dress?'

'I shall,' declared Caroline with a degree

more confidence than she felt.

Mary shook her head. 'I wish I might sort this all out. It seemed so simple when we began. I hoped that you would seduce Hugh away from the Ingleby. Period. I never envisioned it would become so complicated.'

Cautiously Caroline queried, 'Complicated? What, pray tell, is so intricate regarding this?'

'I doubt that Diana Ingleby will forgive you for stealing away both Hugh *and* Giles, my dear goose cap.' Mary again picked up her cup, took a sip, then held the cup as though to draw warmth from it. In her silvery blue muslin round gown with a delicate white bonnet trimmed in blue ribands, Mary looked like a fairy escaped from an enchanted garden. She made Caroline feel like a Long Meg.

'But I haven't stolen anyone,' protested Caroline, her ire rising. Why must everyone harp on her being such a green girl? She was aging rapidly . . . by the hour, as a matter of fact.

'Not yet, but she does not know our plans, and we can scarce inform her, can we? She will see you, however. And I wonder will Hugh be with her . . . or me?'

'What are your plans now, dear Mary?' On the mantel the little cherub swung back and forth inside the clock dome, the faintest of ticks clearly heard in the silence of the room.

The cup and saucer clinked as they were abruptly set on the table. Mary jumped up to pace about the room before she came to a halt at Caroline's side. Slowly Caroline rose to face her, studying the sweet face framed in the prettiest bonnet anywhere.

'I am not sure anymore. Not sure at all.' With these unsettling words she hugged Caroline, silently begging her to understand and bear with her. Then Mary turned and slipped from the room, leaving Caroline standing on the middle of the rug with her mouth slightly ajar.

Moments later Lady Winnington hurried into the room. 'What did she say, if I'm not being vulgarly inquisitive?'

Caroline slowly walked to the same window where Mary had stood gazing out at the street below. 'She said she does not know!'

'My, my,' said Lady Winnington in an exceedingly pensive voice. She sank onto her favorite chair, absently poured a cup of tea, then sipped the restorative. 'That is an unexpected turn of events, is it not?'

The afternoon dragged by with both ladies offering possible solutions and discarding them just as quickly as they were presented.

By dinner no decision had been reached.

'I shall simply wear my tartan dress and do what I agreed to do to the best of my ability,' Caroline declared over the vegetable soup. 'If all these other people cannot make up their silly minds, it cannot be helped.'

★　★　★

When the tartan carriage dress arrived Friday morning from the mantua maker, it was everything Caroline had hoped it would be. It skimmed over her figure in a flattering manner. A pert bow nestled beneath her bosom, and a narrow scarf draped across her shoulders in a dashing way. The sleeves hugged her arms, with tiny pearl buttons marching up from each cuff. Pearl buttons also decorated the top of the bodice in a neat line down the front. It was cleverly constructed and rather difficult to put on, but once dressed, Caroline was vastly pleased with the results.

She possessed a Marie Stuart bonnet which had three jaunty feathers on it. On this she now attached a small bow of the tartan.

'Quite fetching, Caro,' drawled Edmund from the open door.

Picking up her gloves and plain red silk reticule, Caroline turned to face him, her fears not totally concealed. 'Thank you, dear brother. Do you know where Adrian has been keeping himself? I fear he will tumble into some manner of pickle before the day arrives for you both to go home.'

'No, can't say I do. Aunt said you are about to take a drive in the park with Rutledge. Didn't know you flew so high.' He lounged against the frame of the door with youthful arrogance.

She drew a deep breath before replying. 'I cannot fathom why a mere drive in the park should be deemed so dangerous. I'm not *such* a green girl, you know.'

He raised his eyebrows in astonishment. 'Dangerous? What flummery. He ain't a pattern card of respectability, but near enough.'

Annoyed she had spoken with so little thought, Caroline marched past him and down the stairs. In the hall, she informed Simpkins she would be in the morning room while awaiting her escort.

Like every other servant in the house, Simpkins knew full well who was expected to arrive to take young Miss Beauchamp for a drive in Hyde Park. It was quite an honor to be able to announce the Earl of Rutledge, a real Top-of-the-Trees.

Darting a hesitant glance at her aunt, who

sat placidly attacking her piece of frazzled tapestry, Caroline firmed a trembling mouth, squared her shoulders, and said, 'I had best go.' The statement came out a whisper.

'Yes, do, dear child. You will be home before you know it.' As a remark intended to comfort, it left something to be desired.

Gloves carefully covering the hands rarely revealed, except to those closest, Caroline bravely set forth down the hall. Her chin tilted up, eyes defiant, she glided forward, one hand outstretched. 'Lord Rutledge, I am so pleased to see you. 'Tis a glorious day for a drive in the park.'

'I take it this is your new carriage dress.' He studied her silently, walking slowly around her before coming to a halt a foot from where her face now flamed with anger. He nodded. 'It fits.'

She fairly blazed before she happened to note his eyes. That amused glint lurked in the depths of gray once again. The wretched man was laughing at her!

'Lovely,' she responded. 'It would be so depressing to drive out in your charming phaeton and be unfit.' Her voice purred with her delight in besting him.

She didn't miss the quick compression of his lips and wondered what other outrageous thing she might think to say.

'Shall we depart? I should not want anyone to miss the sight of such a friend to the royals,' he said. He offered his arm, and she accepted. In moments they had strolled down the steps of the house on South Street to where his pearl gray park phaeton stood with the matched pair of grays in harness.

Caroline had to admit it was a beautiful sight, sighing with true pleasure. She glanced up at him, then smiled. 'Exceedingly fine, sir.'

A grin flashed across his face, to be replaced with a bland look Caroline couldn't fathom. She allowed him to assist her into the carriage, then watched as he joined her, taking the ribbons with that air he possessed in such abundance.

They headed toward the park, slowly passing Thornhill House as they went. From behind a row of trees, the stately home rose, Corinthian pillars giving it a classical touch. Caroline's eyes lit up. 'Neat but not gaudy,' she commented.

As a compliment it was by far and away lacking. Women had gushed paragraphs of praise on the exquisitely proportioned house, the color of its stone, and the beautiful grounds. The entrance hall reaped the highest encomiums, while the grand staircase had been declared the absolute peak of design. The gallery and great drawing room were beyond description, women had declared in effusive puffery.

Startled, he looked at her in affront, then again compressed his lips. Caroline wished he would laugh out loud. She had heard it once and quite liked it.

'Aye.' He turned the corner into the park, then said, 'I'm pleased to see you were not overwhelmed by it.'

Encouraged by his lack of ire, Caroline continued, 'Mind you, I have been told the music room is somewhat wanting for acoustics, but then, some ears are more delicate than others. I myself couldn't say, as I've not seen it nor attended a concert there.' Her hands fiddled with the red silk reticule in her lap, wondering if she had gone too far this time.

'That shall be corrected.'

Caroline glanced at him, curious to know what was intended by that answer when he spoke again:

'I saw your brother Adrian yesterday.'

She was not encouraged by the tone of voice. 'And?'

'He does live in the clouds, doesn't he?' Lord Rutledge shook his head. 'I located him near Cornhill Street where a chap is digging the foundation for a new building. Adrian was all over the place, trying to prevent the brick from being laid so he could poke about in the muck.'

'Oh, dear,' said a highly dismayed Caroline. Further questioning was postponed as they neared an oncoming carriage. Lady Jersey approached in her elegant equipage, a woman Caroline didn't recognize seated with her.

Discreet bows were exchanged. Lady Jersey took note of the tartan dress and smiled. So this was what the contretemps had been all about. She said, 'Lovely carriage dress, Miss Beauchamp. And it goes so well with your charming bonnet. Do you not agree, Rutledge?' Her eyes narrowed while she awaited the reaction from the most toplofty of Whigs to this clear affront from one who apparently bore Tory sympathies.

Lord Rutledge cleared his throat. 'Now that you mention it, I believe it does.'

Caroline choked back a laugh. As a compliment it equaled hers regarding his house. She longed to say with great solemnity that her dress fit, but knew Lady Jersey would think her totally daft. She turned to face Rutledge, trying to look severe and failing dismally.

'How kind of you to notice.'

Sensing that there was some unspoken intrigue here, Lady Jersey signaled her carriage to proceed. She studied the pair opposite with assessing eyes before they disappeared from her view. 'What a luscious *on-dit*,' she exclaimed to her friend, who nodded in amused agreement.

The pair in the pearl gray phaeton rode on in silence until hailed by other friends, equally curious as Lady Jersey as to how a Stuart tartan came to be in a Whig carriage.

In a moment of peace, Caroline impulsively declared, 'I am sorry, my lord. I had no idea.'

'Don't spoil it, Caroline,' he said. 'It's quite out of character, and you aren't in the least sorry. In fact, I suspect you are enjoying this enormously.' There was no clue as to how he felt. Nothing to tell her if he was truly angry with her. But he had been laughing earlier. What an exasperating man he was.

'Well!' she said with a huff. 'If I say I am sorry, you may well believe I am. I do not say things I do not mean.'

'Shall I store that away in my memory?' The teasing quality of his voice failed to mollify her.

'I do not care what you do with it. I resent being called a care-for-nobody when I am not.' Then she espied a familiar carriage and her breath caught in her throat. 'I do not credit what I see,' she said softly.

'Our friend Hugh has the lovely Mrs Ingleby up with him. I wonder how she managed that,' he said in a voice so soft Caroline barely heard his words above the sound of the carriage wheels on the park drive.

'How could he!' she choked out in mortified accents. She had gone to such great pains to lure Hugh away from Diana so that Hugh might return to the fold, so to speak. And the cabbage-head had turned to Mrs Ingleby rather than his wife! To make matters infinitely worse, Caroline espied Mary in the distance, riding her pretty mare. Edmund, Henry Kenyon, and Sarah Thurlow made up the rest of her party. There was no way that Mary could fail to see her husband with the widow. How utterly stupid of him.

Nearly speechless with anger, Caroline clenched her hands lest she throw something at Hugh, not that there was anything at hand that would be a good missile.

'Don't put yourself into a stew, Caroline. Surely he isn't worth that?' The low voice at her side counseled wisdom, but he didn't know the half of it.

She ignored the quizzing look from the earl. Caroline was out of reason cross with Hugh. How could he jeopardize his marriage with such foolishness?

The carriages drew alongside, Lord Rutledge executing the briefest of bows, Hugh doing the same. Caroline bestowed an icy glare on both the occupants of the other carriage, then turned to the earl. 'I see several friends with my brother. Could we not move forward to greet them?'

It was a snub of the harshest sort, not a cut direct but close enough.

Mrs Ingleby ignored it. Apparently the woman was impervious to Caroline's insult, for she tilted her head, saying, "That tartan turned out lovely, Miss Beauchamp. The Tories ought to adore it. Pity the Whigs have so little sense of humor about these things. Is that not true?'

It was impossible to tell who was intended to answer the question, if, indeed, anyone was. Caroline turned to the earl and silently pleaded with him to move on.

'Good day, Stanhope, Mrs Ingleby. Enjoy the weather.'

Weather! Caroline glanced at Lord Rutledge.

He shrugged. 'One must say something.'

'Must one? Really!' declared Caroline, almost wishing she might have a glorious case of hysterics. She glanced at Rutledge, then became caught in the gray depths of his eyes.

'If I might venture to say so, it is odd that a mere friend should reveal such ire in this situation.' The amused glint in his eyes had disappeared. In its place was a dampening chill. She felt as though something precious had been lost, only she wasn't sure what it was. He broke eye contact with Caroline and looked across the park. 'His wife seems to be having a pleasant enough time.'

Caroline turned her head in time to see Mary laughing at something said by Henry Kenyon. Perhaps she had missed the vision in red seated so boldly in the Stanhope carriage? And pigs might fly.

Whatever Mary did feel regarding the sight of her husband with the elegant widow was carefully concealed from the world behind a gay smile.

While the group chatted away with great amiability, Caroline studied the man at her side as best she might. He had turned from an intriguing man with teasing eyes into a lump of ice in the twinkling of an eye. Or was it the flash of a carriage? Good grief, he must think her enamored of Hugh! Of all the vexatious things. He mistook her anger at seeing Hugh with the Ingleby for jealousy. What utter nonsense that was!

Edmund rode close to her side of the carriage. 'Must talk with you, Caro. There's trouble.'

'About Adrian?'

Edmund merely shook his head and quietly

said he'd meet her at the house as soon as could be.

The group broke up, and Lord Rutledge continued the drive. Caroline had little to say. Her pleasure in the outing had been totally destroyed. Not that she had eagerly anticipated this afternoon in the least. Stares were ignored, comments on her carriage dress deflected, and the weather much discussed. When Lord Rutledge deposited her before the house on South Street, Caroline thanked him prettily, then rushed inside.

Edmund was waiting for her in the hall. 'This way, Caro.' He motioned her into the dining room, unoccupied at this hour of the day, and closed the door.

'What is it, if it isn't about Adrian? Does it concern this dratted dress of mine? I vow I shall place it in the back of the wardrobe and forget I own it.'

'Ain't neither one. 'Tis our aunt. I think something too smoky by half is going on.'

'Have you windmills in your head?' cried Caroline in dismay. 'She's a pattern card of propriety!'

'Then why is there a print in the shop windows with someone who looks deucedly like her and a caption that says, 'The Winning ton?' It shows her with bank notes coming out her sleeves and stacks of those blasted rouleaux on the table beside her. She's leering at a bunch of old dames playing cards. I tell you, there's real trouble afoot here.'

Caroline stared at Edmund in horror as she considered what he had just said. Then she recalled the scene this morning, polishing such an unusual mass of coins and so many banknotes to be ironed. 'Oh, dear heaven. What shall we do?' She pulled out a chair and sank down on it as though suddenly boneless.

'To the rest of the world we'd best pretend we don't know a thing is wrong. But one or t'other of us had best haunt her steps.' Edmund also drew out a chair and joined his sister in shocked contemplation of their proper aunt gone wildly mad.

'You have the right of it, of course.' Caroline shook her head in sorrow. 'I fear 'tis all our fault. I handed her the draft Papa sent up for our keep, but it must have fallen far short if she has taken to gaming to keep the house running and pay bills. Should we go home?'

Edmund slowly shook his head. 'I don't think the old gel is short of blunt. I'd give a pony to know what is going on, though. The only way we can ferret out the truth of the matter is to remain here.'

Caroline met his frank gaze and slowly nodded. 'I suppose so.'

She wished she'd not become involved in all this nonsense with Mary and Hugh. If she had attended to Papa's wishes, she'd have found a nice young man and been well on the way to being betrothed by now. A vision of Lord Rutledge skimmed through her mind, and the censorious look in his eyes was enough to haunt her for the rest of her life.

'Cheer, up Caro. It can't be *that* bad.' Edmund patted her awkwardly on her shoulder, then left the room.

She stared after him, thinking he didn't know the half of it.

8

All through the process of dressing for dinner Caroline had been mulling over the situation. Ought she simply ask her aunt what had prompted the print now presumably circulating the streets and salons of London? Or should she hope for a confidence?

The enormity of the problem began to penetrate as Caroline considered the many possible repercussions. First, there probably would be no more vouchers for Almack's. That would be followed by a dearth of invitations to the various functions. No lovely balls, assemblies, or routs. Only dreary musicales, tedious lectures, and hopeful visits to the opera and theater remained. What young gentleman of any potential would be permitted to dangle after Caroline now? Not where scandal tarnished.

But what could they do?

She left poor Daisy wondering if she had done something horrid, for all her mistress ignored her, and slowly made her way to the drawing room. Lady Winnington was there, seated on her favorite chair with that mangled piece of tapestry in her lap quite neglected.

'Good evening, ma'am.' Caroline studied her aunt. Somehow the dear lady did not look like a gamester in the least. She appeared the same sweet, faintly eccentric woman Caroline had grown to know and love since coming to London. Yet how did one explain the increased profits from the card games she enjoyed?

'Do you have any plans this evening, dear?' Lady Winnington seemed at ease, although she did fidget a bit with that loathsome tapestry.

Did Aunt Fanny wish to head for a gaming table? Determined to dog her steps, Caroline shrugged, 'Whatever you plan is simply perfect as far as I can see. Are we not to attend Lady Carpenter's assembly?'

'Yes, I believe we are.' The reply was thoughtful, almost abstracted. 'Do you know where Adrian is gone? He left the strangest message. I expect he is off digging.'

Not concerned with her wayward brother at the moment, Caroline persisted, 'Does she provide cards for her guests?' It was best to know what lay in store. Usually Aunt Fanny remained at Caroline's side, but once in a while she strayed, when she felt Caroline to be safe. Although why her aunt had felt that way when Rutledge had Caroline in tow that night at Almack's was more than she could see.

'Why, I believe she does. Surely you do not intend to play at cards, my dear!' Lady Winnington looked startled, for, prior to this, Caroline had displayed no inclination toward whist in the least.

'Oh, I might,' declared Caroline airily.

Any riposte to this piece of nonsense was forgotten when Edmund entered the room, heading directly for his aunt. 'I say, dear lady, you are looking first-rate.' He gave Caroline a cautious glance, then returned his attention to his aunt. 'How do you go on this evening? Any place I might join you?'

Lady Winnington stared at him, then turned her head to study Caroline.

If her own face appeared as guilty-looking as Edmund's, there was no hiding the trouble.

'I am pretty well up to snuff, so you needn't think to tip me a rise,' declared the older lady, much to Caroline's amusement. 'There is something too smoky by half going on in this room. First Caroline declares her interest in cards, which she had never had in the least before. Now you, you young scamp, want to attend Mrs Carpenter's assembly with us? Doing it much too brown, my dears. Will you tell me what is really on your minds?

Dinner will be delayed until I get to the root of this.' Knowing how much Edmund liked his meals, she obviously felt this to be a prime bribe.

Brother and sister stood facing each other, not quite knowing how to reveal the awful news, when Simpkins appeared in the doorway.

'Lord Rutledge to see you, my lady.' The butler bowed most correctly, indicating by some means that while this visit at the dinner hour might be odd, it was desirable.

After requesting his lordship be shown up, Lady Winnington set aside the tattered piece of needlework and rose from her chair. 'Why do I feel this is not a mere social visit? Could it be that two gloomy faces bring a premonition?'

'Lady Winnington,' offered Rutledge as he entered the drawing room, bowing most correctly. He was dressed to the nines, wearing a deep blue Bath cloth coat, biscuit pantaloons, and a cream waistcoat of a most elegant design. He carried a roll of papers under his arm.

'Rutledge.' Lady Winnington gave the papers a curious look, then caught a fleeting expression of horror crossing her niece's face.

Over to the far side of Lady Winnington Edmund made a strangled sound as he also seemed to recognize the papers. 'Oh, I say,' he muttered.

'Would someone be so kind as to inform me what is amiss?' Lady Winnington gestured to the sofa, indicating his lordship be seated.

He looked at Edmund. 'You have not told her?'

That young man shook his head, seeming to want to sink through the floor or something equally pleasant. 'No, sir.'

'Fanny, you have been up to something, else these wouldn't have been done.' Lord Rutledge peeled off one of the papers. Caroline stepped forward to see if what she most feared was true. It was.

'My, my,' murmured Lady Winnington. 'Doesn't look much like me, but the name is inescapable, is it not?'

'Do you mean to tell me you have become a gamester?' cried Caroline in horrified accents. 'It passes all bounds of belief!'

Her aunt gave her a wounded glance, then sat down rather abruptly on her chair. 'Oh, dear,' was all she could say.

Rutledge placed the stack of prints on the table, then casually strolled over to the mantel, where he leaned against it with studied ease. 'Henry Kenyon told me. We purchased all the prints that could be found. I believe I have successfully persuaded the printer to destroy any copies that might turn up and I have the plate, so no more can be made.'

'I am much in your debt, Giles. How foolish of me to think I might pass this off with no flutter over it.' Lady Winnington studied the print, then added it to the stack of others in the table. She appeared uneasy, definitely embarrassed, and yet looked as though she had no intention of revealing the whole of it.

'But . . . but you are a pattern card of propriety, dear ma'am. There cannot be any truth to this print. Can there?' asked Caroline, gazing at her aunt with the hope that all would be denied.

'I fear I have had phenomenal success at the whist tables of late. One might be forgiven were they to suspect something havey-cavey afoot, I suppose.' She pleated the muslin of her gown with nervous fingers, then glanced up at Rutledge. 'I meant it for the best.'

'You had better open your budget, dear lady. If we are to help you out of this predicament, we must know all.' Rutledge spared a glance for Caroline. She seemed thunderstruck, like a princess who discovers her fairy godmother has given her an ugly frog rather than a prince.

'It was for Edmund, you see,' declared the gamester with demure simplicity.

That simple statement brought an eruption from both Caroline and Edmund. 'What?' they cried nearly in unison.

'Well,' said Lady Winnington, 'I wanted to give him the money for his stud. I knew my man of business wouldn't let me hand over such a large amount without a squabble, and I do so hate a squabble over money. So I decided to win it for him. His racers ought to be luckier if the money is from winnings, don't you think?' She turned to Rutledge for confirmation of her theory.

'But, ma'am, what made you think you could win such a prodigious amount?' asked Caroline, her eyes large with amazement.

'Well,' explained Lady Winnington with childlike delight, 'I always win when I play to benefit someone else. I discovered it some years ago, when I wished to help Mrs Banting out of a muddle. Since then I have not done it so very often, not wanting to raise an alarm, you know. But I did so desire Edmund to have his future. For you must know that with seven children — for the moment, at any rate — his father will be pressed to provide the necessary funds for him and all those other hopefuls. It seemed the best thing to do.'

There was utter silence in the room for

several minutes. The little cherub swung back and forth on his swing beneath the dome of the mantel clock, ticking out the seconds.

Then Caroline, seeing the utter incredibility of it all, tried to stifle a giggle, albeit a nervous one. Edmund appeared as though choking on something. Rutledge was the last to yield to the absurdity of the situation. In moments the trio was laughing immoderately, while a baffled Lady Winnington sat in an indignant huff on her chair, looking at the others as though they were a collection of zanies.

'Forgive us, dear lady.' Rutledge sobered hastily. 'We had expected almost anything but what you just stated. A system for winning, a clever method for figuring odds, almost anything but the truth of it. 'Tis said that one wins best when playing with unneeded funds. Perhaps this is a variation?'

Rutledge strolled away from the mantel to stand by the papers, staring down at them as though wishing they might vanish. 'The trouble remains, however. A number of these prints were sold — how many we do not know — before we arrived on the scene. Henry is a good lad and won't utter a word of the tale. But others may. How do we deflect the stories?'

'Heavens, I have no idea.' Lady Winnington

turned to Edmund. 'This was to be my last evening, as I have a sizable amount to give you.' She named the sum and the room again fell into stunned silence. This time there was no laughter.

Caroline crossed the short distance to fall on her knees beside her aunt's chair. Shaking her head in wonder, she reached out to bestow a gentle hug, then sat back on her heels. 'Whatever can we say? You are overwhelming, dear ma'am, even if it was a bird-witted start to conceive such an idea.'

The tall, thin young man who had stood gaping at his aunt collapsed on the sofa in amazement, his heart's desire handed him so neatly as to stun him. Edmund said in awed accents, 'Th-thank you, Aunt Fanny. I hope I am not such a gudgeon as to say nay to such a gift, but 'tis a prodigious sum of money.'

'You can settle details later,' interposed Rutledge. 'The fact of the matter is that there is bound to be gossip. Need I remind you all how destructive that could be?'

'Horrors,' said Caroline softly, recalling her earlier fears.

'You had best join us for dinner. We can perhaps find a solution while we eat our meal.' Lady Winnington crossed to ring for her butler. When that good man appeared, she issued some lowvoiced instructions.

The four collaborators shortly sat down to an excellent meal. That they scarcely did justice to the food could be well understood.

While pushing a morsel of beef around and around her plate with her fork, Caroline wondered, not for the first time, just why Rutledge was offering his assistance in the matter. No clue had been offered. Most likely it was due to a fondness upon his part for the dear lady.

'I believe I may have a solution,' offered Rutledge hesitantly. Considering how sure of himself he was most of the time, Caroline glanced at him in surprise.

If he took note of her reaction, it wasn't apparent. 'We shall all go to the Carpenter party. Edmund, you shall escort the ladies. I will follow shortly. Lady Winnington shall play at cards — whist, did you say? And play for yourself this time. If people see you lose — and I fear you'll have to dip rather deep — they will consign that print to the dustbin where it belongs.'

The silence that met this suggestion was a thoughtful one. Caroline placed the morsel of beef in her mouth, a tiny furrow creasing her brow while she chewed. Edmund nodded slowly.

'By Jove, I do believe you've hit on the

answer,' he said with great admiration in his voice.

'Can you do that, Aunt Fanny?' asked Caroline in a soft, sweetly caring tone.

'Well, I do not see why I cannot,' declared her aunt with slow deliberation.

'Fine.' Rutledge began to consume his food with a deal more enthusiasm. Caroline tucked into her orange creme with a lighter heart. Edmund asked for a second helping of roast partridge. Only Lady Winnington seemed lost in thought.

'It was such fun, you know. I had high hopes of raising just a bit more.' She glanced at Lord Rutledge with a hint of apology in her eyes.

'I was thinking, ma'am. It does little good if young Edmund has all this blunt and he knows not how best to spend it wisely. What do you say if he has a few months at my stud in Sussex? Edmund? Would you like to tutor under my head trainer for a time?'

'Learn from one of the best there is? I should rather think I would, sir.' Edmund had the look of a boy who has had the entire Christmas pudding placed in his lap.

'You put that money in the funds at a healthy rate of interest, and there'll be no need to add to it by any gambling,' advised Rutledge.

Seeing that the matter was as good as settled, the group ended the meal on a happy note, all leaving the dining room together, what with the lack of time for the two men to linger over a glass of port. Adrian was quite forgotten.

Edmund stood rather awkwardly to one side of the entry hall. 'I don't quite know how to thank you, Lord Rutledge. It was an enormously kind thing of you to do. On behalf of my sister and my aunt, I do want to say . . . well . . . thanks.'

Lady Winnington walked up to pat Rutledge on the arm, peering up into his face as though she might read an answer to her question there. 'You are one in a million, dear boy,' she said. 'This foolish lady is much in your debt.'

'I shall remember that if need be, madam.' Rutledge had that customary glint in his eye when he turned to Caroline.

Ignoring the fluttering in her heart, Caroline extended her hand. 'I trust we shall meet you later. I should like to add my appreciation as well, sir. It seems you are always rescuing one or the other of us from our folly.'

'Precisely,' murmured Rutledge, much to her confusion. 'And I fear the job's not over with yet.' He departed moments later, leaving

Caroline still wondering what he'd meant.

With the gentle dignity that was such a part of her, Lady Winnington collected her pair, then murmured instructions to each while driving to the Carpenters' elegant home. She walked up the steps with a grand tilt to her head and a serene air about her, as though all the gossiping tongues of London were not waiting to cut her to ribands.

'Quite a lady,' said Edmund to his sister while they strolled along in the line to greet the host and hostess.

'She is that,' replied Caroline, wondering what the next few hours were to bring. Would Lady Winnington be able to pull it off?

That the hostess had been told about the print was apparent. She smiled stiffly, then said in freezing accents, 'The card room is along that way, dear Fanny. I trust you'll have no difficulty locating it.'

A little half smile curved Lady Winnington's lips. 'I wish I always did win, Clara dear. It would solve so many problems, would it not?' She gave the lady an audacious wink, then placidly proceeded on her way.

Caroline longed to giggle at the gasping woman who had limply extended her hand. Rather, she curtsied politely, then proceeded into the room with the intent of joining Sarah Thurlow and Henry Kenyon.

Within minutes it became clear that word of the print had filtered about the room with amazing speed. Good gossip was hard to come by and this was utterly delicious. A respectable woman to whom no hint of impropriety had ever been attached became grist for a goodly number of envious mills.

One or two people snubbed Caroline and her brother as the two strolled through the crowd. Caroline pretended not to notice. But it was a harbinger of what might come if Aunt Fanny was not able to convince the ton that she was indeed innocent of any implications of cheating. A woman might flirt with a man other than her husband, but heaven forbid she play fast and loose with cards.

At last they met their friends. Caroline gave a strained smile to Sarah, then turned to Henry with her thanks for his part in the attempt to clear her aunt. 'It was good of you to seek out Lord Rutledge. Then to assist him to buy up the prints was beyond anything helpful. I fear people love such a scandal broth as this.'

He accepted her appreciation with slightly reddened cheeks and a stammered. ''Twas nothing.' Then he added, 'I had to explain what was afoot to Miss Thurlow,' in a low aside to Caroline.

'Do you know she won the money fair and

square and did it all for Edmund? It is a prodigious sum of money. She feared Papa would not be able to set him up with his stud, so she decided to win the money for him. Is that not excessively kind of her?' Caroline spoke softly lest the people close by overhear her.

'Most generous, I should say,' replied Miss Thurlow in approving tones. She glanced to where Edmund now stood chatting with some friends, looking as though there was nothing amiss. 'He must find it difficult to maintain such calm. Let us join him, Henry.'

Caroline did not fail to miss the curious intimacy of expression that existed between Henry and Sarah. So that was the way the wind blew in that quarter? Sarah was a dear, sweet child. But that was what Caroline found vexing. Sarah was younger. And about to be betrothed. And Caroline looked fair to being on the shelf.

'Miss Beauchamp, I believe the musicians are about to strike up a waltz, if my ears don't deceive me. Will you be my partner?' asked a now familiar voice. Lord Rutledge gazed down at her with that terrifyingly bland expression. Only the glint deep in those beautiful gray eyes revealed his possible feelings to her.

She squared her shoulders a trifle, then

nodded politely. 'It is my pleasure, sir.' She gave him her hand, then suffered one of his to curve familiarly about her waist.

If anyone gave a second thought to such a frigidly polite exchange, it was that Caroline Beauchamp was a brave young woman to risk a dance with Rutledge. One or two of the tabbies commented on the fact that Rutledge usually confined himself to widows like Mrs Ingleby or married women such as Viscountess Stanhope. Few bothered to listen, for they were busy speculating on the latest *on-dit*.

'How strange it is, to feel eyes watching, wondering,' said Caroline. She was spun about in a delicious whirl, and smiled up at her partner with momentary delight.

'Bear up, my dear. No point in taking a green melancholy over this. I have a feeling your aunt will do us all proud. She is no green girl, you know.'

'And I am, I suppose.' Caroline did not take umbrage with Rutledge over this point. This business with Mary and Hugh had shown her there were many fine points to be learned regarding society's ins and outs. Glancing down at the pale green dress that her aunt thought so wicked, she smiled, 'At least I live up to my position.'

'And quite nicely, too,' he said in a warmly approving tone. 'I believe I like that dress even more than I did the first time when you wore the rose tucked in the neckline. You have such lovely' — his gaze swept slowly across her bare shoulders, lingered in the vicinity of her bosom, then returned to meet her eyes — 'taste.'

Caroline had the choice of being outraged or pretending an amusement she did not feel. She chose the latter course. With a determined smile she said, 'You are a complete hand, sir.' Her brain was seething with possible set-downs, none of which she dared to utter.

'Let me see,' he mused, 'I am perfectly horrid, an utterly impossible creature. Am I correct?' There was a hint of that quite enchanting smile in his eyes. His dimple flashed briefly. 'There is most likely more.'

Her pulse quickened abominably and she felt strangely breathless as he whirled her about once again. 'How well you put it. I could scarce have said it better.'

'Saucy minx.' His gaze fell upon Lady Winnington as she made her way through the chattering throng, and he sobered. 'As to the rest, we shall know before long, shan't we?'

When Lady Winnington drifted into the room set aside for card playing, there was more than polite interest in her progress. One after another person found a reason to pass by her table once she was seated. Mrs Banting, alerted by a whispered word and a nod or two, had joined her. Soon the play was intent. It became obvious quite shortly that whoever had started the rumor about Lady Winnington's streak of luck had windmills in his head. The lady did not seem to make a correct judgment half the time, and the other had a bad draw of the cards.

Following the waltz, Rutledge and Caroline walked toward where her brother stood with Sarah and Henry. As they wound their way among the guests, Caroline and Lord Rutledge overheard one stout matron say to her friend, 'What utter rubbish, to be sure. I could have told Lady Babbingson that Fanny was not the sort to cheat. She ain't a bad player, mind you. Just uneven. One time she may be up, the next she's in Queer Street. Not that she don't pay her vowels, mind you. A good sort is our Fanny.'

'I believe your idea has done the trick, my lord,' said Caroline in a pleased whisper.

'It would seem so.' They joined the trio standing a trifle defiantly in a prominent part of the room.

'I do believe it would be appropriate for us to drink a small toast to dear Lady Winnington — in her absence, I fear,' said Caroline. 'That lady is accomplishing her goal most admirably.' Caroline's eyes twinkled with relief and happiness that she would not be consigned to her country home without further enjoyment of the London Season.

Not concealing his thankfulness, Edmund offered Caroline his arm. 'I could use a swallow of something stronger than lemonade. Join us, sir?' Edmund bowed politely and with great deference to the slightly older but much more polished gentleman at Caroline's other side. Dashed if the fellow hadn't been quite civil about this whole mess. Then offering to allow Edmund to get valuable experience at his own stud in Sussex, well! He was a true Top-of-the-Trees in Edmund's book.

'Thank you, perhaps later on,' said Rutledge in his customary cool tones.

After their departure, Lord Rutledge had the sudden feeling he had been relegated to the group of ancients who clustered about a pillar discussing the olden days with fond reminiscences.

It was a pity he hadn't gone with them, thought Caroline later with deep regret. She had missed his wry humor greatly. The champagne had been flat and tasteless without his company to sparkle it up. She searched for her aunt, hoping her duty in the card room was over by now. A voice close behind Caroline brought her up short.

'Caroline, would you dance with me? Or better still, walk along the hall or someplace? I need to talk with you.'

'Hugh,' declared Caroline with annoyance. 'I do not know whether I ought to even give you the time of day. For you must know you have quite sunk beneath reproach. How could you take up Mrs Ingleby in your carriage? And after our careful plans!'

'Keep your tongue between your teeth a moment and I'll explain how it was,' said Hugh with a distinctly unfriendly curtness. 'If ever a man has been so put upon.'

Facing him, Caroline began to seethe. She didn't miss the frosty look bestowed on her by Lord Rutledge when he saw Hugh at her side. The wretched man undoubtedly thought the worst. Even as Hugh tugged at her hand, Rutledge was bidding his hostess good evening and walking from the room. Probably to comfort the widow . . . or was he to attend sweet little Mary and console her?

'This had better be something special, Hugh. I warn you I do not have an abundance of patience, and I have had quite enough of your court promises. I fulfilled my part of the arrangement. When I drove out with Lord Rutledge I hoped you would have the good sense to seek out your wife. But what do I see? You, with the widow in your carriage while your pretty wife is on her mare. I declare, you are the most shatter-brained man I know.'

The man at her side stopped to give her an exasperated look. 'Mrs Ingleby's carriage broke down just as I came up to where she was. I couldn't let her be stranded there, now could I?'

'I would be inclined to check that whatever-it-was on her carriage most carefully, were I you. A hunch tells me that it was all a hum. Heaven knows what Mary thinks of it. For my money she is about to turn to Lord Rutledge and with good reason.'

'I didn't like the business with Mrs Ingleby in the least. The next time it will go better, I assure you.' Hugh spoke with the complacency of a man indulged from his infancy.

'For a man who is supposed to be pretty well up to snuff, you do have a screw loose in your brain box. I should continue with this farce? What will it be next time? Shall Mrs Ingleby suffer an injury to her ankle, pray tell? I can see us meeting you and finding you with her in your arms. Botheration!'

Caroline normally would not have waded into Hugh in such a stiff manner, but that look from Rutledge had cut her deeply.

'I expect you are wishing me at Jericho by

now.' Hugh's contrition was genuine. He did want his wife and this had been his best hope. Now it seemed Caroline Beauchamp was about to desert him.

Stricken at the tone of his voice and the look of dejection as he hung his head, Caroline relented. She truly wished to see her friends united by more than name.

'Very well. We shall think of something.'

When Caroline joined her aunt and brother, it was with a heart full of misgivings. However, she had promised, and she never broke her word if it could be helped. Consequently she was rather quiet on the drive back to South Street.

'I believe I silenced those wagging tongues. Pity Rutledge didn't stay on to see our triumphant exit. Wonder where he went?' Lady Winnington was in high spirits with her success.

Caroline was about to speculate aloud when her brother spoke:

'Imagine he went to White's. Often is found there.'

There wasn't a great deal of comfort in the words, for Edmund couldn't be sure, but Caroline took what ease she could. She did not examine why she cared where Lord Rutledge had gone too closely, for it might reveal something she was not prepared to face at the moment.

As usual, Baxhall stopped the hackney directly in front of the house. Simpkins hurried out to assist Lady Winnington. He paid the driver, then returned to the house to see all was in order and what his employer desired.

In the act of ascending the stairs to the drawing room, Lady Winnington paused, turning slightly to face her butler. 'Was there a message from young Mr Adrian, Simpkins?'

'He was home earlier, madam. I believe he said something about meeting a Mr Samuel Lysons in regard to a dig.'

'That was all?' asked Caroline, concerned, for she had never heard of this Mr Lysons. 'Did he merely go out or did he take some baggage?'

'That I could not say, miss, for when he left the house I was in the kitchen supervising a problem that had cropped up.' He gave his employer a look of apology for being so remiss as to fail to catch something of possible import.

'I see. Thank you, Simpkins. I feel sure Adrian will return before long.' Lady Winnington requested a tea tray be brought up to the drawing room, then continued her way up the stairs.

Once seated on her favorite chair, she met Caroline's gaze with her concern clearly to be seen in her eyes. 'Does your brother often go haring off like this?'

'As Lord Rutledge put it, Adrian ever has his head in the clouds. I wonder if he knows the time of day at times.' Caroline looked to Edmund for a possible clue to his brother's whereabouts.

Edmund shrugged and said, 'A prime wool-gatherer, that one. Always has been. I don't know anything about the chap Simpkins mentioned. Stands to reason if it has to do with that infernal digging.'

'I'll wager Rutledge knows that man, or at least who and what he is,' said Lady Winnington quietly. 'If Adrian is not home by morning, I shall send a note to Lord Rutledge seeking his excellent advice.' Catching sight of Caroline's sudden dismay, her aunt added, 'For he has solved all our problems most neatly. Do you not agree, Caroline?'

Hearing the sharp note in her aunt's voice, Caroline could only nod her concurrence. Her aunt might discover that Lord Rutledge had washed his hands of the lot of them after seeing Caroline with Hugh this evening. Not that Rutledge had given her a chance to explain what was going on. Odious man.

Tea was brought and cups poured. Each of the trio was absorbed in thought. Edmund wondered how soon he might post down to

Sussex. Lady Winnington sighed a bit wistfully for the delight she'd known while playing and winning for Edmund.

Caroline sipped the hot beverage while trying to sort out the muddle she'd fallen into. It surely would take more than Rutledge's acknowledged wisdom to pull her out of this mess!

9

Adrian was not to be seen the following morning. Indeed, the entire day was to pass without his crossing the threshold to the house on South Street.

While Lady Winnington was inclined to call upon Lord Rutledge for his undoubtedly expert assistance, Caroline attempted to dissuade her.

'Only think, dear aunt. Would you not feel foolish if Adrian is up to some silly start and Rutledge is given a disgust of us for sending him on a fool's errand?'

Her aunt studied Caroline with shrewd eyes. Since there were no coins to polish this morning — no winnings having been taken in last evening — the two sat in the morning room. Aunt Fanny had a cup of tea at her elbow while she perused her mail. Caroline restlessly paced about the small room, pausing from time to time to stare out the window in the direction of Thornhill House.

'He might have stopped here to inquire, however,' Caroline muttered after some time. 'Merely to set your mind at ease, ma'am.'

'Naturally. We cannot lay claim to his

attentions, dear girl. Rutledge is a very busy man. Do you have any idea of the extent of his properties? Here in London alone, he has a sizable amount of land.'

Just then Simpkins appeared in the doorway looking as shaken as one ever might think to see that unflappable gentleman. He bowed, then said, 'There is a shockingly irate person to see you, my lady. Something to do with Mr Adrian, I believe. Shall I tell him you are not at home?'

Clearly Simpkins had a low opinion of whoever was calling, for he referred to him as a person, not a gentleman. The distinction was vast.

Exchanging a surprised glance with her niece, Lady Winnington rose from her comfortable chair to walk to the door. 'Come with me, Caroline. I suspect we are about to discover what it is that has been keeping your brother so frightfully busy these days.'

In the center of the entry stood a bull-necked man with red cheeks, pale blue eyes, and possessing a stout form that bespoke hearty meals with ample ale. 'Ye must do something wi' tha' good-fer-nothing jackanapes! Beggin' your pardon, ma'am. Th' young gen'leman is set to dig up Tower 'ill! Ye canna' allow 'im to do it.' He raised a threatening fist, then dropped it when he recalled it was Quality he addressed. 'Th' Runners 'ill be called, for sartin, ma'am!'

'My, my,' said a coolly distant Lady Winnington. She attempted to question the man a bit more, eliciting little of value other than apparently Adrian was convinced there were Roman ruins of an early wall or some such thing beginning at the Tower and running beneath the city.

The man was politely thanked for his message and warning, for goodness knew what might happen to Adrian if he succeeded with his plan and the Runners carted him off to Bow Street!

Once the door was closed behind the message bearer, Lady Winnington hurried back to her morning room, crossing directly to her small writing desk. With unusual urgency she plumped herself on the chair to scribble a note on hot-pressed paper scented discreetly with sandalwood. She found a wafer in the small drawer, affixed it, then rang for Simpkins.

'See to it that this note is promptly delivered to his lordship, if you please.'

The butler took the note, then disappeared with the efficiency of a genie.

Off to one side, close by the windows, Caroline stood with an unhappy face. 'I do wish you had not felt it necessary to call upon

Lord Rutledge, dear aunt.'

'Don't see why not. Depend upon it, Rutledge will have the answer to our problem. He always does.'

'I was not aware you were such good friends,' said Caroline with more than a little curiosity.

'Knew his mother, God rest her soul. Lovely woman. Father, too. Such a shame they were killed. An intruder, you know, or perhaps you didn't? A robber entered the home, most likely thinking the pair were gone. When the villain found them at home, he shot them. Rutledge was up at Oxford at that time. Nearly finished with his schooling. It was a terrible shock for the boy.'

'I had no idea,' murmured Caroline, her tender heart aching for the young man who had had his family so brutally taken from him. She had been blessed with both parents all her life, and many brothers and sisters. What it was like to grow up so alone, then bereft, was beyond thinking.

Lady Winnington had discovered a map of the city among her papers and was studying the area about Tower Hill when Simpkins ushered in the Earl of Rutledge with all due ceremony.

'Lady Winnington, pray tell me what has you in such a flutter?' Rutledge studied the unhappy face of a lady he quite liked with what appeared to be forbearance.

The gentleman was superbly dressed, Caroline noted. A dark blue coat with a pale lemon waistcoat of a fine design was worn over dove gray pantaloons. Those Hessians were so highly polished, Caroline fancied she might see her reflection in them. His hair was a trifle windswept, and he appeared disgustingly fresh, as though he'd arisen early for a morning canter in the park. *He* had not tossed in his bed for hours last night. And Caroline was positive his pillow had not been dampened with tears.

''Tis Adrian. We have a better notion as to what he is up to this morning. Not half an hour ago a man presented himself at the door to complain about the young scamp. Seems the boy wants to begin digging at Tower Hill!'

'Good grief!' exclaimed Rutledge.

'Adrian believes there is the ruins of a wall or some such thing to be found there,' offered Caroline in her sweet, musical voice. 'Although why anyone should care about the Roman remains to the extent of digging up perfectly good buildings is more than I can understand.'

'I declare,' inserted Lady Winnington in an aggrieved tone, 'that boy is enough to put a saint out of temper.'

'Hm' was the reply from his lordship as he strolled to the window. From where he stood he could look out to see the side of Thornhill House peeking through the trees beyond the brick walls of the mews. He glanced at Caroline, then walked to where Lady Winnington stood with her hands clasped in concern.

'We had best get him away from there at once,' he declared in a decisive tone. 'Caroline, if you will put on your bonnet and pelisse, we shall catch up that pudding-head brother of yours before he finds himself in the basket. Somehow I doubt the Lord Mayor of London will take kindly to digging up one of the chief sights of the old city.'

Horrified at the prospect of her dearest brother — for after all, she did care for the harebrained lad — being carted off to Newgate or some other equally terrible place, Caroline did as bidden with no argumentation.

Within a brief time she composedly presented herself in the entry, her bonnet neatly tied beneath her chin and her favorite reticule dangling from one hand. Her peacock blue pelisse was quite new and fashionable. The bodice and lower portion of the sleeves were exquisitely covered with applied decorations in a floral pattern, the cap of each sleeve cleverly interlaced with woven strips of fabric. Her bonnet matched the silk of the pelisse, the ribands a deeper tone of the blue, as was her reticule. All in all she felt she was quite able to cope with an irate citizen.

Intimidation was something she had learned from her mother. When dealing with people of the lower orders, one commanded the situation by not only looking one's best, but displaying a cool disdain if need be. She gave Rutledge a quelling look as he surveyed her.

'I believe we can depart,' he said. That glint had returned to his eyes once again. 'I am impressed, Miss Beauchamp. You are not only quick but also quite charmingly dressed for the occasion. I doubt the Lord Mayor will have the least heart to tackle so imposing a lady.'

Not trusting herself to speak, she merely nodded, then swept out the front door before him. The grays had been put to a silver-gray barouche. Caroline gave a sigh of pleasure. Even the serious task at hand could not diminish the thrill of driving out with the elegant Lord Rutledge in his carriage.

Traffic clogged the streets this afternoon, as it did most days. Caroline remained commendably silent while Rutledge concentrated on threading the carriage through the crush of elegant carriages, delivery carts, and foolhardy pedestrians that converged upon every intersection they passed. At Ludgate they approached the vicinity of St Paul's Cathedral, maintaining a respectable pace, thanks mostly to his lordship's skill with the ribbons.

Clipping along up Cannon Street, Caroline broke her imposed silence. She called out to where he sat in front, 'I do hope we shall arrive in time to prevent Adrian from being hauled away on some charge or other.' She nervously mangled the ribands of her reticule while wondering how she might inform her dear parents of the disaster should it befall.

Occupied with negotiating a deft swing around a dray, Rutledge did at first not respond to her comment. Once clear of the obstruction, he replied with a deal of patience, 'Fools seem to have a guardian angel on their shoulder, Miss Beauchamp.' He turned his head for a moment to survey her where she sat in lonely splendor.

She took note of the more formal address. He had called her Caroline before; she was reduced to Miss Beauchamp today, a clear sign of his disfavor. If she could manage to crown Hugh with something that might knock some sense into his head, she'd gladly make the attempt. Still, she reflected, that did not prove that Rutledge would show strong interest in her once she was freed of the problem of Hugh and Mary.

She reminded herself, with a good internal shaking, that Lord Rutledge performed these sundry tasks to please her aunt, for whom he appeared to have great fondness, no doubt as a substitute mother of sorts. Caroline was certain he had nothing but an aloof contempt for her. Unfortunately. The glint in his eyes she had caught sight of earlier had disappeared, which was understandable given the traffic. But she questioned whether it might return. She was sorry, for she had quite enjoyed their verbal sparring matches.

When they entered Tower Hill, it was an easy task to pick out Adrian. He was the center of a heated argument. The imposing collections of buildings that made up the Tower of London ranged behind him, Adrian earnestly sought to persuade the gentleman at his side of the importance of his mission — to salvage the remains of Roman London from utter destruction. That the gentleman in question was not the least impressed was obvious to anyone with eyes in his head.

Within minutes Lord Rutledge had handed the ribbons to his groom, joined the pair in discussion, soothed a distinctly ruffled set of feathers, and hauled a protesting Adrian back to the barouche.

'I say, sir,' he said with politeness even though hard-pressed to control his annoyance. 'I feel most strongly that the chap ought not destroy the remains I am certain are to be found below the site.' He permitted himself to be thrust into the carriage, plumping himself down while rattling away on the merits of his position.

Lord Rutledge seated himself at Caroline's side, listening to Adrian with a patience she could only marvel at.

The barouche slowly returned through the streets to the house on South Street, driven by an extremely prudent groom who was not about to risk damage to his lordship's fine carriage. It also was quite possible that he felt it might be better if the young gentleman calmed down a bit before presenting himself to his aunt.

Once in Lady Winnington's home, the trio mounted the stairs to the drawing room to find her seated and showing signs of great impatience, the tapestry lying neglected in her lap.

The poorly treated tapestry dropped unheeded to the floor when her ladyship jumped to her feet. 'You are safe! Oh, I knew I might depend on you, Giles, dear. Whatever would I do without your reliable shoulders to lean upon? What happened?'

'Lord Rutledge drove us there in a trice, dear aunt. Most safely, too.' Caroline caught a glimpse of Rutledge on the far side of the room, the glint restored to his eyes again. 'He had the matter sorted out and Adrian in the barouche before I could contemplate how to proceed.'

Lady Winnington turned on her adored nephew to issue a scold. 'Pray do not ever put me in such a quake again, my boy. To think the Lord Mayor himself might have brought charges against you is more than I can tolerate,' she concluded at the end of a set-down that had Adrian looking dazed if not a little confused. It seemed the young man simply could not understand the feelings of those not caught up in his enthusiasm.

'I believe I might be of assistance here, Lady W.' Rutledge turned to Adrian. 'How would you like to excavate what is suspected to be a Roman villa that is located on the edge of my estate in Sussex? Not long ago one of my tenants turned up some fine examples of mosaic while digging a drainage ditch.'

Adrian perked up, his eyes came alive with eagerness. 'Oh, I say, sir,' he said with a deference that would have been agreeable to the Regent himself. 'That would above all be wonderful. When may I leave for Sussex?'

'You waste no time, brother dear,' said Caroline, chuckling at his eager expression.

'Leave be, Miss Beauchamp. There is no crime in enthusiasm . . . for the proper sort of thing,' drawled Rutledge provocatively. He turned to face Adrian again.

Caroline felt her face warm and wondered precisely what he had in his mind. Did he recall her response to his improper kiss in the intimacy of his cozy room that day it rained? Or did he have the business with Hugh on the brain? Either way, it was rather disconcerting to have had him look at her so.

'No doubt,' she replied as coolly as she could.

'I think it an excellent notion, your going down to Sussex. The sooner, the better, as I see it,' declared Lady Winnington with commendable frankness.

Without considering her words, Caroline added, 'You shall have your hands full of Beauchamps if you aren't careful, my lord.'

'True,' he answered, his gaze lingering on her a moment before he turned back to Adrian. He withdrew a card from his waistcoat pocket, scribbled something on the back of it, then gave it to Adrian. 'I shall send a detailed set of instructions down with you when you depart. As your good aunt says, you may as well go promptly. I trust you will proceed with all caution once on site.'

'You may rely on me to do the proper thing, sir.' Adrian studied the card, then nodded. 'I shall prepare myself immediately.' Without further ado, he marched from the room, leaving an aghast Aunt Fanny staring after him.

'I fear he forgets his manners when he becomes absorbed in antiquity,' offered Caroline by way of an excuse.

'There are worse things, my dear.' Rutledge appeared on the verge of saying more, then was forestalled by the entrance of Simpkins.

'Lord Stanhope presents his compliments, madam.' The butler bowed in response to the nod from her ladyship, then exited to return with the guest.

Caroline could have stamped her foot in vexation at the change that came over Rutledge upon hearing Hugh's name. What had been a near return to the pleasant gentleman she had observed more than once now became that icy, positively odious man she utterly detested.

'Lord Stanhope, how lovely,' murmured Lady Winnington, the only person in the room who appeared to greet him with any degree of civility.

Hugh was clearly surprised and not a little taken aback to discover his foe in Lady Winnington's drawing room. He nodded with extreme reserve.

Former friends reduced to the barest politeness! Caroline wished she could shake some sense into their heads, but that was beyond hope, it seemed.

'If you will excuse me, dear lady. I shall tend to that pressing matter with Adrian immediately,' said Rutledge. He bowed over Lady Winnington's hand, bestowed a frigid nod on Caroline, then left the room.

'Heavens, coping with the twins is enough to bring on a fit of the dismals,' declared Lady Winnington with disgust. 'Why do you not take those books to Hatchards that I may know a moment's peace? This has been an exhausting day.' That her ladyship should so forget herself to make such a statement when a guest was present alarmed Caroline.

Truly contrite that her family's affairs should have such an insalubrious effect upon her aunt, Caroline hastily agreed. 'Of course. Will you walk with me, Hugh?' It was less a question than a command.

'Naturally.'

Since Caroline had not removed her pelisse upon returning with Rutledge, she took but a moment to collect the two books. Shortly she left the house with Hugh at her side. 'May I inquire what brings you to my aunt's house? Although we aren't there, precisely at the moment, are we?'

'What was Rutledge doing, and what has he to do with Adrian?'

She explained as briefly as possible, and was satisfied to see Hugh nod with approval. 'Dashed generous of Giles to take the lad on like that. Not every man would, you know.'

' 'Tis a pity you two cannot get on. You did once,' she reminded him.

'That was before he made a dead set at my wife.'

'And whose fault is that?' Caroline countered.

'At any rate, you seem to be making headway with drawing him from Mary's side,' said Hugh with satisfaction. 'Witness his presence today.'

'I doubt he will return after seeing you enter my aunt's drawing room. Really, Hugh!' she cried softly. Her exasperation with her friend was balanced with a desire to see Mary restored to his side. She was fast coming to believe the two truly deserved each other.

'Now, now,' replied Hugh with a complacency that Caroline found most annoying. 'You forget how fetching you are.'

They neared the bookshop, so Caroline

kept her voice to a near whisper. There were a number of the *ton* coming and going from the popular establishment. 'I do not see how you can say such a taradiddle.'

'He's bound to feel himself obliged to remove you from my influence. After all, if he sets himself up to tend to Mary, 'tis only natural.'

Vexed beyond bearing, Caroline flounced off from his side. She returned the books to the desk, then marched to the shelves where the novels her aunt so enjoyed were to be found. Glad that Hugh had found a friend to chat with, she took calming breaths while she perused a number of books.

'My dear Miss Beauchamp,' purred a husky voice at her side, 'we meet again.'

When Caroline gave a startled glance to her right, she encountered the beautiful Mrs Ingleby, arrayed in a lovely red pelisse dashingly trimmed in black braid. Red feathers curled around the brim of the smart black silk hat she wore.

'Good afternoon, Mrs Ingleby.' What could the elegant widow possibly have to say to Caroline?

'You are certainly an eager little girl, are you not?' said the Ingleby with a wry inflection in her voice.

'I don't know what you mean,' whispered

Caroline, hoping no one would overhear the conversation.

'I do not like to have my particular friends lured away from my side, Miss Beauchamp. Remember that, if you please.' The widow whirled about and walked from the shop.

Able to take a deep breath in relief, Caroline wondered what else could possibly occur to cut up her peace this day. She selected two volumes she thought her aunt might enjoy, then hurriedly made her way to the counter. In minutes she was out of the bookshop and marching down the walk, Hugh at her side.

'That was quick.'

'I'll thank you to let Mrs Ingleby know I do not appreciate her threats. I was never so taken aback in my life,' declared Caroline in an undertone. 'I warn you, Hugh. Arrange your marital affairs soon, else I wash my hands of you and Mary. I suspect it could all be settled in a flea's leap if you were not so hen-hearted.'

'I will do what I can,' promised a contrite Hugh. It was clear he felt badly about the confrontation from the demi-mondaine who had thrust herself at Caroline. It ought not to have occurred, especially at Hatchards.

She parted from a subdued Hugh at the front door, then ran lightly up the stairs to her aunt's room, where she was normally found resting before dinner.

A rap on the door brought a summons to enter. 'Such a day,' Caroline said, handing the books to her aunt.

'I own the boys have had me quite in a fret. How glad I am that Rutledge has solved our problems. Thank you for the books. Perhaps I may get to read the others sometime.'

Casting an amazed look at her aunt, Caroline broke into reluctant laughter. 'You are a clever one. What shall you think of next!'

'I believe Rutledge is quite fond of you, child. Why else would he put himself to such bother for your brothers? Believe me when I say a gentleman doesn't look after young scamps in trouble without reason.'

'No, no,' denied Caroline in return. 'He does it all from fondness for you.' She couldn't deny the ridiculous leap of hope within her, however.

'Aye,' responded Lady Winnington with wry accents. 'The lad has spent more time on my doorstep the past weeks than in the past year.'

Caroline sniffed with disbelief. Not even her high hopes would permit her to believe that sort of rubbish.

The evening went off without incident.

Apparently word had not spread about her brother's nonsensical doings. The crowd at Lady Babbingson's musicale was thin. Worried her aunt might be overtiring herself, Caroline persuaded her to leave early. Never would Caroline have allowed that the evening seemed sadly flat without the appearance of the Earl of Rutledge.

★　★　★

Come morning, Caroline slipped from the rear of the house by way of the mews to ride out in the park. She was about to ask if Davy might accompany her on her solitary ride when she saw a change of expression on the groom's face as he glanced behind her.

'I trust Lady Babbingson provided her usual musical treats last night?'

'Lord Rutledge, good morning,' replied Caroline with equally frigid politeness, spinning about to face him. 'The musicale quite charmed one.'

'So you left early?' A hint of tolerant amusement crept into his voice.

Caroline gave him a look of rebuke. 'I feared my aunt was becoming overly tired. She has endured much since we arrived on her doorstep. Although, to be honest, she did not bargain for such as my brothers when she offered to present me to society.' A twinkle crept into her eyes as Caroline considered all that had transpired since her siblings had come to Town.

'You are about to ride out. Ride with me; my groom can follow us to preserve your good name.' Rutledge's voice was impatient, his manner curt.

Flushing at the implication that she had little name to preserve, Caroline's smile faded. She permitted Rutledge to throw her up onto her mare, then rode ahead of him along the mews in the direction of the park.

It was one of those misty mornings in late spring, not a rain or even drizzle but the sort of thing that would burn off with the advance of the sun. As she trotted along through the cool, damp air, Caroline found her ire fading. How she and her brothers had imposed on this poor man at her side. Whether or not he had any regard for her, she must convey her appreciation along with her proper regrets.

They were walking along rather sedately beneath some splendid oaks when she impulsively turned to face him. Studying his expression, she dared to say, 'You have been excessively kind to us, my lord. Please accept my thanks for all you have done. I know your efforts have made life much more agreeable for my poor aunt. I daresay, were my parents to know the whole of it, they would be exceedingly vexed with Edmund and Adrian. I — well, I thank you very much.'

Her cheeks pink with emotion, Caroline glanced at him, then stared straight ahead.

'You're refining too much upon it.' He coughed with what Caroline suspected was a touch of embarrassment.

A proper gentleman is modest, well mannered, and considerate. Rutledge had of late demonstrated all those traits, particularly around her aunt. He revealed other traits as well, she reflected, but those came out when alone with her.

Uneasy with the direction of her thoughts, she touched her boot to her horse, urging the mare to a canter. She was more than a little aware of Lord Rutledge as he quite effortlessly rode alongside.

They slowed once again, coming to a stop near the Serpentine. Caroline stared off across the water, wondering how many more weeks she would be allowed to experience the London Season with her understanding aunt. She slid from her horse to walk slowly along the water's edge. Rutledge followed suit.

'Did I tell you how well that green habit becomes you, Miss Beauchamp?'

Impetuously, Caroline looked directly at

him and said, 'You called me Caroline before.'

'I have your leave to do so again?' he asked politely.

Vexed that she had perhaps appeared a bit forward in his eyes, Caroline had no choice but to nod in agreement. 'Of course.'

'Does Hugh still call you Caroline as well?' The question was out before he considered how it might sound. He cursed his tongue for making him seem the veriest fool.

Not appearing to be the least amused by his position, Caroline gravely replied, 'As an old friend who is married to my closest friend, he retains that right.'

'Somehow I had the feeling there was a greater, ah, regard existing between you.' He slanted a glance at the glorious figure not far from where he stood.

Thinking of how she longed to lace into the caper-witted bungler, Caroline could not refrain from chuckling. It was a light, musical sound, one her escort seemed to find delightful. 'Not in the least,' she blurted out in refreshing frankness. 'I could cheerfully throttle him at times. I am persuaded that Mary has a deal of patience, but perhaps that is because she loves him.'

'You feel such an emotion is required in

marriage?' He took a step closer to her side, then stopped.

'Anything is to be preferred to marrying without affection,' declared Caroline fervently. 'I would remain a spinster to my dying day rather than accept the hand of a man I did not love.' She bent over to pluck a stem of grass. She rolled it between her fingers, continuing to gaze across the water. 'I suppose this is not the accepted mode, but fortunately I have a competence that will permit me to live modestly by myself, should it come to such a thing.' She glanced at him then. 'My days in London are numbered, as I well know. If I fail to attach a gentleman, I shall return to my parents.'

'You sound surprisingly cheerful about the prospect.'

'I adore my little brothers and sisters. Elizabeth and Anne are precious dears, and Thomas and William are becoming fine boys. I could never rail at the thought of guiding them.'

'You help your mother, I take it?'

'I do.' Her simple reply held no boast, rather a mere statement of fact. A half smile curved her soft lips as she turned to lean against her mare. Stroking the gentle animal, she added, 'I should be fairly content with what I have there, you know. When one knows nothing else, one must accept what life brings.'

Later she was to wonder if he would have kissed her had they not been hailed by Henry Kenyon and Sarah Thurlow.

The pair rode up full of zest and laughter. Caroline thought they seemed to have the world by the tail this morning. And well they might, for they seemed much in love. She glanced at Rutledge to see if he observed what she had noticed, but couldn't tell, for his face was that bland mask again.

Only when he came over to help toss her up in her saddle did she see that glint in his eyes once more. A slow smile curved her lips as she returned his look.

Perhaps there was yet hope for her, for she knew that if she could not have her heart's desire, she would have nothing at all.

The four continued to ride through the park, with the grooms trailing respectfully behind at a distance. When Caroline and Rutledge returned to the mews, she felt in great charity with the world.

'You are to attend the opera this evening?' said Rutledge, pausing at the door that led to that shaded walkway Caroline recalled quite vividly.

'I believe so.' She expected she might see

him there, but not so much as a hint was given her as to his intentions. She walked quickly along the mews, then let herself into her aunt's garden with a lighter heart. Perhaps. Just perhaps.

10

The peace and quiet of the breakfast room where Caroline and her aunt lingered at their nuncheon was shattered with a crash and a flurry of feminine chatter in the entry hall. Caroline exchanged a startled look with her aunt, then rose to hurry to the front entry.

Three boxes, two trunks, and four valises were being placed in a pile near the door while an agitated young woman fluttered about, checking and rechecking. Simpkins stood to one side in affronted dignity, looking about ready to have a spasm while the footman struggled with the baggage.

'Margaret?' inquired Caroline cautiously. Although her face was concealed by an enormous bonnet, the voice was most familiar. Her cousin had married Baron Justin Fancourt the year before. Caroline had thought her to be quite happily settled in the country with her pleasant husband.

'Oh, Caroline, how glad I am to see you.' The figure whirled about and rushed to Caroline, arms outstretched. 'And you, dear Aunt Fanny.' The brave smile of greeting abruptly dissolved into a flood of tears.

'What has happened, dearest?' Concerned, Caroline drew her slender little cousin along into the morning room. The last of the nuncheon was quite forgotten in the excitement of an unexpected guest.

''Tis Justin, the brute. I shall never return there again. I declare, Caroline, 'tis the outside of enough, the way he treats me.' Margaret held up a fragile wisp of linen to her pair of lovely hazel eyes, then sniffed.

Caroline tenderly urged her dab of a cousin onto a comfortable chair, then stood back to study her. Margaret was wearing a charming pelisse of ruby velvet that set off her creamy complexion and black hair to perfection. Ruby Morocco slippers in the latest cut peeped out from beneath a delicate pink India-muslin traveling gown. If Margaret was being ill-treated, it had nothing in connection with the way she dressed.

Lady Winnington plumped herself down on a chair close to Margaret's, reaching out to gently pat her arm. 'Poor dear. You must stay with us until you can resolve your troubles.'

Privately Caroline thought her cousin was undoubtedly over-reacting from some mere slight. She studied the figure in the chair, then abruptly asked, 'When is the baby due?'

Margaret gasped, looking at Caroline with horrified eyes. 'Caroline, I am ever so shocked! How can you be so indelicate?' She sniffed, then added in a petulant tone, 'And what makes you suspect such a thing?' She smoothed out her pelisse, taking care to arrange the folds of the pelisse and her gown just so before continuing. 'I did not think it was in the least noticeable.'

A wry note crept into Caroline's voice as she answered: 'You forget I have six younger brothers and sisters. I have assisted my mother during most of those confinements in one manner or another. I have learned the signs well.'

'Justin refused to permit me one last trip to Town before I am confined to Fancourt Abbey. I *had* to get away! I want to order several suitable gowns for the coming months. Heaven knows I shall look like a whale at the very least. I want to look like a pretty whale, if I may. And I longed to attend the opera, browse among the shops, ride in the park, just once more. It was positively wicked of him to deny me my little treat.' She sniffed, then batted tear-dampened lashes at her aunt and cousin, looking for all the world like a wee kitten begging for a drop of milk.

Unable to deny what seemed such a reasonable request, Lady Winnington said, 'And you shall, dear girl. Since the boys have gone, you shall have that room. It has such a pretty view from the window.'

'I thought Fancourt to be of sterling character,' declared Caroline in a soft, reflective voice. 'I cannot imagine him to be so cruel.'

'Well, to be fair, he did not wish me to travel alone. He feared the highwaymen, if you must know. Then he found it necessary to take a trip to one of his estates off in Devon. But he sent me a letter to say he is to be quite delayed. By the time he returns, it would be too late. I would be beached!' With those breathless words Lady Fancourt leaned against the back of her chair, appearing beautifully done to the bone.

The analogy between her cousin and a whale was a little hard to accept. Margaret looked to be one of those women who even in the last months of their pregnancy would appear scarcely halfway along. Caroline took a turn about the morning room, pausing to glance out the window at where ivy crisscrossed in a neat design on the brick wall that backed upon the mews. She turned back to face her cousin, warily watching her while presenting the evening's plans.

'We intend a visit to the opera this very night. I expect you will be too exhausted to attend with us. Will you mind being alone?'

The scrap of somewhat damp linen was

whisked into a pretty ruby velvet reticule; the figure in the chair straightened perceptibly. 'I don't doubt but that if I may rest a few hours, I shall be able to go with you. It would cheer me immensely, I believe. I would only sit here and mope if I am left alone.'

'You must not mope, dear child,' remonstrated Lady Winnington. 'I am firmly convinced that an expectant mother must think beautiful thoughts. Caroline's mother is certain that is what has made all her children so handsome.'

'See,' coaxed Margaret in the sweetest possible voice. 'It would be very bad for me to be left at home. I shall rest on your soft, comfortable bed until supper. I well remember how cozy your home is, dear aunt. My abigail will undoubtedly have things ready for me by the time I get to my room. Oh, how can I thank you, dear aunt? And you, too, sensible, kind Caroline. I vow, I cannot be in better hands.'

Somewhat doubting that, given the tangle she found herself plunged into at the moment, Caroline nodded, bestowed a cautious smile on Margaret, then extended her hand. 'Come with me, then. I shall help you to your room and see to it you are comfortable for your much needed nap.'

'As to that, I did have a pleasant journey,

for I used the britschka Justin insisted we buy. Since it converts to a sleeping carriage, I lounged most of the way in the greatest comfort imaginable. So you see, I shall be fine in a trice.' She popped up from her chair, looking far brighter than one would expect from a woman who had traveled into the city from the wilds of Kent.

Caroline exchanged a look with her aunt. Her raised brows above an expressive face conveyed more than mere words could possibly at the moment. It seemed that far from being an ogre, Justin feared for his wife and her safety more than the average husband. Indeed, Caroline could only hope that she might someday be so fortunate to have such a caring husband. If, indeed, she ever found one.

Some time later when Margaret had been tucked in, after being persuaded to enjoy a cup of beef broth and a wafer-thin sandwich of lean ham on fresh white bread, Caroline sought out her aunt.

'You realize this presents a few problems, dear aunt, the least of which is an irate husband, should he return home to discover a missing pregnant wife.'

'Caroline,' complained Lady Winnington, 'must you be so outspoken? 'Increasing,' 'in a delicate condition,' or 'in an interesting way' is more ladylike, my dear. One does not wish to be thought vulgar. Is she well along, then? I should not have thought her so brazen as to present herself in public were she so.'

'Perhaps four months. 'Tis hard to say with one so slim. Fortunately, the present styles permit her to conceal it well. If she wears a dress with full gathers below the bosom, I daresay no one will be the wiser,' Caroline paused by the window to stare out while fiddling with the fringe hanging from the drapery.

'I had thought our dear little Mary would be anticipating an heir to the Stanhope name by now,' reflected Lady Winnington.

'That is prodigiously difficult when he wanders, ma'am.' Caroline sighed, then began a restless pacing about the drawing room, where her aunt awaited a few friends for a comfortable coze. Glancing at the cupid swinging so gaily away in perfect measure, she stopped, putting a dismayed hand to her cheek.

'What is it?'

'Tonight. The opera. I had forgotten Hugh is to escort me . . . at my request. I hope Rutledge has the task of taking Mary. But what of the widow Ingleby? I neglected to tell you that I encountered her at Hatchards while exchanging those books. She was not best pleased with me. In fact, she seemed excessively vexed. I need not explain why to you, I know.' Caroline bestowed a worried look on her aunt. Both knew only too well how the gossips would adore some contre-temps to banter about over tea.

'You don't think she might create a scene? While she is not of the best *ton*, she assuredly knows better than to behave so. She walks a thin line of acceptability as it is now. Would she dare risk what reputation she has left?' Lady Winnington put aside the crumpled piece of tapestry that served to occupy her hands when she wished to appear busy.

'I do not know,' said Caroline softly, wondering what the evening promised to bring. She had a strong suspicion it was more than music.

'It will be interesting to see what our dear Margaret shall say to the situation. She was a madcap before she married Fancourt.'

'It would seem to me she has changed very little on that score, dear ma'am,' replied Caroline dryly.

With the entry of three of Lady Winnington's friends, the subject veered to other channels. The coming marriage of the royal princess, the scandalous Lord Byron, and the climbing debts of the Regent were thoroughly discussed over delicate China tea and lemon wafers.

Caroline slipped away as soon as she could, knowing that her presence kept the ladies from indulging in the more risqué gossip.

At their early supper, for Lady Winnington did not wish to miss one note of the opera, Margaret joined Caroline and her aunt, looking the merest child. As fresh as a bowl of just plucked strawberries, she floated down the stairs in a rich pink jaconet trimmed with rows and rows of exquisite lace.

In her pale green silk lutestring with ivory ribands, the dress she had worn when Lord Rutledge had made those rude comments, Caroline felt almost sedate. Even though she admitted to her own decolletage, there was something rather daring about the pink jaconet. And on a matron, no less.

'Do not give me that look, please, Caroline. It reminds me too much of Justin when he first saw this gown,' complained Margaret when she caught sight of Caroline's face.

'For a mother soon-to-be, you scarce look the part, my dear,' admitted Caroline with a reluctant laugh. Margaret seemed to adore being outrageous.

'How lovely of you to say so. I vow, it has quite made my evening.' Margaret gave a happy little skip, then crossed the hall into the dining room.

The meal was enlivened by stories of life at Fancourt Abbey. Justin was indeed a patient man if one listened carefully to the tales embroidered by Lady Fancourt. Margaret's love for mischief had not diminished one whit. It appeared to be one trait shared by all in her family, decided Caroline.

If Hugh was dismayed to discover he had three women to escort to the opera this night, he gave not the slightest indication of such. With a fine degree of courtesy he assisted Lady Winnington into the carriage, then Margaret and Caroline.

He managed to sit next to Caroline, favoring her with an approving look. Fortunately, he didn't recall she had worn this gown before. Caroline did not ascribe to the notion that one could wear a gown only once. She had spent a considerable sum on this one and intended to get full usage from it before consigning it to the heap.

There was no opportunity to exchange information, much to her regret. Margaret kept up a lively flow of entertaining chatter.

The Stanhope driver brought them along Pall Mall at a goodly pace. They soon approached the corner at Haymarket where the Royal Italian Opera House — also known as the King's Theatre — rose in elegant simplicity above the throngs of carriages and masses of pedestrians.

It was a mere stone's throw from Carlton House to here. Caroline wondered if the prince would dare present himself this evening. The poor man was in more than a spot of bother over the Canova sculpture mess, not to mention his mounting debts. The last she had heard, the work on the commemorative statue was to proceed. His attitude toward debt was a dangerous thing, given the general poverty that spread across the nation. One heard rumors of revolution, whispered in shocked accents. Rioting and rick burning disturbed the countryside; the stories of these acts roused fears in the hearts of many.

'I neglected to ask you what the program is to be this evening, dear aunt. Something special?' Margaret could not fail to take note of the crush of carriages, the air of anticipation that clung to the people who entered the opera house tonight.

'Sir Henry Bishop has adapted Scott's novel *Guy Mannering* for the stage. I enjoyed the book so much, I can scarce wait to see it performed,' declared Lady Wilmington with a delighted smile.

Once the carriage drew up before the opera

house, the ladies were assisted from the carriage with the same pleasant courtesy. Caroline wished she might warn Hugh that his wife probably would be here this evening in the company of his former friend. With the press of people all about them, though, Caroline dared not say anything.

They wove their way through the throng with increasing difficulty. Caroline cast more than one concerned look at her cousin. The promise of hearing Scott's words to music drew the crowds.

Once they reached the relative peace of Lady Winnington's box, Caroline drew a breath of relief. She urged Margaret onto the most comfortable seat while closely watching her for any signs of distress. Thankfully, the young woman seemed none the worse for the experience. Indeed, Margaret seemed to bloom under the eye of the *ton*.

In the pit below, the dandies strolled back and forth, preening while all the time searching the boxes with sharp eyes, hungry for a tidbit of potential gossip. The benches filled rapidly with those who could not afford the horrendous price of the more comfortable and private boxes.

Caroline edged over to the partition to discreetly peer around the interior of the theater. Within the confines of each red-draped box sat the members of the *ton* and those who aspired to such heights. The Fashionable Impures, as those ladies were obliquely called, also bought boxes so they might display their rather blatant charms. It always irked Caroline to see men clustering about those women like so many drones around a queen bee. Not that she was supposed to know about such things. She often smiled in wry amusement at the things young women were not supposed to know. She suspected others, like herself, possessed a great deal of awareness but maintained a prudent silence.

Gorgeous gowns and fabulous jewels fit to bedeck a queen could be viewed in any direction. For one who enjoyed watching people, it was quite a sight.

'Do you see anyone in particular?' inquired Hugh. He stood slightly behind Caroline, next to where Margaret gracefully reclined in her chair.

Noting that Margaret and her aunt were engaged in a spirited discussion of the merits of Lady Jersey's latest gown, Caroline replied, 'I see Mary over there on the second tier, and if I make no mistake, it is Rutledge with her.' Squinting just a bit, Caroline gave a decided nod. 'Yes, it is her 'dear Giles,' as she calls

Rutledge,' she added with deliberate intent.

Tired of this constant feeling of being at war with her friends, Caroline hoped to prod Hugh into action. Heavens, for someone who looked as he did, he was the most hen-hearted person she knew.

An upward glance at Hugh revealed her barb had indeed struck home. Pleased, she went on, 'I have not seen Mary for some days. I cannot imagine what occupies her time so, other than the drives in the park with Rutledge. Although I believe that is a new gown she wears tonight. Quite lovely, do you not think? Undoubtedly she has been involved with the modiste.' Caroline suspected Hugh knew enough regarding ladies' gowns to know a dress could not possibly take up that much of his Mary's time. She was highly gratified to see a flush of dark red creep up Hugh's handsome cheeks.

'She does look very pretty this evening,' Hugh admitted. He seemed about to say more when the curtain rose to begin the first act of the drama.

Caroline subsided on her chair, indicating to Hugh that he ought to follow her example. There was no need to display him for all to see. Mary and Rutledge, Caroline was certain, had observed his presence in the

Winnington box. That was all that was necessary.

Farther down the tier of boxes sat the incomparable Mrs Ingleby in the company of Lord Mortland. His coach had drawn up to the opera house just after the Stanhope equipage had pulled away. The sight of Hugh escorting Caroline Beauchamp did little to cheer the lady. Wearing her favorite shade of red in a daringly cut gown of net over silk faille, she regally made her way to the Mortland box. Once seated, she observed the insipid child married to Stanhope enter the Rutledge box on the far side of the theater, a box where Diana desired to reign.

A feeling of ill-usage took strong hold of Diana Ingleby. Before the appearance of the Beauchamp chit, things had gone quite as Diana wished them. She had enjoyed the attentions of Rutledge from time to time, though never as intensely as she might have hoped. And later when she desired to set up a bit of competition, she had managed to snare the pleasure of Stanhope's handsome gallantry.

Then something happened. What, Diana didn't know for certain. But first Stanhope had defected, then Rutledge strayed. And she instinctively sensed Caroline Beauchamp had something to do with it, although how, Diana couldn't imagine. The mere thought of that little nothing, even if she did have a passing figure, attracting Rutledge to her side made Diana want to laugh. Only it had gone beyond laughing. The whey-faced Viscountess Stanhope was a polite attention — Diana hoped. But deep inside she acknowledged that Caroline Beauchamp had several assets on her side — virginity, unblemished reputation, and family — that Diana could not match.

She sincerely wanted to lure Rutledge to her side, with the ultimate goal of marriage in mind. She knew the value of her beauty, and she possessed an admirable amount of money, something few in her position could claim.

Neglecting to consider her marginal respect-ability, a thing which made her totally ineligible as a future bride to the Earl of Rutledge, she saw only her beauty. Surely a womanly coun-tenance and opulent form was to be preferred to a mere blushing girl. She also forgot that Caroline Beauchamp had not turned pink when confronted with the elegant widow.

While the drama unfolded upon the stage, Diana Ingleby considered how best to handle her situation.

Caroline pretended to enjoy the opera, actually more of a drama with a bit of music here and there for effect, but her mind wandered far from the story being presented. How unlike her to be such a worrier. Usually she permitted things to happen as they came, figuring there was little she could do to change the course of events. Tonight she worried, knowing there was nothing she could do, that events were most definitely out of her control.

A less optimistic young woman would have indulged in a fit of the blue devils, or have vapors at the very least. All that revealed Caroline's inner turmoil was a sadly twisted handkerchief clutched in restless hands.

When the intermission arrived, she turned a polite, attentive face to the others, responding with what she hoped was appropriate enthusiasm to the treat being given by her aunt.

Lady Winnington cast a narrow glance at Caroline, then patted Margaret's arm. 'You are not feeling any ill effects, I trust? Should you have the least little twinge, you must tell me at once and we will return to South Street.'

'I have never felt better. I daresay Caroline has something on her mind, for she looked quite abstracted when I turned to her during the performance.'

Smiling brightly, Caroline denied this

heresy. 'Nonsense, Margaret. Look, do you see what the Duchess of Richmond is wearing this evening? What a beautiful gown, and I vow her hair is dressed most becomingly. And Lady Melbourne is here tonight as well. How she has the courage to show her face with the scandal of her daughter-in-law is amazing. Caro Lamb is most assuredly a mad woman to behave as she does.'

And how the *ton* adored scandal. Caroline glanced at where Mary sat at Rutledge's side, then at Hugh. If this silly couple did not resolve their troubles immediately, she would assuredly wash her hands of them. She vowed to call upon Mary the next day to inform her that the end had arrived. Caroline wished to forget the entire proposition, Mary could well try seducing her own husband, if that was what was needed!

The curtain rose again to begin the final act of *Guy Mannering*. With great effort Caroline set aside the fears that plagued her to absorb the drama unfolding on the stage.

The singing was pleasant, the acting fair, certainly not bad enough to bring down the scorn of the audience upon the heads of the performers. Caroline had seen this only once, when disgusted with the acting, people had thrown fruit at the stage, hissing and booing in the most frightening of ways. She had hastily departed the box with her aunt, and managed to leave the premises before things became totally beyond control.

'Well,' declared Lady Winnington as the final curtain fell and they had applauded the stars of the performance sufficiently, 'I believe that was lovely.'

'Thank you for the treat, dearest aunt. I feel ever so much better. Once I get in a bit of shopping and perhaps a drive or two, I shall be more amenable to the thought of Fancourt Abbey once again.' Margaret rose to her feet, assisted by a politely attentive Hugh. She flashed him a brilliant smile. Caroline could well see what had attracted Justin Fancourt to his wife.

Lady Winnington and Margaret went first, followed by Caroline, then Hugh. They had safely negotiated the stairs and were slowly making their way to the front of the building when they saw Mary and Lord Rutledge coming toward them. As if that were not difficult enough, Diana Ingleby could be seen descending the last of the steps on the arm of Lord Mortland.

Destiny seemed to decree that the three pairs meet. Caroline tried to ascertain what Mary might be thinking. She thought she knew well enough, but Mary had behaved oddly the last day or two. Had she changed her mind?

Rutledge's handsome face appeared sculpted from stone. Only those gray eyes revealed emotion. Caroline searched them as they neared one another. Had she totally sunk beyond his regard? And all to help a friend. This was not the moment for bitter reflection, however. To Caroline's right was the Ingleby.

'Well, what an interesting little group we have here. Lord Stanhope, I am surprised to see you with Miss Beauchamp,' said Diana in a carrying voice. 'I thought your taste to be far above the infantry. But then, when one views your other choices, well, I guess 'tis all of a part.'

She turned her glittering eyes upon Caroline, surprised to discover that young miss calmly returning the look, chin lifted in defiance, eyes flashing with unmistakable challenge.

'You do manage to get about, do you not? For a sweet young girl who is supposed to be so unblemished of reputation, how does it pass you are permitted to lure your dearest friend's husband? I vow, I find society vastly diverting.' The widow cast a glance to the side, where avid ears listened for every word, hoping to be the first to repeat the *on-dit* on the morrow.

'And you, Lord Rutledge, how immensely kind of you to escort the neglected bride. I declare, she still has the virginal look of a miss about her.' Continuing, Diana's wrath got the better of her common sense. 'How long shall that continue, I wonder?' Her malicious smile was noted by all around, and a few titters of uneasy laughter ran through the nearest of the crowd. 'Perhaps you will undertake to assist there as well?'

Mary's gasp at this attack was not missed by anyone. She seemed so pale as to swoon. Caroline felt distinctly ill. How could she have permitted herself to become entangled in such a caper-witted bit of stupidity?

'Well, I'm sure you shall be the first to broadcast whatever you know to the entire world, Mrs Ingleby,' declared the petite Lady Fancourt to the five involved in the scene that was rapidly getting worse by the moment. 'But then, featherheads are known to hold little of value in them. Just so much air, you know.' She waved a dainty hand in the direction of Mrs Ingleby, glancing at her escort in derision.

Lord Mortland had stepped back in amused silence.

'Shall we go?' said Margaret in a plaintive

voice. 'I am exceedingly tired.' She placed one delicate hand to her brow, indeed appearing as though she might faint.

Roused from stunned immobility to concern, Hugh quickly moved forward to escort the delicate-looking Lady Fancourt from the opera house. Caroline tossed an anguished glance at Mary, then followed Margaret and her aunt from the building, and out to where the Stanhope carriage had just pulled up.

The silence within the carriage was as thick as leftover pea soup. The sound of the wheels rattling over the cobbles on Pall Mall was quite distinct, echoing about the interior in a dismal way.

'That was quite a performance,' commented Lady Winnington. Whether she referred to the opera that had been presented or the scene in the lobby was unclear.

'I believe London is more dangerous than I recalled,' offered Margaret in a small voice.

Fortunately, Caroline avoided conversation by the mere expedient of their arrival at South Street. She hurried into the house, politely thanking Hugh, denying him entry.

'I shall talk to you later, Hugh. Not now.'

Once the rattle of the carriage faded into the night, the three women walked up to the first floor, entering the drawing room by unspoken consent.

Margaret crossed to drop into a chair, exhaling a long sigh of relief.

'Thank you for your help,' murmured Caroline. She stripped off her gloves, dropping them onto a table along with her tiny mesh reticule.

'I still cannot credit what my ears heard,' said Lady Winnington, pulling her shawl more closely about her as though to fend off a chill.

'I believe that has put paid to my ever contracting even a respectable marriage. Scandal is not considered a desirable feature in a prospective bride,' stated Caroline in dry, crisp accents.

'For once I cannot argue,' replied a defeated Lady Winnington as she seated herself near the fireplace. 'This will be no nine days' wonder, to quickly pass. No, indeed. Did you see the expression on Rutledge's face?'

11

A gentle, misty rain fell upon the city. The gray skies echoed the mood inside the house on South Street. Caroline sat by the breakfast room table nursing her cup of chocolate, though in truth it was quite cold.

'I insist you come out shopping with me,' declared Margaret in her most winning manner. 'I should like your opinion on my gowns when I go to the modiste, and you know it is always great fun to have a friend when one is hunting for all the little fripperies.'

'If you wish, of course I shall go with you,' replied Caroline in a colorless voice. She placed her cup on the table, then drifted across to stare out the window at the brick wall behind the house. Water dripped from the ivy, resembling nothing so much as a dismal green cascade.

'It is not the end of the world,' said Margaret.

'I know that. I suspect I shall come about in short order. At the moment I find my optimism has deserted me. But I will go along while you purchase these gowns you must have.'

'Good,' said Margaret, giving her cousin a sharp look. 'It is regrettable that Mrs Ingleby felt it necessary to pour out her frustrations in that foolish manner. Pray those whose itching ears listened so avidly will find something more fascinating to spread abroad than this minor trifling.'

Caroline rounded upon her cousin, a hurt look upon her face. 'It is not you who must face those same people today and in the days to come. Aunt Fanny agreed with me last night. My chances of a respectable marriage are put paid.' Then, regretting her harsh tone, she half smiled and more softly said, 'You are kind to care enough to try to cheer me out of my dismals. I fully expect to receive a note rescinding my voucher for Almack's, you know.'

'It's as well Brummell left early last night. You do not have to fear his acid tongue, although I do not know how much influence he carries anymore.'

Caroline had not paid the least attention to the dandy last evening. Indeed, she had been aware of little beyond the drama that enveloped her. 'They say that your past deeds return to haunt you later. Perhaps the snubs and Turkish treatment he has dealt out will fall on him.'

'Come, enough of this maudlin stuff. I am

anxious to get to the shops. May I tell Simpkins to order us a carriage?'

Reluctantly Caroline nodded her agreement to an outing she felt certain would be a test of her durability. This time of day, even with the mist, there would be women out and about. It could be worse, she supposed, though she was not quite sure how.

When they left the house, Margaret was in a determinedly good mood. 'See, the clouds are parting, and I do believe a spot of sunshine is about to peep out. We shall have a lovely day.'

As usual, Baxhall took the ladies to the shopping areas of the city, wending his way through the masses of carriages and pedestrians with great skill.

At the modistes, Margaret settled quite happily on a dainty chair. Caroline attempted to concentrate on the selection of several gowns suitable for the remaining months of Margaret's pregnancy.

'Cheery striped lutestring for one, I believe. The stripes will make me seem thinner,' Margaret explained.

Reluctantly smiling, Caroline nodded. 'True. And what of this simple blue with the pretty pattern on it?'

'Well . . . ' Margaret grinned and conferred with the modiste while Caroline stared absently out of the window.

The bell rang when two ladies entered the pleasant little shop. Caroline glanced at them, then stiffened her spine. They had been at the opera last evening. She dimly recalled seeing their faces in the crowd.

'Lady Fancourt, how lovely to see you again. What brings you to town?' Caroline was totally ignored.

'A bit of shopping and a desire for a touch of London. Were you at the opera last night? I vow I enjoyed the presentation of Scott's work exceedingly. How lovely the weather is improving. I long for a nice drive in the park once again. One misses these little things while in the wilds of Kent, you know.'

One of the women gasped when Margaret deliberately mentioned the opera. Eyes were carefully averted from Caroline. Rather than continue the conversation, both of the women suddenly decided to leave the shop, vowing to return later. The implication was quite clear. Caroline apologized to the modiste, who shrugged the matter aside, saying those two were always late in paying their bills.

The problem of the gowns came to a quick settlement, and Margaret hustled Caroline from the shop with flustered speed.

'I have never received the cut direct before. Amazing how a little thing like that can hurt so.' Caroline's voice was light, amused. There was no outward clue to the blow that had been dealt to her pride or her heart.

'Do you wish to go directly home?' Margaret was devastated that her good intentions had brought such shocking results. 'I vow, it was the horridest thing to see the look on those nasty women. Pity they didn't fall on their noses when they left the shop, for I do not know how they could see where they walked.'

'No,' declared Caroline softly. 'I cannot possibly receive worse. Come, let us find all those fripperies you want so badly.'

With a sad heart Margaret led the way to Grafton's, where she found a pretty fan to beguile and distract her husband, several lovely handkerchiefs, and patterns for some chair covers she intended to do in tapestry work. 'The dining room chairs are in a woeful state, if you must know. I believe I shall like a design of flowers on each.'

There were no further confrontations as Margaret skillfully steered them away from any potential source of trouble. Still, it was a time fraught with tension, and both were relieved to find Baxhall waiting to take them to South Street once more.

'It was a great piece of impertinence, you know. Those women were of no significance in the least. For them to behave in such a manner, well!' Margaret drew Caroline into the house with her while Simpkins hurried out to handle the payment of Baxhall.

'I am foolish beyond permission if I believe I can resume my modest place in Society after this farce. I suspect I am in Queer Street, as Edmund would say.'

'Why do you suppose Lord Rutledge has been so kind to Edmund and Adrian?' Margaret asked as she slowly walked up the stairs to the drawing room, where she expected to find her aunt.

'If you have any notion he nurses a secret passion for me, disabuse yourself of it. I believe he dotes on our aunt, for he rushes to aid her when she summons him.' Caroline proceeded to inform her cousin of Adrian's mad start and the aborted trip to Bath. By the time they entered the drawing room, Margaret was giggling over the story.

'Dare I hope your visits to the shops were uneventful?' Lady Winnington asked, watching the two young women cross the polished wood floor to reach the new Oriental carpet that covered the area by her sofa.

Sobered by the reminder, Margaret stopped. 'I fear you are wrong. Lady Torrance and Mrs Alperson were utterly horrid. They had the nerve to give Caroline the cut direct!'

'As bad as that,' murmured Lady Winnington. Her distress was acute. 'I know not how to proceed.'

'I refuse to permit this to throw me into a stew. I think it a great piece of work about nothing,' declared Caroline quite bravely.

'You have been seeing Hugh a good deal as of late, dear girl. Anyone who did not know the truth of the matter would have legitimate cause to think the worst. What a pity Mary cannot settle the matter for herself.'

'What is this? A mystery? I declare, you must tell me the beginning, for it is terrible to come into the middle!' Margaret said. She drew up a chair close to the sofa, motioning Caroline to sit beside her aunt. 'Now, the whole of it, if you please.'

'It is like this, cousin.' Quickly Caroline detailed Mary's request for help in bringing her errant husband home, especially freeing him from the association with Mrs Ingleby. When Caroline revealed Hugh's similar request, that Mary be drawn away from Rutledge, Margaret could stand no more, but sank back in her chair, giving way to immoderate laughter.

'Oh, dear,' she gasped at last. 'What good this trip is doing me. I shan't have the megrims once I return to Fancourt, for I shall think on this tangled web and go into

255

whoops.' She made an attempt to still her laughter, but kept giggling at the thought of Caroline luring Rutledge.

At the sight of her cousin so utterly disbelieving her ability to attract the handsome lord, Caroline was greatly tempted to reveal that brief touching of lips in his cozy study the day of their ride. A glance at her aunt's expression halted her confession.

Instead she reached over to give her cousin a playful tap on her knee. 'I can see that I shall receive spurious sympathy at best from you.'

'You must admit the situation is excessively droll.'

'To own to the truth, I could have done well without it.' Caroline sat primly on the sofa while her aunt crossed to ring for tea.

When Lady Winnington returned to the sofa, she studied her two nieces, so very different in personality and looks. 'If I might venture to say so, we still have the problem on our hands. Merely because it is an amusing tangle does not whisk it away.'

'I know,' replied Caroline soberly. 'It quite sinks my spirits. I cannot face the thought of returning home with not the least hint of an attachment.'

'Nonsense,' retorted Margaret. 'We must fight back. Can you not appeal to Lord Rutledge?'

'What? Allow me to remind you that Rutledge was there last night, and Aunt Fanny took most particular notice of the expression on his face. I scarce believe he would be the one to petition for help!' Caroline subsided as the footman entered the room with the tea tray. All remained silent while he set things out, then once he had departed, speech burst forth again.

'Nevertheless, he has played a part in this farce and he did help out with Edmund and Adrian.'

'That proves nothing,' declared Caroline stoutly.

The brangling might have continued indefinitely without the interruption that followed.

'Hullo, good to see you are at home. Margaret, you here?'

'Adrian!' Caroline cried. 'Has something happened? Why are you here instead of in Sussex? You have not been hurt in all that digging about, have you?' Caroline anxiously examined her younger brother for signs of ill-treatment.

'Not in the least.' Adrian grinned with good humor at his sister's concern. 'I need to talk with Rutledge about what I've uncovered on his land.'

'Oh, dear.' Caroline backed away to plump

herself down on the sofa.

Seeing the general exchange of guarded looks and frowns, Adrian asked, 'What's going on here? You look as though someone has died.'

'In a manner of speaking, you are not far from the truth,' Caroline replied. 'It is just too jumbled to explain in any detail, but I have quite sunk beneath consideration, and I very much doubt if Lord Rutledge will give you the time of day, should you inquire,' she concluded with asperity.

'We shall see about that.' Turning to his aunt, he inquired, 'About my room . . . '

'Margaret is in there now. Should you deem it necessary to stay, it will have to be one of the rooms on the top floor.'

'Very well.' Adrian gave his unhappy-looking sister a thoughtful gaze. 'I shall see what can be done about this matter.'

'Can you tell us what you have discovered? Or must it be a secret?' Margaret asked, poking him with her slippered toe.

With boyish enthusiasm Adrian dropped onto a chair, reached for a macaroon, then forged into his explanation. 'I have uncovered the corner of what I suspect to be a truly great Roman villa. Judging from the size of it so far, it should be a wonder to behold. There is a section of mighty fine mosaic, and I've found coins and pieces of pottery, too.'

'But?' urged Caroline, intrigued with his story and fearful he would find himself crushed by her behavior.

'I need more men to dig, and permission from Rutledge to do that digging. The tenant is not best pleased with my tearing up the land for a lot of what he calls nonsense.'

'So you must see his lordship. I wish you luck.'

'No time like the present,' declared Adrian. He seemed undaunted by the prospect that faced him. He excused himself most politely.

When he had left the mom, Caroline jumped up to wander over to the window. On the street below she could see Adrian walking briskly toward Park Lane. When he turned at the corner, she said, 'He has gone to see Rutledge now. I can only hope that the man's animosity toward me will not extend to my brothers.'

The three women exchanged wondering looks, then silently considered what must be done next.

★ ★ ★

Lord Rutledge lounged deeper into the soft leather of the chair behind his imposing mahogany desk to consider the problem facing him. What was he to do about that impossible girl next door? Picking up a quill from his desk, he fiddled with the thing until exasperated that no solution presented itself immediately.

'She ought to be punished.' Yet something stopped him from taking any form of retribution. She had faced the Ingleby bravely, he admitted with reluctance. But it had been an impossible situation. Scandalous. Tossing the quill aside, he rose from his chair to stroll over to the window. Beyond the trees that rose along the perimeter of his land stood the brick house where Caroline Beauchamp was right this moment, unless he very much missed his guess.

A discreet rap on his door was followed by the entry of his butler. 'A young gentleman to see you, milord. A Mister Adrian Beauchamp.'

'Show him in.' What the devil was young Beauchamp doing back in the city? Rutledge had been certain that scamp wouldn't be heard from for months at the very least.

Adrian was dutifully respectful, sufficiently so to give Rutledge the depressing sensation he was near being elderly.

'Sir, I have a report on the Roman villa. I believe it to be far larger than you suspected and of greater value.'

Intrigued, Rutledge motioned the lad to a chair, then returned to his favorite leather one behind his desk. 'Tell me what you have found.'

With no diminishing of his earlier enthusiasm even with the repetition of his tale, Adrian revealed all that had been uncovered and why he had decided to come to Town.

'Did you see your sister when you stopped by Lady Winnington's?' The query slipped out with casual nonchalance.

Not suspecting any ulterior motive for the question, Adrian replied, 'Yes, sir. She was in the drawing room with my cousin and aunt. Dashed gloomy it was, too. Told her they acted as though someone had died. As matter of fact, she mumbled some nonsense about having sunk beneath consideration. Even said she doubted you would give me the time of day. Got windmills in her head!' Adrian declared with strong affront.

'In a bad mood, what?' Rutledge suspected Adrian was putting the thing far too mildly. If he didn't miss his guess, that young woman was suffering at the moment. It puzzled him why he felt disturbed by the thought.

She deserved to be banished from polite society. He admitted a married woman or widow might pursue a man whether he be single or wed. But for a young girl making her bow to society, it was unthinkable.

'Are you putting up with them while in Town?' Rutledge asked. He hated the thought of subterfuge, but he wanted to know what was being contemplated at the house across the mews.

'In the attic. My cousin Margaret has taken over my room for the nonce.' Adrian made a wry face, but seemed good-naturedly resigned to his fate.

Rutledge frowned. Attics were cold and inclined to be damp and not comfortable in the least, even for a young buck who could sleep most anywhere. 'My good fellow, I've bedrooms in abundance. You'll stay with me, for after all, you are in a sense working for me. We shall inform your aunt immediately, before she has you settled in there.'

Taken aback at the invitation Rutledge had just extended, Adrian could only nod and murmur something about his lordship being most kind and all the stuff one says at such an offer.

Never would Rutledge admit that he desired to see for himself how Caroline Beauchamp fared following the disastrous evening at the opera. They were about to depart for the Winnington house when the butler admitted a particular friend, Lord Lansdowne.

Dismayed to see Rutledge obviously about to leave, Lansdowne detained his friend long enough to impart his startling news. While Adrian was nonplussed, Rutledge shook his head in wonder. The three sauntered down the front steps of Thornhill House conjecturing what the event might mean to a good many people.

They parted once out on Park Lane, Lansdowne to mount his horse and ride off toward Hyde Park with the hope of catching someone who didn't know the latest scandal. The others strolled around the corner to the Winnington house.

Simpkins ushered the two gentlemen up to the drawing room, where Caroline, Margaret, and Lady Winnington still sat in desultory conversation.

Caroline jumped up, ready to come to her brother's defense if necessary.

'Lady Winnington, Lady Fancourt, Miss Beauchamp.' Rutledge bowed most properly. 'We came over to inform you that young Adrian will stay with me while in the city. After all, we have much to discuss regarding the excavation.' The dismayed glance between Caroline and her cousin was amusing.

'That is very kind of you, Lord Rutledge. I am certain my brother appreciates your hospitality,' said Caroline stiffly.

'Fine. Perhaps you can arrange to have a footman bring his things over later.' Rutledge turned as if to leave, then paused. 'By the by, have you heard the news?'

'What news? Caroline and I were at the modiste's this morning, but learned nothing new of import.' Margaret perked up, hearing a note in Rutledge's voice that promised a rare bit of gossip.

'Brummell left the opera early last night and drove, some say, to Dover and a hasty sail to France. His debts were pressing and he could not hope to meet them.'

'So he left?' Caroline sank down upon the chair as the ramifications of this event began to sink in.

'Lord Lansdowne told us not minutes ago. I have no reason to doubt his word.'

'I didn't intend to cast doubt upon your knowledge, sir,' replied Caroline hastily. 'But you must admit that for me it is a most fortuitous occurrence.'

'I had already realized that,' said Rutledge. Really, the chit looked incredibly lovely even in her distress. Last night she had worn that revealing gown that made him want to hide her away from the eyes of the *ton*. No man should see her so revealed. Except, perhaps, himself. This afternoon she was modestly garbed in a round dress of fine white cambric trimmed in sapphire ribands.

Caroline turned to her aunt to explain her odd reaction to the news. 'If such a startling thing has taken place, Society will be far and away too absorbed in this scandal to pay the least attention to my most unimportant self, or for that matter, the business of Hugh and Mary and Mrs Ingleby.'

'True,' said Lady Winnington. 'It would help if you were seen out and about as though you have not a care in the world. I don't hold with hanging your head as though you did something wrong.'

Caroline's anxious glance at Rutledge did not appear to register with her aunt. 'Aunt Fanny,' cautioned Caroline.

Curious what the old lady meant, Rutledge wondered how he could find out. Even the most devoted of relatives had to admit that Miss Beauchamp had been improper in her behavior.

'It is time for the daily drive through the park. Why not join me, Lady Fancourt? Miss Beauchamp? You as well, should you desire, dear Fanny.' Rutledge cast the older lady a twinkling smile.

'You know how I feel about horses. Never go out unless I must and then I avoid an open carriage. No, not me. But the girls should,' she declared decisively. 'Margaret said she wished above all things for a drive in the park before returning to Fancourt Abbey.' Turning to her pleased niece, she added, 'Get your things, I think this will do nicely.'

Not quite understanding what her aunt meant, Margaret left the room, followed by a puzzled Caroline.

The park was lovely after the gentle rain. The sun peeped around clouds to bless the occupants of the carriages that flowed in a never ending river through the park. Nearly every coach, landau, and phaeton paused to impart the latest news, the decampment of Brummell.

Hisses of 'Shocking!' gasps of 'Well, I never!' and those who proclaimed, 'I knew it would come soon enough,' echoed along the road.

Caroline shared a look of unease with her cousin as they rode with Rutledge in his gray phaeton. Although intended for two people, he had insisted that since Margaret and Caroline were such slim creatures, there was no problem.

Margaret quickly agreed, for she wished to say she had ridden in the Rutledge carriage. Caroline felt it was easy for her to agree, since Margaret hadn't been required to snuggle close to Rutledge, feel the warmth of his body, nor watch the strain of his biscuit pantaloons over those muscular thighs. A sudden nudge in her ribs drew Caroline's attention from the man at her side.

'Look, there's that spiteful Mrs Alperson. I wonder if she will acknowledge you now that you are up in Rutledge's carriage,' whispered Margaret in a voice that Rutledge must have heard.

Caroline cast a despairing glance at her dearest cousin, then at the approaching landau. It was old-fashioned but in excellent repair, the Alpersons being people of good name but careful with their money.

The grays were slowed to a halt, and Lord Rutledge tipped his gray beaver hat with a courtly flourish. 'Mrs Alperson, Lady Torrance. I believe you are acquainted with Miss Beauchamp and her cousin, Lady Fancourt? Lovely day, is it not? I imagine you are agog with the news of Brummell.'

'Shocking,' declared Mrs Alperson with a darting glance at Caroline as though to convince herself she was seeing what she actually saw — Caroline Beauchamp in Rutledge's carriage as though last evening had not occurred.

'Poor man,' said Margaret with a wistful smile. 'He must be devastated to leave his clubs and friends behind. Too, too sad.'

'Oh, yes, indeed,' agreed both ladies hastily.

They nodded, then signaled their driver to proceed. Not only did they have the import of the Brummell departure to absorb, but the apparent restoration of Miss Beauchamp to favor. It was all most exciting.

'Thank you, sir. I believe we have made our little statement. If you wish, we can return now.'

'Nonsense, Miss Beauchamp. Lady Fancourt desires the full drive and she shall have it.'

With that Caroline subsided into silence for the remainder of the trip, much to Rutledge's frustration. If he had thought to worm out the tale from either of these women, he was disappointed.

Caroline suffered the drive, thinking this had to be the slowest she had ever traversed the park. When the carriage stopped before Lady Winnington's house, Caroline breathed a sigh of relief that her ordeal was finished. She had reckoned without Rutledge and her cousin.

Determined to reach Miss Beauchamp in some way, Rutledge racked his brain for an excuse to see her again. She must be drawn away from Hugh for Mary's sake. Satisfied that Hugh would not be interested in the Ingleby after last night's fiasco, all that was needed to complete the reunion of his friends was the removal of the lovely Caroline. Inspiration struck.

'Miss Beauchamp,' he said softly after Lady Fancourt had been handed down from the carriage by Simpkins. 'Would you care to join me this evening? I go to Holland House. I can assure you of a glittering assemblage. Though if you are of Tory sympathies, you perhaps might not dare.'

'Dare or care, Lord Rutledge?' Caroline gave him a look that bordered on pert.

'Oh, do go along,' urged Margaret, shamelessly eavesdropping. 'I vow I am so tired I shall go to bed immediately after supper.'

There was little Caroline could do other than agree, especially after Rutledge had been so obliging regarding the carriage drive in the park. Of course, it had been for Margaret's sake, she reminded herself, but it had been kind.

'I shall be pleased to attend.'

A time was arranged and Caroline helped from the carriage. As she entered the house she could have sworn she heard Rutledge whistling to himself as he drove toward the mews.

'It is all over town, the business about Brummell. I daresay you will hear nothing else talked about for days. One speculates what the Regent will say!' Lady Winnington fanned herself while she studied the two girls who had entered her morning room.

'Rutledge invited Caroline to Holland House this evening. Wherever did he get the quaint idea you are a Tory?' Margaret drew off her stylish bonnet, revealing a fatigue that concerned Caroline not a little.

'Oh, some silly nonsense regarding a tartan dress. Come, let us get you into your bed for a lovely nap. Ladies who are increasing must be careful not to overdo. And I think you have had quite enough excitement for one day.'

Margaret allowed herself to be tucked into bed and cosseted with the affection she craved.

Alone, Caroline wandered to her room to change her carriage dress for something suitable for the evening. Not the pale green lutestring, she decided.

* * *

Set in the countryside beyond London proper, Holland House was more than a little intimidating. Caroline had never been invited there before. Green girls were seldom asked. Lady Holland was not accepted by some of polite society. She had fallen madly in love with Lord Holland while touring on the Continent and eloped with him while still married to Lord Webster. Their closeness was no secret and they even had a son before marriage, although it was spoken of in whispers when Caroline had heard of it. Once divorced, Elizabeth married her beloved Henry and now attempted to rule the Whigs. She was shunned by Lady Jersey and her set. Someone had neglected to inform Lady Holland that she ought to be properly cowed by such a cold shoulder.

Once inside the house, Caroline quelled her trepidation with some difficulty. She had not flown quite so high before.

Lord Lansdowne and Lord John Russell turned to greet them as Rutledge guided her into the drawing room. Lady Holland sat on a thronelike chair where she appeared to prefer to receive her guests. Caroline curtsied properly, while noting there were far more gentlemen in the room than ladies.

Scraps of outrageous conversation had filtered even to Caroline's ears, and she wondered if she was to be regaled with bits and pieces of such this evening. On the far side of the room Lord Palmerston engaged in earnest conversation with John Allen, the historian. Near them she could see Tom Moore and Charles Greville chatting with some amusement.

The departure of Brummell was mentioned

271

in passing, but since all assembled were devoted to the king and Brummell had so foolishly criticized the royal person, there was little sorrow that he was no longer around.

The dining room was a cheerful place with crimson damask walls and a sideboard positively glittering with old plate. A china closet overflowed with a collection of lovely specimens from the Orient.

Conversation ranged from the problem of Catholic emancipation to Miss Austen's novels, which Lady Holland declared to be excellent. Madame de Stael she deplored as totally out-classed by her rivals. There was little doubt who controlled the talk at the table. Lord Holland, while seeming capable in his own right, yielded to his wife. However, it was stimulating, and Caroline followed everything as well as she was able.

After dinner, Rutledge took Caroline on a stroll through the house, pausing in the library. 'Well, what do you think of the Whigs now?' queried Rutledge. His voice was low and intimate.

'Lord Holland is a charming man. I can quite see what attracted his wife.'

'And his wife?' Rutledge inquired further. He had been pleased with Miss Beauchamp's conduct during dinner. She had acquitted herself well, with Russell on one side of her,

Lord Holland on the other, at the over-crowded table. Rutledge had sat opposite, where he could observe the faint blush of pink on her cheeks when noticed by Holland, and the delicate laughter at some sally by Russell. Yes, she had fit in amazingly well.

'I suspect her rudeness covers good intentions. She orders her guests about like servants and I find that odd, you know. But she is exceedingly clever, and one can forgive a great deal under those circumstances, I expect. I doubt she would ever extend beyond good nature and good breeding. My aunt is much impressed by Lady Holland's fondness for flowers, especially the dahlias.'

Far from revealing a young woman totally unfit to be the wife of a peer — as her behavior with Hugh might indicate — Rutledge discovered that Caroline Beauchamp was utterly charming, possessed of a great deal of poise, and well liked by those to whom he introduced her.

Clearly she deserved a second chance. Or did she? He was much puzzled about which direction to move regarding this young lady.

12

By the following morning Lord Rutledge had reached a decision. After considerable thought over a bottle of his finest brandy, during which time he sought to reconcile his most peculiar feelings toward Miss Beauchamp with the knowledge he must teach her a lesson, he steadily drew closer to the conclusion that it could not be avoided. Dash it all, she might be beautiful of face and exquisite of form, but she was totally wrong!

Naturally, as an arbiter of fashion and manners, he would be a logical one to instruct this green girl. Although, he mused while sipping his third cup of coffee, she had not seemed so very green when kissed. He couldn't forget that kiss. It certainly did not fit with the image of an innocent miss.

Her gowns were another matter in which she needed tutoring. Giles had wanted to throw a shawl over her neck and shoulders when he saw Russell last night, from his place next to her, studying the beautiful expanse of skin and the hints of charms revealed. That neck had cut across her bodice too low by half, and the tiny sleeves had been split to reveal her soft, slender arms.

When he and Caroline strolled about the house he had glimpsed slender feet in deep rose slippers peeping from beneath the ankle-length skirt. The net of her pale rose dress had rustled most seductively as it swished over the silk sarcenet of her gown.

Of course, her dashing carriage dress of Stuart tartan was another point of contention. Even though she had not exhibited any sign of being a militant Tory, it was unthinkable that a young woman should display such partisanship. Last night had been a test of sorts, and though she had passed, Giles found doubts still lurking in the back of his mind about her.

And then his thoughts drifted back to that pale green thing she had worn to the opera. It had taken great determination not to plant a fist on Hugh's fatuous face when Giles had seen him standing so close to Caroline, looking down at her as though she was something to eat. Why didn't the man pay that sort of attention to his wife?

The matter at hand at the moment was how to teach Miss Caroline Beauchamp a lesson she'd not forget! He rose from his breakfast table to wander through the house until he saw the brick wall of the mews. He must think of something utterly devilish and appropriate. Let the punishment fit the crime!

Caroline Beauchamp's offense was to dangle after a married man, the husband of her supposedly close friend. Since squiring Mary about town, Giles was totally convinced she loved that scoundrel of a husband she was saddled with. How could a young woman of Miss Beauchamp's seeming sensitivity be so cruel as to flirt with Hugh right under Mary's eyes? Giles, for one, couldn't understand such behavior.

'Good morning, sir. Dashed fine day out, isn't it?'

Giles turned to discover Adrian Beauchamp standing uncertainly in the doorway, looking at him with a guarded expression. The boy was neatly dressed with collar points of moderate height and a waistcoat that was almost too plain. Clearly he sought not to offend in any way.

'Fine, fine,' replied Giles absently. 'We must settle this business about the digging, I expect. 'Tis plain you are anxious to begin work.'

Eagerly stepping into the room, Adrian grinned hesitantly. 'By all means. I thought perhaps a few more men and your instructions to your tenant regarding the site might suffice, at least for now until we see the true extent of our find.'

The restraint of the young scholar was admirable. Giles nodded. 'Why don't I write a letter to my man in Sussex that you may carry with you?' Without waiting for a reply, Giles briskly strode to a desk, where he dipped a quill pen into the standish of ink and began to write in his bold hand the message he wished to convey to his steward. Once finished, he sanded, folded, and then sealed the missive with wax, imprinting it with his seal. 'I believe this will do quite well.'

When Adrian accepted the paper, he flushed slightly, bowing his head in humble appreciation of the largesse of this man to whom he owed so much. 'Yes, rather, thank you.'

Seeing the lad to be modestly appreciative, Giles wondered if he might have a clue as to what approach might be useful with his sister.

'I trust your sister is finding her Season most enjoyable?' said Giles in the blandest of tones.

Startled at the abrupt, puzzling change of direction in the conversation, Adrian blurted out, 'I suppose so, but I think she worries about a suitor for her hand. Hates to go home without at least a hint of an attachment, you know.' Clearly, Adrian did not remotely consider Lord Rutledge in that capacity.

'I imagine she was sent to Town, as are most young women today, to catch a husband.' Giles strolled down the room, absently noticing that the fringe on his carpet was wearing badly and needed replacement. Had he a wife, she would have tended to this sort of thing.

'Quite so, sir. You see,' Adrian added in an alarming burst of honesty, 'with the six of us behind her, she feels the necessity of a good match.'

'Hmm.' Giles paused before the window, looking out across his lawn in the direction of South Street and the Winnington house. For a chit that desired to be wed, she had a particular notion of how to lure a suitable mate. A married man, happily or not, was of no help. Divorce was out of the question. Perhaps she was merely attracted to Hugh's blond good looks.

Personally, he thought blonds insipid. Diana Ingleby came to mind with her chestnut locks and flashing blue eyes. Since she was beyond what was acceptable, he needed to look elsewhere. The image of a brunette with sparkling green eyes that saucily teased rose before him, but she, too, was not worthy of his name. He supposed he needed a wife one of these years. Now he merely wished to teach that blasted

Beauchamp chit a lesson she'd not forget in a hurry.

'I imagine she's a dutiful daughter?' Giles clasped his hands behind him, rocking on his heels in a show of nonchalance.

'Yes, sir. Mama says she is a good manager, knows how to care for a home most properly. But Caro hasn't said one word that I've heard about any chap she's set her cap for yet, or any man who is paying her court. Papa won't be best pleased if she comes home without forming a *parti*, I'll wager.' Then recalling his good manners, the young man clamped his mouth shut and said no more. He owed his sister something, after all, for he surmised her friendship with Lord Rutledge had been influential in helping with his dig. Perhaps there was something in the wind from that direction?

'Do not let me keep you if you are anxious to be off.'

Accepting the dismissal in good cheer, Adrian stammered his earnest thanks once again, then bade farewell to his host and benefactor.

Alone once again, Giles mulled over young Adrian's words. The sprout has said something about her father not liking it if she came home empty-handed, so to speak. Would being denied an eligible *parti* teach her that much needed lesson? It was definitely worth consideration.

* * *

'I do wish you could teach me how to keep my wools from getting tangled while I work on my tapestry, Caroline. I vow, 'tis the most dreadful muddle,' exclaimed an exasperated Lady Winnington as she sought to unravel a thread on the back of her much maligned tapestry.

In a soothing voice Caroline replied, 'I suspect it is best to work with only one color at a time, and then to be certain that the wool is not snarled at the back with each stitch. I find it so vexing to be making progress, then turn the piece over to find I've neglected to check for that.' Caroline took the offending piece of needlework from her aunt, and patiently began to sort out the various strands of wool that gave the back of the piece the appearance of a flattened bird's nest.

'I find it helps to keep a finger at the point where I insert the needle,' said Margaret from her chair by the window. 'That way I can feel if there should be a knot or one of those aggravating snarls that do so love to mess up things.' She studied the new canvases upon which she intended to work a lovely spray of roses and forget-me-nots. It was always a problem to know precisely where to start the design. 'Caro, help me, will you?'

Gratefully setting aside her aunt's incredible jumble of wool, Caroline rose to join her cousin. In moments she figured out the matter, then paused to stare out the window.

'You have said very little about your dinner at Holland House last night. What is she like? Really.'

'Margaret,' cautioned Lady Winnington.

'I have heard such fantastic stories. Is she actually so rude as to order her guests about?' Margaret threaded her needle with a lovely shade of wine red, then began the first of her roses.

Caroline nodded, smiling slightly. 'She told one gentleman to ring the bell, and he rather sarcastically asked her if she wished him to sweep the room as well.'

'Never say so,' breathed Lady Winnington in horror.

'Was the table crowded? Justin told me that people tend to multiply and she simply pushes them together. True?'

Shrugging, Caroline said, 'We did sit extremely close. I could scarce cut my meat for fear I'd jab Lord John Russell with my elbow. 'Tis a good thing I was at the end of the table next to Lord Holland, or it would have been a near thing.'

'I wonder how it was that Lord Rutledge happened to ask you to go with him? Judging by the expression on his face the fatal night at the opera, I'd have wagered he would have far rather strangled you than take you to dinner.' Margaret studied her cousin's face as it flushed an exquisite pink. Why couldn't she blush so beautifully? Justin said she reminded him of a beetroot when she colored up.

'He was all that was polite. I fear I cannot satisfy your curiosity, my dear.'

'Did he introduce you to anyone who was, er, interesting?' said her incorrigible cousin, her hazel eyes dancing with mischief.

'I gather you mean, did I meet a hopeful husband? No. I found most of the assemblage overwhelming. Brilliant men are rather intimidating, I think.'

'Does that include Rutledge?'

'Margaret, you go too far,' said Lady Winnington. 'Caroline is not to be examined as though she is in court. Whether or not she feels anything for Rutledge is for her alone to know, at this point, anyway.' She spoke with cool reserve, sending a chastising glance to her niece with the hope it might actually have some effect.

'Well, are you to see him again?' persisted Margaret with the tenacity of a terrier.

'How should I know!' exclaimed Caroline, suddenly losing her patience. 'I expect our paths will cross. 'Tis almost inevitable. I believe I shall go for a walk.'

Margaret watched her cousin flounce out of the room with amazed eyes. 'How unlike dear Caroline to lose her temper like that. She is exceedingly touchy about Rutledge, is she not?'

'Leave be, Margaret,' was Lady Wilmington's reply. While she had noticed the same curious reaction, she wondered if it was more pique than passion.

In her room, Caroline changed from her white muslin morning dress to one more suitable for a walk in the park. From her wardrobe she pulled her new 'coberg' walking dress, named in honor of the princess and her new husband, Prince Leopold of Saxe-Coburg. It was a round dress of fine French cambric, which she wore under a pelisse of amber-shot sarcenet elegantly ornamented with a blue satin riband.

Once Daisy had assisted her into the outfit, Caroline reached for her new Oatlands hat, named for the home of the Duke of York where the royal couple honeymooned, and tied it on with a blue-and-white-checkered riband. She admired the hat excessively, quite liking the bunches of passion flowers that bobbed from atop the brim. Her light blue half boots were the latest thing, as were her Limerick gloves. She studied the final effect in her looking glass, wondering if she were mad to be so concerned over a mere walk in the park.

'You look a real treat, miss, and that's the truth,' declared Daisy. The maid followed her mistress down the two flights of stairs and out the door, pausing only to collect her cloak as a protection against a spring breeze.

Caroline averted her face from the mews and Thornhill House before she crossed Park Lane to enter the park grounds. It was a pity, for she might have seen his lordship astride his favorite mount. She also might have noticed that when Rutledge espied her, he wheeled about and hastily returned to the stables.

It was one of those odd, indifferent days when the weather can't seem to make up its mind what it wants to do. There were clouds and bright spots where the sun deigned to shine most briefly. However, the breeze carried the scent of spring flowers. Caroline thought it a very good notion to plant flowers in every spare bit of ground in and around the city, for although most laughed at the idea, she felt it would make living here far more bearable were the smells to decrease.

She nodded to an acquaintance and had the pleasure of a return acknowledgment. Rutledge was undoubtedly responsible for her return to grace. First the ride in the park and later the dinner at Holland House undoubtedly had done the trick, although Lady Jersey would sniff with disdain. But even that powerful lady hesitated to scorn someone merely because they were aligned with the Hollands.

Caroline poked the tip of her umbrella at a leaf, piercing it as neatly as could be right through the center. Did she wish it was Rutledge?

'Miss, there's a gentleman in a carriage comin' to a stop close by. Was you expectin' to meet someone?' Daisy said. She possessed a romantic heart that hoped each day for a fine gentleman to capture her sweet mistress and carry her off to a magnificent home, where she, Daisy, would most naturally serve in as a grand abigail. She would no longer be called Daisy, like some parlor maid, but assume her last name as title, Ashby. She sighed wistfully at the thought.

'No,' declared Caroline in a cool tone. But she couldn't resist a peep from beneath the brim of her new bonnet. 'Rutledge?'

The Earl of Rutledge had handed the reins

of his carriage, a lovely gray curricle, to his groom, and was now striding across the grass directly toward Caroline. She stopped in her tracks, puzzled as to why he would seek her out in this fashion.

'Miss Beauchamp, what a surprise to see you without a cluster of beaux. May I beg the favor of your company for a short drive about the park?' His rich voice was most persuasive. Tall and well formed, with that raven hair beneath the impeccable gray beaver he wore, he was nigh irresistible.

Still she hesitated, for some peculiar reason other than that her maid would not be able to accompany her in the curricle, which was not intended to carry three.

The pair of greys were restless. Rutledge extended his hand in a beckoning gesture. 'Come, my man shall lend you respectability if you are concerned over such.'

She darted a suspicious glance at Rutledge's face. It was devoid of any sarcastic intent as far as she could see. The idea of a drive on a lovely spring morning with Rutledge in that divine open carriage proved a lure too difficult to resist.

'Daisy, tell Lady Winnington I have gone for a short drive in the park.'

'Yes, miss.' Daisy's eyes were huge with awe not only for the carriage but for the handsome young groom who perched behind the front seat. She watched her mistress being handed up into the vehicle, then seated with solicitous care on the dove gray velvet cushions. As the carriage began to move, the groom, at a nod from his master, jumped down to walk swiftly to Daisy's side.

'I'll walk you there, Miss Daisy.'

Forgetting to protest that he ought to have remained with the carriage for propriety's sake, Daisy gulped, then timidly tucked her hand into the crook of the arm so gallantly offered her. Dressed in gray livery trimmed in silver, this smart young man was more than an answer to a maid's prayers. He was overwhelming. They slowly strolled across the park, Daisy not minding in the least that they took the longest route possible.

Unaware of this event, Caroline settled happily back against the soft squabs to enjoy her drive through the spring green of the enormous park, London's favorite.

'You look quite splendid this morning, Miss Beauchamp.'

'You are too kind, Lord Rutledge. I do admire your carriage. I have noticed all your equipage is in gray, as are your servants. 'Tis most effective. I applaud such restraint. Some members of the *ton* are inclined to more gaudy effects. Such deplorable taste, I believe.'

'I'm pleased that it meets with your approval.'

There was no missing the hint of sarcasm in his voice now. Caroline threw him a confused look, tightening her grasp on her blue parasol. A sense of unease began to creep over her.

The curricle bowled along at a fast clip, faster than Caroline had ever gone while in the park. Rutledge took three sharp turns, causing Caroline to clutch her side of the carriage. What was happening? When they took an unfamiliar gate from the park, she grew alarmed.

She decided to ask the suddenly taciturn man at her right side what, precisely, was going on! 'Lord Rutledge, where are we going?'

'For a drive,' came the laconic reply.

'I am aware of that, sirrah. I want to know our destination, if you please.' Her accents were like winter frost on the air.

'I don't.'

'Don't what?' she snapped back at him, her heart beginning to pound in a dreadful manner.

'Don't please.'

At that bit of errant nonsense, she turned

her head, fixing him with a stern look. 'If you do not stop this carriage at once, I shall — shall pull on those reins as hard as I can.'

She could feel him tense. Daringly she lifted her gaze to meet those dark gray eyes, a feat that took courage. She began to breathe easier as the curricle slowed to a mere trot, then halted. She looked about her, recognizing their location. They were in the country beyond Holland House, somehow having gone around the Kensington turnpike tollgate.

The sign in front of the inn before which they stopped proclaimed it to be the White Hart Tavern.

Expecting the groom to take charge of the horses, she glanced behind. It was then she discovered they were alone!

'I trust you have an explanation, sirrah.' She glared at the amused countenance of the man at her side. 'You well know 'tis not proper for me to be alone with you with no maid or groom attending.'

'No need to ring a peal over my head, Miss Beauchamp. I know what I'm about.' The confidence in that deep voice irked Caroline to no end.

'That is more than I can say,' muttered Caroline, deciding she had best remove herself from the carriage before seen by anyone. Once inside the inn it might be possible to take concealment in one of the private parlors.

'How wise of you, Miss Beauchamp. This is a highly traveled portion of highway. One never knows who might drive past.' This was said in the suavest of tones. Like scented oil one pours into the bath, it smelled.

Suspicion reared in her mind. 'Are you trying to ruin me, Lord Rutledge? I cannot fathom why. What have I ever done to you or yours?' She stood, arms akimbo, gallantly defying the tall man who so casually faced her with his threatening words.

'Inside, if you please. We do not desire the world and his wife to know our business, do we?'

She wanted so much to stamp her foot and say that she did *not* please to go with him. Common sense demanded she obey. Marching along at his side, she made it clear she was angry, even though she didn't open her mouth until they were safely inside a neat little parlor.

Rutledge closed the door behind them, then strode over to confront her. He lifted his hands to remove her pretty Oatlands hat, tossing it carelessly on a settee near the wall.

'I beg your pardon,' cried an affronted

Caroline, unsuccessfully attempting to grab her hat.

'Well you may, for I have had to spend a considerable amount of time figuring out what's to be done with you.'

'You need not have bothered, my lord. I prefer to see to myself, thank you very much.' Caroline gave an indignant sniff, then backed away from this intimidating man. Distance seemed the best course at the moment.

He slowly followed her, one daunting step after another, until he stood not a foot away. Caroline hated that she cowered against the window, but that's what she did. Positively disgusting, her lack of fortitude.

'You, my sweet young woman, deserve to be punished. And punished you shall be. When it is known we have spent the day closeted in this room, you will no longer be plagued with the worry of an eligible *parti*. There will be no gentleman' — he emphasized this word most nastily — 'who will give you a consideration for the position of wife.'

'I do not understand,' she said frowning, then edged away to one side so that she might not feel quite so threatened.

'It is perfectly clear to me.'

'Then explain, for I think you have windmills in your head.'

'Miss Beauchamp,' he lectured, 'a young,

unmarried lady of any consequence possessing refined manners does not set up a flirt with her best friend's husband. Poor Lady Stanhope is utterly devastated to see you at his side, with that fool gazing down at you as though you were a cream cake.'

'Oh, I doubt he does that,' protested Caroline, trying to imagine Hugh looking at her other than that brotherly way he had.

'Take my word for it, Miss Beauchamp, he does,' declared Giles, thinking of that silly look Hugh had worn the night of the opera before all hell broke loose. A man ought to look at his wife that way, not some young chit.

'Why is it my fault?'

'Deny you encourage him?'

'At least he is no longer dangling after the widow Ingleby,' she countered, somewhat illogically from his viewpoint.

'What has that to serve to the question?'

Exasperated beyond belief, Caroline turned to study the scene out of the window. It afforded a view of a kitchen garden, where a serving maid gathered herbs and vegetables for the evening meal. 'I should like a pot of tea, I believe.' She wished to stall for time while she considered whether or not she ought to reveal the truth of the matter to Rutledge. She was getting extremely tired of this plan Mary had concocted.

Though she sympathized with her friend, Caroline had decided — and this had put the cap on her conviction — that Mary had better solve her own problems with her husband. Only she hadn't had the opportunity to inform Mary of her decision to drop the entire scheme.

'Hungry?'

Suddenly aware that she was miles from her aunt's home and totally alone with a man who seemed to have a screw loose in his head, Caroline nodded. 'For tea.' It seemed to her Rutledge had a predatory glint in those gray eyes. Or was it amusement? At any rate, she needed time.

He said nothing to her, but crossed the room to ring for service. When the curious girl came, she saw only Caroline's discreet back, the hat hurriedly slapped on her head to conceal her features. The tea, when it came, was hot, and a variety of sandwiches and a salad came with it.

'By way of a lunch,' Rutledge explained with a gesture at the plates of food. 'I have no notion how long we shall be here, you see.'

'Pray don't allow that to disturb your poor addled brain.' Caroline carefully placed her hat on the far end of the table, not wanting a repeat of the careless toss, then gracefully seated herself.

'Now, what has the gorgeous widow to do with any of this?' demanded Rutledge.

'I feared you would not forget that,' murmured Caroline as she poured the tea.

'Explain.' Rutledge sipped from his cup, then took a bite of a generous ham sandwich.

'Mary asked me to seduce her husband.'

The silence following this statement was louder than any thunder that Caroline had ever heard in her life.

'She did what?' exploded Rutledge, thankful he had swallowed his bite of sandwich.

'It's true,' replied Caroline calmly. 'And fool that I am, I agreed.'

'But why?' he demanded. Tea was neglected and the lunch forgotten at this astounding turn of events.

'Well,' said Caroline, beginning to relax now the worst was past, 'she was resigned to Hugh and his bits of muslin, for the silly girl thinks herself to be of no account. Mary is pretty and well mannered, and would make an excellent mother — if she were given the chance.'

'Go on,' insisted an intrigued Lord Rutledge.

A sip of tea, followed by a dainty bite of a sandwich, and, thus fortified, Caroline was ready to continue. 'It was Mrs Ingleby that precipitated the plan. Mary truly feared that woman, for since Mary has fallen deeply in love with her husband, she felt in danger of losing him to the beautiful widow. Hence my attempt to lure the man from the Ingleby's side. I succeeded, too.'

At this brass-faced remark, Rutledge sputtered, looking as though he longed to grab Caroline by her throat. Alarmed, she slid farther away from him.

'I might have been able to unite that silly couple if you had not interfered,' Caroline continued. 'You see, Hugh confessed to me that he has fallen desperately in love with Mary. The stupid man wanted me to lure you from Mary's side. He was beside himself with jealousy and yet did not wish to call you out, for after all, you once were close friends.'

'I don't believe what I am hearing,' declared Rutledge softly. Then he reflected on what Caroline had said and began, much to her amazement, to chuckle. In moments that alluring chuckle turned to laughter, and his lordship had to fish for a snowy handkerchief with which to wipe his streaming eyes.

Eyes wide with astonishment, Caroline's mouth began to curve as she considered the situation as she'd described it. It was rather amusing if one merely looked at the matter impersonally. She chuckled a little, then recalled where she was, with whom, and the dire consequences to follow.

Clearing her throat, she interrupted his merriment. 'So you see, you need not have worried in the least. I wouldn't have Hugh on a silver salver if he was offered to me. What a nodcock, to be so hen-hearted that he was afraid to approach Mary. *If* I ever marry' — and here Caroline bestowed a dark look on his lordship's head — 'I should hope my husband stakes his claim immediately rather than dawdle like that stupid Hugh. What a cabbage-head.'

A trenchant gleam fired in the earl's eyes, but was concealed from Caroline by reason of quickly dropped lashes. 'It would seem we have a bit of a muddle here,' he said reflectively.

'A bit! Well, I declare! I should think it more than that, sir.' Caroline was most indignant. Her future was about to vanish like a mist, and he thought it a bit of a muddle? What a gross absurdity that was!

'Do you not think they ought to be taught a lesson?'

'Such as you are teaching to me,' she answered sweetly.

Rutledge gave the teapot in her hand a wary look, then said, 'Now, think on it. Mary loves Hugh and Hugh loves Mary. I propose we get them together, but in a way that shall recompense ourselves and pay them for all the trouble they have put us to. A lesson, if you will.'

Tea was poured into the two cups on the table, then the empty pot carefully replaced on the tray.

'How?' She absently stirred a spoon of sugar into her cup, while studying the man who sat across from her. What a devious mind he had, to be sure.

'Here is what I propose.'

Caroline leaned forward to listen to the plan set forth. He seemed so certain, so positive it would work. She frowned, wondering. Would it? And what if it did? What about her reputation, which might be shattered to bits and pieces at any moment should someone see her with Rutledge?

'If I go along with this idea you have, I should like to know when and how we begin. For you must know, I have been absent for some hours, and my maid knows you took me up in your carriage. If word gets out of this escapade, I doubt we will be in any position to do anything.' Her words were all garbled and she knew she hadn't made much sense, but she was finding it increasingly difficult to concentrate on anything but the handsome man who sat so close, yet so far from her in this small room in a rural inn. All alone, together.

'Leave everything to me,' he said suavely.

13

'How do we get out of this pickle?' Caroline rose, leaning her hands on the table while she gave Rutledge a direct look intended to make him most uncomfortable.

'I suspect the best thing to do is for me to check outside, then spirit you away from here. We shall retrace our route on those country lanes, avoiding the principal road. I shall have you back at your aunt's house in no time.'

Caroline considered this, then nodded. 'I suppose that must do. At any rate, I have no better suggestion.'

'Pity you don't have a veil or a fichu to conceal your face.' That silver glint sparkled deep in his eyes, and that elusive dimple peeked at her again.

'I scarcely thought I would encounter an abductor when I left the house, my lord,' replied Caroline tartly, but not without a reluctant curve of her mouth. She was beginning to wonder what prompted that particular look in his eyes.

He pushed back his chair, rose, and also leaned forward over the table. Once she might have thought him intimidating. Now she sensed a feeling of unity between them that had not existed before with him or, for that matter, with any other man she had ever known.

'Next time I suggest you go out prepared.'

'There will not be a 'next time,' Lord Rutledge.'

The skeptical look he darted at her implied she had best be on her guard. Rather than comment on her answer, he said, 'I do believe you might call me Giles. It seems more friendly than Rutledge, and I daresay we have transcended our previous relationship to that of a new one. Be ready to leave when I return, Caroline.'

How she longed to ask what this new friendship might be. By the time she had worked up her courage sufficiently to inquire, he had gone. She tied on her new Oatlands hat, smoothed her gloves, and had a militant hold on her parasol when he suddenly returned.

'There is a coach due to pass soon. We have to be gone from here within the next few minutes. I see you are ready.' His eyes expressed gratitude for her easy compliance with his orders, ones which he knew some females with little sense might have resisted.

'I hope . . . ' She left off her remark,

thinking it was futile at best to hope that no one might see her with him, alone, in this inn quite removed from the city.

'It could be worse, you know.' He threw a lovely Norwich shawl over her shoulders, partly covering her head, as though she was suffering from a cold or some such ague. How he had managed to produce this item in the middle of nowhere, she didn't ask. She wasn't certain she wanted to know. Nor did she inquire how the situation might be worse than it was. That, too, was better not discussed.

The curricle awaited them, a young lad proudly holding the horses until the fashionable couple was ready to depart. It was a dashed queer setup, but everyone knew the gentry were given to strange starts.

'We're off!' The boy jumped back, watching the curricle leap forward, the magnificent matched grays straining to perform for their master. The escape was made with marvelous ease. As they whisked around the first of the corners, the coach could be seen approaching in the distance. Caroline drew a hesitant breath of relief.

When Rutledge brought Caroline up before the Winnington house, she sat for a moment, studying him with serious eyes. Then she dropped her gaze to her hands. 'I shall report to you later on the first step of our plan.'

He nodded. 'I imagine we shall be required to confer frequently regarding our progress. It must be carefully done, you know.' He watched as Simpkins marched down the front steps to assist Miss Caroline from the curricle. She paused to hold up the shawl, a quizzical look on her face.

'Wear it in good health,' he said, smiling at her confusion.

'Until later, sir.' Caroline dipped the faintest of curtsies, then fled into the house. She paused once inside, listening. As before, she distinctly heard whistling. It was a joyous, carefree melody. At Simpkins' look of inquiry, she flushed, feeling slightly foolish, then asked, 'My aunt?'

Simpkins gestured in the direction of the morning room.

Handing him the shawl, for she did not want questions regarding that at the moment, she turned away. Without removing her hat or gloves, Caroline hurried down the hall. 'I am returned.'

'So you are,' replied Lady Winnington. Seeing Caroline still dressed for outdoors, she asked, 'Do you not intend to remain?' Nothing was said about the message from Caroline regarding her drive. For one thing, by the time Daisy strolled into the house, it was late. Lady Winnington assumed Caroline and Giles had joined a luncheon party. She preferred to think that, at any rate. One did not borrow trouble needlessly.

'I must visit Mary. There is little point in taking my hat off, then immediately putting it back on again.'

'True. You had a pleasant outing in the park?'

It was difficult to know how to answer that question without revealing some of the plan she and Giles had put together. Nervously fingering her gloves, Caroline replied in an offhand manner: 'Lovely. The weather seems to be improving. I do so like spring. Has cousin Margaret gone out?'

'She is resting. She insists on attending the Aldworth assembly with me this evening. You will go with us, won't you?'

'I think so,' Caroline said absently. Whirling about, she made to leave the room. 'I shan't be long.'

Caroline had said that this morning, and it had been hours before her return. Lady Winnington wondered what had really happened while Caroline was gone with Giles. Clearly, it was to be kept a secret. In Fanny's experience, a secret shared was a powerful bond between two people. She tossed her tapestry onto the table, then slowly walked up to her room so she might also rest for the evening ahead. But she would think about the possibilities of this newfound rapport between two of her favorite people.

Baxhall waited patiently as Caroline paid him, then he promised to return when asked. She hurried up the broad steps of the Stanhope residence, greeting Pennyfeather with a relieved smile at the news that her ladyship was to home.

'Good afternoon, dear. You are in first-looks today,' said Mary, rising from where she worked at an impossibly delicate piece of needlework to greet her friend.

The Oatlands hat was praised and the new ensemble admired before Caroline could approach the subject she needed to present.

Over tea Caroline casually remarked, 'I do believe we can put to rest the specter of Mrs Ingleby. I am convinced that Hugh is firmly detached from that lady. I doubt there was ever anything more than a casual dalliance in the first place. She simply does not seem like the type of woman Hugh would truly find attractive.'

'I saw her with Lord Mortland yesterday. Do you think there might be an attachment there?' There was a studied casualness in Mary's question, but Caroline could not fail to hear the note of devout hope in her voice.

Shrugging her slender shoulders, Caroline sought to reassure Mary while planting a few seeds of doubt in her mind at the same time. 'Perhaps. I can see why she was attracted to Hugh, however. Not only does he possess a respectable fortune, but he is quite handsome.' If you happened to admire blonds. Caroline found her taste leaning more toward dark, dark hair and gray eyes that contained an intriguing glint within.

'True,' agreed Mary, but without a trace of complacency. She sipped from her teacup while watching the woman across from her.

'He dances well and can always be relied upon to fetch a refreshing drink when one is perishing from the stuffy rooms at a ball or assembly. You are very fortunate.'

Caroline hoped her woeful sigh was convincing. At the swiftly altered expression on Mary's face, it seemed she might have been.

'I hope you do not mind, but in the interest of drawing Hugh away from the Ingleby, I agreed to his suggestion that we join an outing of some sort soon. The weather appears to be turning for the better, which can only help. I cannot recall the name of the people we go with, but it is bound to be great fun.'

'Lovely,' murmured Mary with a distinct lack of enthusiasm.

'Are you to have the escort of Rutledge tonight?'

'Yes,' replied Mary with a sigh. How any woman might regard an evening spent with Giles in such a lackluster manner was beyond Caroline. But then, she was beginning to find Hugh a trifle wearying. And Mary had proclaimed herself to be passionately in love with the man. There was no accounting for taste, it seemed.

'I shall see you there, then. Your husband has promised to escort me, so you need not worry about him in the least. You haven't changed your mind, have you? I mean, having Rutledge at your beck and call might put some women to calculating on how to eliminate their husbands!' Caroline forced a gay laugh while observing Mary most carefully.

'Oh, no,' Mary denied quite vigorously. It was the most animated Caroline had seen her this afternoon.

'Fine.' It was a relief to know there were to be no complications. How deflating for Rutledge to know there was a woman who could totally ignore his charms!

'How is your cousin, Lady Fancourt? I vow I was surprised to see her in London alone.

There is no problem, is there?' Mary seemed genuinely concerned.

'Not actually. Her marriage was well-known to be a love match.' Here both young women sighed. 'Margaret is increasing and simply insisted she must do a bit of shopping, attend the opera, and take a carriage drive in the park before retiring to Fancourt Abbey for her confinement. I fully expect her husband on our doorstep any day. She has only her gowns to be ready, and she ought not to mind should he insist on her removal from the city.' Caroline watched to note the reaction to this bit of homespun news.

'How fortunate for her, to be breeding. I should dearly love a baby.' Mary looked as though she would heartily enjoy a good cry. Caroline decided she had done enough damage for the nonce, and rose to leave.

'I shall see you this evening?'

Mary touched her forehead as though warding off a headache. 'I expect I shall.'

How Caroline longed to give her friend a push at her husband. If Rutledge was right, and their plan proved correct, perhaps Mary would have that dear little one before another year was out.

Once the door had closed upon Caroline Beauchamp, Lady Stanhope informed Penny-feather that she was not at home to anyone and rushed up the stairs to her room. The butler shook his head in a worried manner, and went about his duties with a grim countenance.

The Aldworth assembly was declared a sad crush by the time Lord Stanhope presented Lady Winnington, Lady Fancourt, and Miss Beauchamp to their hostess. Mrs Aldworth was in high alt that her little gathering should have produced such a response from the *ton*.

Across the room, Caroline caught the eye of Lord Rutledge and smiled. While he was most circumspect, she hoped that fascinating glint had flared in his eyes. She was sure it revealed an inner amusement. How lovely to find, if only for a brief time, someone who shared her sense of the ridiculous.

'Hugh, dear, you must join me in a waltz. There are few as skilled and polished in that dance as you.' She gave him a demure smile, batted her eyelashes, then placed a trusting hand on his sleeve.

Lady Winnington gave her niece a stare that masked whatever thoughts roamed in her head. Caroline could only guess.

'I count it my good fortune,' he said politely.

'Oh,' confided Caroline to Hugh while she led him away from her relatives, 'talk about good fortune. I have been invited to a marvelous picnic out in Richmond. With the Almonds, or someone with a nutty-sounding name.'

'The Chestnuts?' inquired a bemused Hugh.

'Perhaps. Your old friend Rutledge was so kind as to invite me. Is that not a coup for me?' She humorously tapped Hugh's arm with her fan, then smoothed down her new gown. It was the latest thing, with a tiny, low-cut bodice of green above a white silk slip overlaid with tulle. Festoons of flowers were tucked in the draperies of tulle, peeping out with bursts of primrose and green. The gown made her feel wonderful. Especially after she noted the glare from Rutledge when he got a better look at it on her.

Knowing full well the hostility that had erupted between Rutledge and Caroline, and not being privy to the cause due to his estrangement with his former friend, Hugh became suspicious. 'Dashed odd, is it not? For Rutledge to invite you to some outing, and to people you do not know?'

'You have a little villa in Richmond, do you not? Perhaps they are mutual friends. You could inquire of him, I imagine. Or is your argument too deep-seated for that?' Caroline bestowed an artless smile on Hugh that made his suspicions deepen.

She was acting mighty peculiar. Telling him to seek out Rutledge when she was safe in assuming he'd do nothing of the kind was a bit smoky. Dashed smoky.

'No,' replied a thoughtful Hugh. 'I shall have a word with him later. Can't have you flitting off to someplace not the thing, you know.'

'I know I can depend on you. If I had an older brother, I vow he could be no more considerate of me.' She gazed up at him with the trusting look of a little girl at her saintly father.

Running a finger around a collar that suddenly appeared to have become too tight, Hugh nodded, then excused himself for the moment.

'What are you up to, dear girl?' inquired a fascinated Lady Winnington, pausing while on her way to the card room.

'Mending things, I hope,' said Caroline enigmatically.

'I see,' replied her aunt, seeing more than Caroline ever suspected. 'Well, you look utterly delicious, and more than one woman here tonight is gnashing her teeth at your ensemble. Not to mention the attention you have been getting from Rutledge and dear Hugh.'

'Dear Hugh is a nodcock,' muttered

Caroline in an unguarded moment.

'No doubt he is,' replied Lady Winnington, unperturbed at the comment. 'I see Rutledge is coming this way. I will take myself off to the card room. Shall I play for you this evening?'

Knowing what was implied by this remark, Caroline recklessly shrugged. 'I may have need of a few extra shillings one of these days. Do as you see fit.'

'One does like to win occasionally, am I not right?' Lady Winnington nodded to Rutledge before whisking herself to the next room.

'I thought that pale green thing you wore was indiscreet. Must you dress for all the world to see your charms?' complained Lord Rutledge in a soft voice close to Caroline's ear. That he was standing where he could not help but have an excellent view of any charms revealed was not pointed out to him.

The demure smile that spread across her face was slightly at odds with the coquettish look she shot him. 'I see little difference between my gown and the one my cousin wears.'

'Ah, but she is wearing it,' was his reasoned reply, as if that explained everything.

'You, sir, are utterly impossible.' Caroline lowered her voice, then added, 'I went to see Mary this afternoon directly after you left me. I informed her that I am firmly convinced

Mrs Ingleby is no further danger to her marriage, then told her that Hugh is to take me on an outing soon, but was maddeningly vague about it. I shall see her again to plant a few more seeds of doubt and worry.'

'What about your particular gallant?' Rutledge shot a look of pure dislike at his former friend, Lord Stanhope of the blond locks and handsome figure.

'I have made Hugh aware that you have invited me to a picnic this coming Friday at some villa in Richmond. I couldn't recall the name of the people in either case. I told Hugh I thought it had something to do with nuts.' She peeked up at Giles with a wicked little grin.

'Minx,' said Rutledge. 'Is every dance spoken for by now?'

'I have scarce had time to be approached by anyone, between you and Hugh at my side. You tend to be rather off-putting, you know.' She formed an adorable pout with that rosebud mouth, and Rutledge found it exceedingly difficult to concentrate on what he had intended to say.

'Good heavens.' Caroline straightened, her brow forming a faint crease, the smile disappearing. She stared at the door like a ghost had suddenly appeared.

'Well, well. Fancourt has come to claim his

wife. He looks positively murderous. I would not be your cousin.'

'He will do nothing. He wants his heir far too much to injure Margaret in any manner. If he has a bit of patience, she will happily return with him to Fancourt Abbey and none the worse for the trip.' Caroline studied the tight-lipped man who had paused to greet his hostess and make his apologies. Now he walked around the perimeter of the room with a cautious tread, like a spy fearing detection.

'Lady Fancourt is, ah, in an interesting condition?'

Caroline gave him a resigned look. 'Pregnant.'

He shook his head in dismay. ''Tis a good thing no one can overhear your shocking speech. They would think you a blue-stocking at the very least.'

She gave him a withering glance, then glided forward to greet her cousin-in-law. 'Justin, how very good to see you again. Margaret is in fine feather and anxious to see you.'

'I'll wager she is no such thing, else she'd have waited for me. I finished in Devon as soon as I could and rode pell-mell for home with scarce a stop.' He glanced at Rutledge with a masculine look that defied Rutledge to breathe a word of his anxiety over his adored wife.

'I believe she is sitting with the dowagers over there.' Caroline gestured toward an arrangement of chairs against the wall. Margaret was indeed sitting there, looking like a gay butterfly come to rest amid a bed of faded flowers past their prime. In a gown of soft sarcenet with a pink bodice and an exceptionally full, deep blue skirt, she sat as though holding court. A sequinstudded fan glittered as she waved it about in emphasis, and her toes could be seen tapping in time to the music.

A slight softening of his eyes was the only clue that Caroline had spoken truly. Justin Fancourt would never harm a hair on his Margaret's silly head. 'I shall tend to that lady at once,' he said in a polite monotone.

'He sounds grim, but he has a heart like a down pillow. 'Tis no wonder Margaret adores him so.' Caroline watched Justin stroll across to present himself to his wife. She was not quite as sanguine about Margaret's obedience to her overzealous husband and his desire to wrap her in cotton wool.

Rutledge made no reply to this candid remark. He watched as Fancourt deftly removed his wife from the clutch of dowagers, then escorted her onto the floor, where a sedate minuet was forming. He had a strong suspicion that a storm cloud had just descended upon London.

Returning his gaze to Caroline, in particular to the expanse of creamy skin presented to his view, Rutledge bent over slightly, speaking softly once again, 'I fully intend to purchase a selection of the finest fichus for your wear, Miss Beauchamp.'

Stiffening her spine, and unknowingly giving Rutledge more reason to wish her covered, Caroline replied, 'We are cooperating to help our friends, Lord Rutledge. Nothing more than that.'

'Remember what I know about you, Caroline.' With that rejoinder he strolled from her side, making it possible for several other young men to seek a dance with her.

She spared a confused glance as Giles left her. When he spoke her name, it was a caress. But what he had said was more like a threat!

A flushed and upset Margaret hurried to her side following the conclusion of the stately minuet. 'Justin is here. What shall I do? I am not ready to return to Fancourt Abbey yet.' She gave Caroline an unhappy look before smoothing her face when she sensed her husband approaching.

'Justin, never say you plan to whisk dearest

Margaret from us yet,' declared Caroline in a flirting manner.

'You do not understand — ' began Justin.

'Oh, pooh. You would think no other woman in the world had expected a baby before. If she is careful not to overdo, and takes the ride home in stages, I do not see why she must part from us immediately. It isn't as though she was out until all hours and dashing madly about.' Caroline met Justin's gaze with a frank one of her own. 'She has been of great help to me this past week. I would dearly appreciate her presence for a few days longer if you can manage it.'

'We shall see,' he replied in a most discouraging manner.

When Rutledge appeared to partner Caroline in a waltz, she observed her cousin being led from the room. It looked as though a cloud hung over their heads, although others might not have noticed.

'I fear Margaret and Justin are in for a bit of bad weather,' Caroline said.

'I thought the same when I first saw him. Is it always thus with her?'

'Only since her 'condition,' as you insist I refer to it.' Caroline wished to forget the family troubles for a while. She would find them waiting when she and Aunt Fanny returned later this evening.

'You do not approve that a husband should be solicitous? Somehow that does not fit with the image I have of you once married.' Rutledge whirled her about much as he had that first time they had waltzed, only this time there was an added something Caroline couldn't put her finger on.

'Between you and Hugh, there is little chance I shall reach that state,' Caroline was goaded into saying. Once the words had left her mouth, she wished them unsaid. It didn't help when Rutledge merely chuckled.

On the far side of the room, several of the noted gossips of the ton observed the unusual amount of attention being given to Miss Beauchamp by the estimable Lord Rutledge and tongues wagged full spate with speculation. Among the gentlemen, four of the wagering kind decided to place a bet on the book at White's.

Lady Winnington overheard this latter arrangement, and as soon as she ended her game of whist, she took herself off in search of her niece. It was one thing to help a friend. It was quite another to become the subject of the prattle-boxes who had nothing better to do with their time than tear someone apart.

She watched the two in question as they concluded their waltz, then decided to say nothing to Caroline. If Rutledge heard about the wager, he would tend to the matter. It would not do to worry Caroline unduly about something that was probably of no import anyway.

Joining her aunt, Caroline confided, 'Did you know Justin came and swept poor Margaret off with him?'

Lady Winnington frowned. This turn of events was even worse than the business of the betting. 'Perhaps we had best take our leave.'

Once her dance with Rutledge was over and she had taken care of the matter with Hugh, the party had ceased to hold great attraction for Caroline. She watched Rutledge lead Mary out in a country dance and decided it might be as well to depart as Aunt Fanny desired.

'I believe you are right, dear aunt. Although I do not fear Justin. I think Margaret was only funning when she said she feared him. Was she not?' Caroline's gaze met Lady Winnington's and the two women crossed to the door. Along the way Lady Winnington paused to speak briefly with Hugh, and he joined them in the quiet exit from the room.

Two pairs of eyes followed their departure. Mary wistfully turned her sad gaze to her partner. 'I believe I should like to go now, Giles.'

'You need to get more fresh air. I shall undertake it.' He paused for a moment, then said, 'I'll think of something.'

Caroline pulled her cape tightly about her in the damp night chill. The footman assisted them into Baxhall's carriage with deference, then shut the door with a snap.

'There were comments regarding the amount of attention Rutledge was paying you tonight.' Lady Winnington searched the face of her niece in the dim light provided by the one lamp inside the carriage.

The weary sigh from Caroline was not the sort from a young miss courted by her lover. 'They love a bit of scandal broth, don't they? Well, no matter, I have well and truly sunk my chances, I expect. Even if the outcome of the opera thing did not succeed in doing so, I imagine I shall do something else just as stupid ere long.' Caroline wondered if the farce planned for their friends would become general knowledge. 'Regarding Lord Rutledge, I feel sure he merely pays notice of me to further our intentions for Hugh and Mary. For I may say that we intend to do something.'

'I see,' responded Lady Winnington with quiet grace. That so powerful a person as Rutledge should conspire with a young miss when he had never bothered to speak to such girls before was to be ignored? Not in her book.

At the house on South Street, light blazed forth from the hall and the small sitting room that faced that faced the street. Exchanging worried glances, Lady Winnington and Caroline entered the house, Simpkins walking to the good Baxhall to pay him, thanking him in austere tones for taking care of the ladies.

Margaret was curled up on a small sofa that was placed between the windows. Opposite her Justin paced back and forth.

Unaware that her aunt and cousin were near the doorway, Margaret declared, 'I suggest you take yourself off to your club, or a hotel, or one of your friends immediately. If you wish, we can discuss this tomorrow. I am going to bed. Alone.'

Justin watched unhappily while his cherished wife rose, then stalked from the room. He gathered his tattered poise about him and walked out to meet his relatives with a grave countenance.

Caroline had tugged her aunt away from the door at the sound of an angry voice. Not wishing to eavesdrop, they made it seem as though they had just entered.

'We shall see you in the morning, Justin?' offered Lady Winnington in a conciliatory voice.

'Ladies who are increasing are often illogical, Justin. They need special consideration at this time. Love and a great deal of patience,' added Caroline, trying not to sound as though she knew the whole of the dispute.

'I shall think of something.' The sixth Baron Fancourt of Fancourt Abbey strode from the house with nary a glance up the stairs where his love was even now hopefully regretting her actions.

'My, my,' murmured Lady Winnington as the door closed behind her nephew-in-law. She said good night to Simpkins, adjuring him to get to bed, then slowly walked up the stairs to deal with her niece.

Caroline reluctantly followed. She was not certain she wished to get involved in yet another entanglement. It seemed to her that one was quite enough!

'I refuse to go with him. The brute! He dragged me away from that lovely party with no thought as to whether I wished to go or not. He belongs in some dank castle, for he is positively Gothic in his notions!' declared a highly incensed Lady Fancourt.

'He only wishes the best for you, dear,' soothed Lady Winnington. Upon seeing Caroline, she beckoned, saying sotto voce that Caro might be more in sympathy with her cousin's wounded sensibilities.

'Aunt Fanny has the right of it, as I am sure you do not wish to hear,' said Caroline firmly. 'Consider how concerned Justin was and have patience with the poor man. As I recall from my father, men feel particularly helpless at a time like this. There's no logic in their heads at all.'

Margaret permitted her cousin to put her to bed, unaware that nearly identical arguments had been used on both her and her husband.

Upon returning to her own room, Caroline gave herself up to the tender ministrations of Daisy, then sank into bed. Life was becoming a deal more complicated than she had supposed it might when innocently leaving her home for a London Season.

14

Overnight a state of war appeared to have been declared at Lady Winnington's lovely Georgian house on South Street. In her room, the charming Lady Fancourt perversely refused to see her husband, while on the ground floor of the house, Lord Fancourt prowled about the morning room in seething annoyance.

'Aunt Fanny, what *are* we to do?' whispered Caroline as his lordship took a turn in the central hall.

That estimable lady shook her head. 'My late husband and I never had cause for such nonsense. I know not how to deal with it,' she confessed.

Friday's planned assignation stretched far into the distant future with the present dilemma beneath her nose. Caroline sighed for what must have been at least the tenth time when Justin wandered back into the room.

'She said,' Caroline ventured, driven by a desperate desire to help, 'that she would return to Fancourt Abbey as soon as she had been to the opera, driven in the park, and ordered a few gowns for the coming months. All this she has accomplished. We await the delivery of her dresses from the modiste at any moment. I feel certain that were you to exhibit patience with her, she would gladly go with you.'

'You do not understand, my dear, do you?' replied Justin with more patience than he had ever thought to possess. 'If I allow Margaret to have her way in this matter, the rest of my life will be spent under the cat's paw. I'm dashed if I'll become a jerrysneak.'

'Somehow I cannot think of you in terms of a poor henpecked husband,' said Caroline, her head tilting so to study him. 'You do not look the part. For one thing, you are far too handsome a man.'

Justin gave her a wry smile. 'Flummery, dear girl, only works if the male is susceptible. I fear I am past that in this case.'

'A little more time, Justin. Another day, perhaps?' she suggested.

He strolled to the window, stared out at the brick wall with the clever pattern of ivy clinging to it, then turned. 'Very well. There are a number of matters I can tend to this day. But warn my dear wife that I intend to reside beneath this roof and in her bed this night. *And* we shall depart on the morrow, gowns or no gowns.' So saying, he strode from the room. In the hall he could be dimly heard giving a terse order to Simpkins for a carriage.

Silence followed, broken only by Lady Winnington's sigh.

'Now *there* is a man!' She sat gazing wistfully at the doorway, her tapestry as usual in a jumble on her lap.

'How can you say such a thing?'

'What would your father have done?'

Caroline stopped in her perambulations about the room to stare at her aunt. 'Why, I suppose he would have demanded my mother come to her senses and leave at once.'

'Precisely. Justin has learned the fine art of compromise. Tomorrow Margaret will gladly drive off with him to Fancourt Abbey, for, if you recall, her gowns are due to be delivered today. She will be content her husband is so thoughtful of her. He will be pleased his wife obeys him. A fine thing, I say.'

'I suppose I had better inform Margaret,' said Caroline, casting an unhappy look at her aunt. 'I do not relish it.'

Lady Wilmington merely smiled and bent her head over the mess of tangled threads on her tapestry, which, no matter how often anyone worked at it, never seemed to alter.

Confronting a cousin who looked remarkably well for a lady supposedly cast into despair, Caroline found herself a bit non-plussed. 'Margaret, Justin has left the house,' she said cautiously.

'No!' Margaret ran over to the window, searching the street below. 'What did he say, precisely!'

'He informed us he had a few matters to tend to during the day, but that he intends to stay here tonight, and in your bed, if I may say so,' added Caroline hesitantly, wondering what to expect at these words of challenge.

'Did he, indeed!' Margaret seemed unable to speak in anything other than exclamation points this morning.

'And, he also intends to leave on the morrow.' Caroline retreated toward the door. She had no desire to get caught in another episode of throwing pillows and anything else that happened to come to hand.

'Oh!' Margaret subsided onto a chair, deep in thought. 'And he actually demanded to sleep here, in my bed?'

'True,' replied Caroline with all due caution.

'Well!' Margaret considered this at length, then rose from her chair. She wore a self-satisfied, incredibly smug smile, much to Caroline's amazement. 'I had best purchase a few remaining things. I should like a few lengths of fine flannel, a length of dimity, some cambric for infant's shirts, and a quantity of soft muslin for the dresses. I wonder, do they have some pretty lace for the caps? Will you go with me to Harding and Howell's? I am persuaded they will have the best assortment.'

Caroline shook her head in wonder. 'I vow, I thought you would be fit to fly.'

'In a rage? No, Justin has asserted himself in the nicest possible way. I should not admire a meek man, you know. I deem it a fine thing that he allows me my pride.'

In a bemused voice, for her aunt had predicted the matter quite well, Caroline murmured, 'I shall be but a moment while I fetch my pelisse and bonnet.'

Thus it was that Caroline went with her cousin to the elegant shop where the contretemps over a length of tartan had taken place not so very long ago.

*   *   *

Not far from this scene, Lord Stanhope sought out his old friend in what he deemed the subtlest way. He strolled to his club, then proceeded to watch and wait until he espied Rutledge enter the room nearly an hour later. With a seemingly casual effort Hugh placed himself so that

Giles would practically fall over him.

'Well, Hugh, and how do you get on?' said Rutledge with an air of forced bonhomie.

'Tolerable, tolerable,' replied Hugh, the firm set of his jaw betraying his unsettled state of mind.

'I rejoice to hear that.' Rutledge made to step around Hugh.

'Won't you join me?' said Hugh, gesturing to a table where a small but choice cold collation was set out. The wine was particularly fine, a fact Hugh knew would appeal to Giles.

Intrigued with the apparent offer of restored amiability, Giles nodded, pulling out a chair to sit opposite his former confidant and best friend. Women! Had it not been for Hugh's good wife and the widow Ingleby, the men's friendship would be as firm as ever. Now Giles only hoped his plans could proceed as intended.

The food was excellent, the wine an outstanding vintage. Both men concentrated on their plates and glasses for some time. They talked most politely about nothing in particular, skirting around the issue that both would have liked to approach. Neither could quite seem to figure out the best way to reopen the channels of communication. Finally Hugh took a plunge.

'I have seen you lately in the park with Caroline Beauchamp. Surely you do not think to settle down?' said Hugh at long last. He was a bit heavy-handed to be totally convincing in his attempt at nonchalance.

'Settle down?' declared Giles as though the words were in a foreign tongue that he'd never learned. He winked at Hugh with a roguish grin. 'Get leg-shackled? Why? There are other ways to get what a fellow wants, as you well know. After all, there is the Ingleby.'

'But Caroline is Quality.' Hugh turned a shade of red, struggling to contain his ire.

Giles shrugged, then smirked in a way Hugh would have liked to punch off his face. 'I daresay there are any number of young things out there that qualify for that title. However, there are a number who know how to delight a man nonetheless.'

'You'd never ruin the girl!' said Hugh, softly, aghast at the change in his one-time friend.

'How can you bring to ruin that which is willing, my dear chap?' said Giles, suppressing a smile at Hugh's reaction. He dropped his gaze, lest Hugh recognize the familiar look in his eyes. It was a good thing they were in a staid, very public place, or he'd no doubt be picking himself up from the floor about now.

'Willing?' queried Hugh in a clearly disbelieving tone. He had known Caroline for some time, and she might have a few odd notions, but playing fast and loose with her reputation was not one of them.

'Well,' said Giles in a musing tone, 'that young lady has agreed to meet me in Richmond early Friday morn, with no chaperon along.' There was an air of satisfaction that could not be pleasing to the man who faced him across the table. 'We are going to have a picnic. A nice long picnic.' Giles gave a wicked chuckle, then pushed back his chair. 'I'd invite you along on our jaunt, but I fear three would most assuredly be a crowd.' With a casually voiced thank you and farewell, Giles disappeared.

Hugh took a hearty swallow of his wine while absently crumbling a bit of cheese between two fingers. Mary would not be happy to discover her closest friend had been deceived by Giles. Not that Hugh intended to squeak beef on Caroline. But he would do something! He was not going to permit Giles to lure the innocent Caroline off to an assignation in Richmond for the purposes of seduction.

★ ★ ★

The two ladies at Harding and Howell's fine emporium were ecstatic at the discovery that all the fabrics desired were to be found at excellent prices. 'Fancy muslin at three shillings, six pence a yard, Caroline,' said Margaret happily.

The price seemed dear to Caroline when she recalled the amount she had paid for her tartan, but then, Lady Fancourt was a good deal more plump in the pocket. And a first baby must have the best of everything, for those little clothes were normally used again and again.

Envy surfaced momentarily. Would the state of matrimony ever be hers to claim? Caroline wondered if her own Season might be extended another year, since both Adrian and Edmund looked to be in a more settled way. Deep in her reflections, she dutifully remained at Margaret's side while she paid for her purchases, then requested a young clerk to carry her parcels to the waiting Fancourt carriage. An obliging Lord Fancourt had ordered their carriage placed at Margaret's disposal while he went about his business driven by the good Baxhall.

'Come along, Caroline. Enough of your wool gathering. I vow you are as pensive as an owl today.' They strolled past the jewelry and the elegant fans, Lady Fancourt pausing to sigh over one in particular that she declared the prettiest thing but of no earthly use deep in the country.

On the steps of Schomberg House, Margaret had the pleasure of bumping into a special friend, Emma Holt, now Lady Twisden, a bosom bow from her come-out days. Both matrons plunged into memories. When they discovered they were both in an interesting condition, nothing would do but they retire for ices at Gunter's famed shop.

It was a pleasure to see Margaret so happy after the misery of yesterday. Of course, it took a bit of doing to keep a straight countenance when Margaret deliberately explained that she was returning to Fancourt Abbey on the morrow because her husband simply could not do without her.

Deciding to wander away a bit from the two so they might exchange confidences, as Caroline sensed they were eager to do, she wandered beneath the trees of Berkeley Square while they sat in the carriage.

'Caroline.' The rich voice startled her. Caroline whirled about to nearly tumble into Rutledge's strong arms.

'Sir! You gave me a start.' She glanced about to determine if she was safe in conversing with him. Not far away her cousin was happily engaged in conversation. Perhaps that sufficed?

'I spoke with Hugh not long ago. I believe I managed to convince him that you are about to hopelessly compromise yourself by slipping off to Richmond for a rendezvous with me come Friday morning.' That wicked glint lurked deep in his beautiful gray eyes. Caroline was lost in them for a moment before his words actually penetrated.

She gulped at the very notion of such an event possibly taking place. 'I see.'

He nodded with seeming approval at her lack of feminine palpitations or behavior of that sort. One hand reached out to lightly touch the Norwich shawl she had draped over her arms before leaving the house. Really, she hadn't been able to resist the silken beauty. It looked well against her lemon yellow pelisse, picking up the colors of the ribands on her chip straw bonnet.

'I am pleased my spur-of-the-moment purchase proved to be useful to you. 'Tis most becoming. You have no fear that someone may recognize it? No,' he answered himself, 'for those people were outbound from the city. Unlikely thing. And there are so many shawls about nowadays.'

'You believe Hugh will take some manner of action?' she said a little breathlessly. She had best avoid the topic of the wild drive out beyond Holland House to the White Hart Tavern. The intimacy shared there had been most innocent, but she would never forget the thrill of being with him.

'I would wager almost any amount he will. I was careful to note you would depart early Friday morn. That way the majority of the ton will be still abed. We shall be able to perform our intrigue with relative ease. I suspect our gallant Hugh will set out to prevent what he anticipates will be your seduction.'

'Oh, dear,' said a slightly horrified Caroline. 'I hope he does not carry a gun. I'd as lief not see you killed, or even injured, Rutledge.'

'Giles,' he prompted softly. 'I am gratified to note that you care for my somewhat worthless hide.'

She feared the flash of her eyes in his direction revealed that she, for one, did not consider his hide to be in the least of no value. 'You are a shocking flirt, my lord ... Giles.' That odious man smiled with monstrous satisfaction at her admiration, even if it was reluctant.

'Your cousin leaves soon?' Giles walked Caroline slowly in the direction of Lady Fancourt, who was showing signs of wishing to depart.

'Yes, on the morrow.'

'Good, the fewer people about, the better. Your brothers are settled quite safely in the country.' At her small frown, he continued, 'There is no other problem I've not heard mentioned, is there?'

Caroline waved her hand in a dismissing gesture. 'No, no.'

'Caroline, I sense otherwise.'

She did not pause to consider that she had mentioned her dilemma to him before. It was most unlike her to spill her worries to another. Her predicament had been weighing heavily on her mind for days. There had been no one she had felt she might confide her troubles to at Lady Winnington's house. Her aunt would as like insist upon taking Caroline for a second Season, even if Papa could not afford it.

'Unless something wonderful happens for Adrian, I shall doubtless be resigned to spend my time at home waiting for a country squire, for I shan't enjoy a second Season.' Caroline had accepted the inevitability of remaining in the country; she had failed in her duty. 'Edmund may do well enough once he gets that stud established, but I fear his inheritance will not be great once Father fires off the rest of his brood. As for Adrian . . . '

'An heiress?'

335

'Of course,' she said with asperity. 'Why did I not think of that? You would need a girl who adores mucking about in the field while searching for bits and pieces of antiquity. All the while having pots and pots of money.'

'Small matter.'

Caroline laughed at this ridiculous man who could make her see a silly side to her vexations. 'Only you could view it in that way. But if I can accomplish some good from my actions, I shall be well pleased.'

'A most worthy sentiment, my dear girl.' He touched her arm lightly to warn her to silence, then ushered her up to where her cousin sat with her friend in the Twisden carriage, the Fancourt vehicle waiting just behind.

'Ladies, a pleasure, I assure you. I shall see you again, Miss Beauchamp.' He sketched an elegant bow, then strolled from their company, the epitome of masculine elegance. Both the seated ladies sighed.

'You fly high, Miss Beauchamp,' chided Lady Twisden, her eyes twinkling when she saw the pink that rose on Miss Beauchamp's pretty face.

'Not in the least. We are but friends,' replied Caroline, thinking it most unfortunate that someone as understanding as Giles

336

Thornhill, Lord Rutledge, was so far above her.

Margaret exchanged a meaningful glance with her bosom bow, then smiled. 'In our experience it is nigh impossible for a young woman to be merely friends with such a handsome man.'

'I am quite of the opinion that it is, in this case, Margaret. Do you wish to leave? You really ought to get some rest.' Caroline placed a concerned hand on her cousin's shoulder. She had not missed the hint of fatigue in Margaret's eyes.

An interesting blush crept across Margaret's cheeks as she hastily rose, subsiding slowly as she bid good-bye to her friend amid promises to write and visit in the future.

Now Margaret thankfully relaxed while being driven to the house on South Street for a welcome rest.

Once they reached the Winnington house, Caroline urged her cousin to seek her comfortable bed and a lovely nap. 'If I might beg the use of your carriage, I would visit with Mary this afternoon.'

'Stanhope's wife? I thought you were on the outs with her,' said Margaret. She gingerly stepped down from the carriage, permitting herself to lean ever so slightly on Simpkins' stout arm.

'Nonsense. We have been close for years. I shall see you later, and do remember to rest.'

Caroline ordered the driver to proceed to the Stanhope address, hoping to find Mary at home. This was normally her athome day, but that did not mean she would receive Caroline. Their friendship had been woefully strained as of late. Caroline would be glad to end this tangle, with the hope that a pleasant understanding might be restored. She had missed their girlish giggles.

'Her ladyship will see you, Miss Beauchamp,' intoned the stately Pennyfeather, ushering Caroline up the stairs to the pretty gold-and-white drawing room with a nearly friendly attitude. How nice to be in his good graces in any event.

Mary sat on the sofa, looking charming in a pale blue round gown of the finest India muslin while stitching away on a piece of needlework. She gave Caroline a cautious survey, as though wondering if she had made a mistake in permitting her to enter.

'You are in first looks, Mary, dear. Blue is definitely your color. And I find that lace cap positively delightful. I must get your pattern.'

'Lord Rutledge was so gracious as to say I ought always to wear this color,' replied Mary, her eyes boldly meeting Caroline's. More than a hint of defiance lurked there.

'He has tact and sagacious kindness, which is more than I can say for my husband.'

'Yet you wish him yours, do you not?' A thread of worry crept into Caroline's voice. Had Mary turned cat-in-the-pan? It wasn't unusual for a woman to change her mind regarding a man, but why now, of all times?

'I suppose I might as well try to milk a pigeon as to fool you, Caroline. However stupid I may be for wanting him, he is my husband and I most devoutly wish him to be truly mine in every way.' Mary crumpled a little, slumping against the sofa in dejection. 'Rumor tells me you have been seen with Lord Rutledge. I thought it was my lot to flirt with him to help lure Hugh to my side.'

Wincing at the implied treachery, Caroline hurriedly sought for words to soothe her friend. She also needed to plant more seeds that would hopefully bear fruit come Friday.

'La, how little things get magnified. He is a shocking flirt,' she said, unconsciously echoing her earlier words to Giles.

'A flirt? He was all that was correct with me.' Mary seemed affronted that the estimable Rutledge would treat her less well than her friend.

'But then, he is trying to assist you with your husband. I suspect there is a slight difference there.' Caroline hoped she mollified Mary by these words. Goodness knew, there was sufficient to do without making Mary jealous.

'Perhaps,' said Mary doubtfully, giving Caroline a suspicious glance.

'It is to be a picnic that Hugh takes me to in Richmond this coming Friday,' revealed Caroline with studied nonchalance.

'Not alone, surely!' Mary sat up straight to send Caroline a reproving stare.

'I thought it a plummy thing, a lovely picnic by the banks of the Thames. He has a friend who owns a home between Richmond and Twickenham. It fronts on the river, or so Hugh declares. It is my intention to persuade him to see you for your true worth. I care naught for myself. Just to see you two together would give me the greatest pleasure.'

Her suspicions flaming to a roaring heat, Mary quietly asked, 'Is it to be a party, then?'

'No, but Hugh has assured me that I shall enjoy myself exceedingly.' Caroline assumed the most innocent of expressions, raising trusting green eyes to smile at her friend.

'I daresay,' murmured a stunned Mary. She was now convinced that her wayward husband actually had it in mind to seduce or, at the very least, toy with the affections of her dearest friend! Not while she still drew a breath.

'Before long, you shall be in his arms, I guarantee it,' declared Caroline with delicate fervor.

'Indeed?' Mary might be forgiven if there was a good deal of skepticism in her voice.

The talk turned to other, less agitating subjects. Caroline rose to leave when two other ladies arrived. Pennyfeather announced them, and Mary bade him show them up in a pretty manner.

'I shall see you later, my dear,' said Caroline before taking her leave.

'Sooner than you dream,' whispered Mary to the departing figure.

* * *

That evening Margaret came down to the drawing room dressed in the prettiest rose-pink gauze gown trimmed with knots of silver riband. Pink and silver silk roses were tucked into her black curls. There was a vast amount of creamy skin revealed above the neckline of her gown. She appeared to be in exceedingly fine fettle.

The new dresses had arrived and been packed away for their departure on the morrow. In fact, she was quite ready to face her husband.

'You look quite ravishing, my dear girl. A new gown?' commented Lady Winnington, surveying her niece with an appreciative eye.

'No. This is what I wore the night I first met Justin. I wonder, will he remember?' Margaret murmured in a barely audible voice.

'I see.' Lady Winnington saw a great deal more than her niece believed. She turned to greet Caroline as her other niece entered the drawing room and asked, 'You enjoyed a pleasant visit with Mary?'

'Yes, ma'am. She was in first-looks today.'

They awaited the arrival of Lord Fancourt with various moods. Lady Fancourt was all nerves, shredding a handkerchief into tiny bits. Lady Winnington was vastly amused by the whole affair. Caroline's thoughts kept drifting to Friday.

She wondered if she would see Rutledge this evening. Her success with Mary had left her unsettled. While there was little chance Mary might actually talk to Hugh, one never knew. Stranger things had happened than for a husband to go directly to his wife to demand an explanation of her conduct. Justin's arrival drew Caroline from her worries.

'Good evening, wife,' he said. Justin entered the room with eyes only for his

Margaret. Lady Winnington exchanged glances with Caroline, wondering if they ought to remove themselves from the drawing room immediately.

'Good evening, Justin,' replied Margaret in a tremulous voice.

Simpkins came to the rescue with the announcement that dinner was served. A sigh of relief escaped from Margaret. Caroline and her aunt went down first. From behind, Caroline could hear Justin speaking to his wayward wife in low tones:

'I believe I have seen that gown before, if I make no mistake.'

'You have.'

'Lovely.'

'Oh, Justin . . . ' There was a soft rustle of silk. Caroline and her aunt didn't look behind them.

Caroline faced her aunt at the otherwise empty table, glancing at the door from time to time. 'Do you think they got lost?'

'Undoubtedly,' replied Lady Winnington with spirit, and ordered the meal to be served.

★   ★   ★

The musicale at the Pilkingtons' town house was composed of as many music lovers as that good lady knew. She had captured Mrs Elizabeth Billington to sing for them and not one invitation was declined.

Caroline strolled along the hall, darting glances from one side to the other. He was not here.

'Come, Caroline, we shall find ourselves some excellent seats before the crush becomes too bad. I am looking forward to this evening very much.' Lady Winnington swept past Caroline with the expectation she would follow without question. She did.

The singer possessed an exquisite voice. It was small wonder that she had enchanted Italy with her singing before returning to her homeland to conquer London.

Caroline forgot her worries while lost in the music. When the moment came for Mrs Billington to take a rest and for the guests to partake of an elegant repast, catered by no less than Gunter's, she felt as though she woke from a lovely dream.

'I gathered you enjoyed that greatly.'

That rich voice coming from so close jolted her like a pot of cold water over her head. 'Lord Rutledge. I fear I did not notice your arrival. She has an amazingly excellent voice, does she not?'

Any pique that his lordship might have felt at being so easily ignored was swallowed in the allowance that the singer was indeed outstanding. 'That she does. May I escort you to the delicacies that await us?'

'I need to talk with you,' Caroline said urgently and as softly as she dared, with the hope he might yet hear her.

'What has occurred, fair lady?'

'I saw Mary again. She now labors under the false illusion that I am to share a picnic by the Thames with her husband this coming Friday. I explained where it was to be located and that I planned to set out early. I also implied there might be a party, but was sufficiently vague as to give her leave to doubt it and fear the worst.'

'Excellent girl,' he said in an admiring tone that was like salve on a wound. They approached the table slowly, and with the proximity of other people Caroline had to lean just a bit closer to this exceedingly disconcerting man to speak.

'I do not like this deception, but I realize it is for their best. Pray that Mary keeps this information to herself and does not decide to break a lifetime of discretion to empty the bag.'

'She does not seem the gossip.' He handed Caroline a plate and began to heap mouth-watering delicacies upon it.

'One never knows about people. For

example, who would ever have thought that you and I would join forces?'

Lord Rutledge appeared to have a sudden frog in his throat, for he coughed extravagantly. Once he was able to speak again, he inquired, 'Where are your cousin and her husband this evening? I had hoped to see Fancourt on a matter.'

'That was most odd. One moment they were behind us on the stairs. Then, poof, they were gone. We ate dinner without them. I expect we shall see them before they depart tomorrow.'

Lord Rutledge had another fit of coughing, this one fortunately milder. 'One of these days we shall have a fascinating little conversation, my dear,' he murmured softly.

'Should you still desire to communicate with him, I expect I can either give him a message or you can write him at the Abbey. I hope it was not terribly important?' Not understanding his intent, she sought to divert the subject again.

'Not terribly, no.'

They joined her aunt and fell to discussing the evening's entertainment.

Caroline ate quite well, considering that she hadn't the vaguest notion as to what she was putting in her mouth. It all tasted wonderful.

The remainder of the evening was delightful. Mrs Billington regaled them with more Italian songs, some English airs, and a few German lieder. Caroline resumed her entranced state again, relieved, she told herself, that Rutledge had settled in the back of the room. It would never do for him to make too great a point of attending to her.

When it came time to leave, he sought her side once again. 'I may have some interesting news for you come Friday.'

'News?' she said blankly. What news could he possibly have for her? They had plans, well-laid plans. There was nothing 'new' to be discussed, she hoped. Or did she? Did deep in her heart, so nicely covered by her pretty green silk gown, linger the absurd longing that this handsome lord declare an interest in her?

Balderdash! Utter rubbish! But, her tender heart reminded her, such a lovely idea.

She drifted out to Baxhall's carriage with her aunt, murmuring agreeable replies to all remarks, even when her aunt asked if she had enjoyed the fried mud. Once home, she floated up the stairs to her room with an optimistic heart.

Until she crashed to the ground with the remembrance that Lord Rutledge could reach far higher than a green girl with only a paltry dowry, and that they had merely joined efforts to bring two silly friends together. Nothing more.

It was a most depressing thought upon which to end the day.

15

'Please write me, dear Caroline, and tell me your news. For I am sure there will be something soon.' Margaret's eyes twinkled with mischief. 'I shall appoint you godmama for this infant.' She placed a gentle hand against her stomach, then looked fondly at her husband. 'The days will doubtlessly go slowly, but before I know it, the boy will be here.'

'You are very certain,' said Caroline with amusement.

'Naturally. Justin wants a boy and he always gets what he wants.' This was said with the placid assurance of a wife extremely well loved.

The peculiar-looking britschka departed early the following morning. Lord and Lady Fancourt omitted mention of the missed dinner, rather extolling the comfort of the house and the hospitality extended. Margaret radiated such happiness, beaming her joy in a manner Caroline could only envy.

The remainder of the week dragged by in blessed peace, with no younger brothers to unsettle her nerves and no further marital contretemps to enliven the hours. It was excessively dull. Evenings were spent at Almack's and a soirée that Caroline deemed flat. Hugh made a point of escorting her to both. Rutledge had not been so much as glimpsed from afar. It was a good thing Caroline had no need to consult with him. Of course, she could steal over to his house through the mews and into their private room should it prove absolutely vital.

He was away, reported the groom, when Caroline casually questioned about the whereabouts of his lordship on Thursday morning. It shouldn't have made one whit of difference, but she felt strangely eased by the knowledge he was not avoiding her while in London.

The sun shone brightly Friday morning, with a few wisps of clouds dotting the pale blue sky. Caroline dressed in her newest ensemble. The amber-shot sarcenet pelisse floated about her as she silently moved through the hall and down the stairs. In moments she was in front of the house, entering the hackney carriage with the good Baxhall awaiting her instructions. She congratulated herself on her foresight to engage the man the day before when she had gone out. It saved time and so many explanations!

A signal from Baxhall informed her that

another carriage had fallen into line behind them A slow smile crept across Caroline's pretty face as she relished the day to come. How she was going to enjoy this. Hugh had bordered on tedious the past two evenings. Did Mary know what she was asking for when she yearned for Hugh at her side? It *had* to be love, for most assuredly it could not be anything else!

Another signal from her driver let Caroline know that a second carriage appeared to be trailing them. Her satisfied smile grew to a grin. Everything appeared to be working like clockwork.

★   ★   ★

In the third carriage of the little procession, Mary chewed her lip in anxiety. Hugh would undoubtedly be furious with her should she spoil his assignation with Caroline Beauchamp. But it was not merely a desire to protect Caroline that placed Mary in the hired carriage this morning.

She felt the time had come to do something herself, rather than ask another to do for her. Life was passing her by, she wanted no more of that. She desired children . . . now. Love . . . now. Her husband . . . now. And neither Caroline nor Mrs

Ingleby nor any other woman was to be permitted to deny this pleasure to her. She firmed her mouth and her determination to see this deed through to the end.

⋆ ⋆ ⋆

Lord Stanhope glared at the ceiling of the Stanhope carriage that immediately followed Caroline's as he lounged against the well-cushioned interior. Poor Caroline. What if Mary had Rutledge, or some other man, leading her astray? Caroline needed a man to look after her, but Hugh was becoming heartily sick of the job. He wanted his wife, a child, and the loving atmosphere of a home, not his club or the boudoir of a mistress. Today would be the last time he would see Caroline, and this was merely to save her from ruin. How Rutledge could behave so enraged Hugh. He really thought he knew his old friend far better than that. Hugh shook his head and left the negotiations of the carriage to his driver while dozing off for a short nap.

⋆ ⋆ ⋆

Not far behind the third carriage, Giles rode his horse. He had explained to Caroline that it would be easier for him to keep sight of all three carriages while astride, rather than confined to his phaeton. He watched the line of carriages wend their way through the light traffic, then out on the road toward Richmond. They had stopped, one by one, to pay the toll at the Hyde Park gate, then continued, a mightily amusing parade to the man on horseback.

Although Caroline doubted if either of the occupants of the carriages behind her would be paying the least attention to anything in back of them, she had agreed with Giles that it would arouse fewer suspicions were he to ride. If she estimated correctly, Hugh would be in the first carriage behind hers, Mary following directly behind him. What surprises were in store today for both of them.

Caroline leaned against the freshly brushed squabs, taking care not to crush her Oatlands hat. Life would be rather dull after all the excitement of the past few weeks. She could return to the respectable balls and the insipid evenings at Almack's like all the other girls who had come to London to search for a husband. What hopes were nightly crushed, what dreams denied each day come the hour for the drives through Hyde Park. Why did it seem that there were far more young women hunting than eligible quarry? Undoubtedly there were men on the lookout for a wife; indeed, she had encountered a few. There was that Lord Bannister and probably Lord Mortland. Both were close to their dotage. From the last seen of Mrs Ingleby after she had so neatly burned her bridges that night at the opera, it appeared she intended to settle for Mortland.

It was unbelievable that Caroline had so forgotten herself as to confide in Lord Rutledge about her foolish worries regarding her future. He had that way about him, however. One felt instinctively safe when at his side, as though he could keep you from any harm, solve all your troubles. Odd, too, how she had scarcely questioned his suggestions, but fallen in with whatever he promoted without one argument.

When had she begun to realize she loved the dratted man? Had the knowledge slowly crept up on her, totally capturing her until she was utterly lost?

She toyed with blue ribbon trim on her pelisse. Oh, it would be deadly dull after today.

The unlikely trio of vehicles slowly trundled through Little Chelsea, then Waltham Green. At Putney they crossed the bridge on the Thames. Caroline wondered at this point if she was doing the right thing. It seemed so final to cross a bridge, even though she knew it was possible to return again. Would she make the drive alone? She wondered if Rutledge would join her so they might chuckle over their friends' fate.

He had promised a fascinating talk, but that was most likely his manner of flirting, nothing serious.

Somewhere off to the right could be found Kew Gardens. It might be an interesting place to view. Perhaps she could get Aunt Fanny to go with her one day when it was pleasant out.

Then came Richmond. There was no turning back at this point. They crossed over the Thames again. Her carriage made a left jog and bumped along a rutted lane that followed the river for a short distance before heading away from it. It was tranquil here. The river flowed along so peacefully.

The gates to Marble Hill were closed today. Poor Mrs Fitzherbert had not lived there for some years, removing to Brighton to be, some said, near her true love, the prince. The Earl of Buckinghamshire had taken possession of the property not long ago.

Now Caroline leaned forward to search for the place Giles had told her about. It was on Folly Lane, so frightfully appropriate. At last she thought she saw the correct house, and she signaled Baxhall to stop.

'You may go to the Star and Garter in Richmond until I send someone for you, Baxhall,' she instructed the driver.

Actually, it was not so terribly far but what she might walk if she needed.

Bracing herself, she strolled forth to inspect the house Giles had arranged to be at his disposal for the day. It was rather lovely, with a neat garden surrounding the building, roses in abundance and pansies in bloom.

A carriage rolled to a halt on the lane behind her. Caroline whisked herself inside the house, thankful she hadn't been required to wait for a butler to open the door for her.

'Caroline? Where are you?' Hugh hurried from his vehicle, then plunged into the house and, ignoring the elegant stairway, charged along the hall until he came to what appeared to be a small salon.

'Hugh, whatever are you doing here?' she asked, the picture of innocence, staring demurely at the rude intruder.

'More's the point, what are you? Do you not know better than go haring off all alone to the countryside for a picnic with a man? Especially Rutledge?' His annoyance had reached its peak. He stopped, hands on hips, to glare at this tiresome chit he felt obliged to rescue.

A smile peeped out, her green eyes sparkled with glee, and she shrugged. 'La, what a piece of work about nothing. You're refining too much upon something quite innocent.

'You forget, I know the man. You ought not be here.' Hugh took a step forward, raising one hand in a sort of plea.

Dropping her pose, Caroline faced him, her heart beating rapidly as the crucial moment neared. 'I have no intention of leaving here, at least not with you. Why do you meddle in others' affairs?'

'That is an unfortunate word to use, Caroline. Have you so fallen as to consider such with Rutledge?'

She shrugged again, feeling rather well pleased in her role. 'You are the one to so construe it as bad. I am here for a picnic, nothing more.'

'But don't you see? Rutledge intends to seduce you!' Hugh wanted to wring the girl's neck by this point.

Caroline pretended to be shocked. 'Hugh!'

'Where is he?' demanded Hugh, casting a hurried look around the small room, as though expecting to see Giles concealed behind a high-backed chair.

'Not here as yet, I fear. Perhaps I shall be forgotten?' She pouted, looking to Hugh like a little girl deprived of a sweet.

'Would that you were so fortunate,' muttered Hugh as he walked out into the hall to inspect the premises. He did not quite believe that Caroline was telling him the truth. Giles was most likely lurking about the place. Perhaps the bedroom? At that thought Hugh bounded up the stairs to check the upper floor.

Caroline grinned as she heard the front door softly open and slippered feet whisper down the hall. The first part of the intrigue had gone rather well. If only she could keep it up.

'So, you are here!' Mary rounded the corner of the small salon to come face to face with her girlhood friend.

Hugh was walking down the stairs when he heard voices in the small salon. Edging along the hall, he stopped in horror as he heard the dulcet tones of his wife!

'Where is he?' demanded Mary in an unusually firm manner for her. 'Give me my husband!'

Caroline shrugged again. Really, her shoulders were getting a lovely working out. 'Find him yourself. I am here to meet Giles.'

'Giles? Oh, Caroline, you need not try to cozen me. You told me you were going on a picnic today, and you did not mention Giles at all.'

'I got them confused,' lied Caroline hastily.

'Please do not protect that man. Hugh doesn't deserve it in the least. He is inconsiderate, has a devil of a temper, and chases after anything in muslin. But he is mine, and I fear I love the wretched man.'

'How interesting,' murmured Caroline, hoping that the squeak she'd heard was the wooden floor and not a mouse. Were Hugh around the corner, he would have heard that declaration of love, albeit it lacked a certain something.

The front door opened again and the firm tread of a man could be heard. A sudden altercation issued forth. Loud voices — familiar ones — shouted. Thuds and bumps and something that sounded like a crack came next.

At first the girls were rooted to the spot, horrified at what they suspected. Then Mary dashed out into the hall, followed closely by a curious Caroline.

Mary screamed as she saw her husband stretched out on the wooden floor, his eyes closed, one side beginning to puff a bit suspiciously.

Rounding on Giles, who did not appear to be in the least ruffled by the confrontation, she cried, 'You've killed him! You brute! And I believed you were my friend!'

She dropped to her knees, cradling Hugh's unworthy head in her lap while enough tears flowed to fill a basin. 'Oh, my dear, speak to me. Say something.'

Hugh stirred, then looked up at his precious wife who had confessed her love for him not moments ago.

Giles beckoned to Caroline and they gingerly stepped past the two huddled on the floor, then slid out the front door, locking it behind them.

'I wonder how long it will take before they discover the door is locked,' mused Giles. He took Caroline's hand while they strolled down the lane.

'They may not care,' replied Caroline. Truly, if she was married to someone she loved and was able to be locked in a house with him, she would ask for nothing more, save food perhaps. 'Someone will come to unlock it later?'

'If they don't discover a way out before then. But then, they may not mind, as you said. Just as your cousin and her husband ignored dinner to retire to their room.'

Bravely, Caroline dared to say, 'I expect it is most delightful.' She didn't quite trust the chuckle that issued from the man at her side. It had a rather wicked sound.

He stopped to face her.

Caroline's heart was beating rapidly, and her lips were so dry she ran her nervous tongue over them, wetting them in an unconsciously provocative manner.

'Oh, Caro, my little love.'

She found herself swept into his arms, right in broad daylight where anyone and his wife might see them, and she didn't care a fig. Rather, she leaned against the strong, so very masculine body to accept what he offered.

His kiss was undoubtedly practiced, and he most likely showed great skill in the way he held and caressed her. How fortunate she was!

Seeming to come to his senses, Giles released her mouth, then merely stood, holding her tightly against him.

'I was right. It is delightful,' declared Caroline in a wondering voice.

Giles threw back his head in a hearty laugh, then shook his head in amazement as he drew her along with him to the bottom of the lane. 'I fear there is a bit more to it than that, my dear.'

'Really,' replied Caroline, her curiosity growing. More to it than that earth-shattering kiss? 'How intriguing.'

The Rutledge carriage waited for them around the corner. It was a traveling carriage with four horses and a pile of boxes and trunks on top. A groom and a driver sat in readiness. Giles ushered her to the door.

Caroline frowned, balking. 'But what about Baxhall?'

'I sent him back to London, well paid for his part in our plot.'

'Were you planning a trip?' she asked. Suspicions were creeping up on her. Perhaps Hugh and Mary were not the only ones to be duped this day. Maybe Hugh was right, she ought not to have trusted Giles in the least. After all, a man as practiced in the art of loving as he might have designs on her virtue, or something equally dire. 'It is not proper for me to drive with you in a closed carriage, you know that.'

'I have some information for you. Get in and I'll explain what I have been doing.' A firm grip on her elbow convinced her that she might as well enter the dratted vehicle before she suffered at his hands.

'You were gone,' she accused in a mild tone while settling herself in the corner. A glance around the interior of the carriage revealed sheer luxury such as she had never viewed before, even in her cousin's britschka. Softest Morocco leather was complemented by gray-figured silk tabaret. The side curtains were made of pale gray silk lutestring. She pulled back slightly into her corner when

Giles reached over to draw them closed across the windows. What did he have in mind, pray tell?

Her feet shifted uneasily on the deep wine-colored Brussels carpet beneath her feet. 'You were saying?' He was staring at her in a way that disconcerted, almost frightened her. She pretended to be unconcerned all the while she searched for a way out of this new predicament.

Giles reached over to remove the charming Oatlands hat, tossing it to the seat opposite them. 'I was going to kiss you once again, but I suppose I'd best tell you my news and be done with that?'

'What news?' she asked warily. She thought it best to ignore the part about the kiss.

'If you recall a certain conversation we had, you will remember saying Adrian needed an heiress.'

She couldn't help but smile at the memory. 'True.'

'I found him one.'

'You are hoaxing me.' This she meant in more ways than one.

'Actually, I did. There is a respectable family on the estate that marches with mine. I knew they'd had a devilish time with their daughter, for she is a blue-stocking of the milder sort. Totally absorbed in Roman antiquities, it seems. Also has a dowry of twenty thousand pounds. So I rode down to Sussex and introduced her to Adrian. It was love at first sight. Her parents were extremely grateful, and I suspect a marriage will follow before you can sneeze twice.'

'Good heavens. How excessively droll.' Caroline eyed the Oatlands hat. If she jumped from the carriage, would it have to be left behind? It was vastly becoming and quite the loveliest hat she had ever owned. Perhaps she might grab it on her way out the door?

He gave her a vexed look. 'You never react to things quite as I anticipate. One thing for certain, life with you will never be dull.'

'So my mother says,' agreed Caroline primly.

'Lovely woman.'

The hat was forgotten for the moment as she turned to face him. 'You have never seen my mother.'

'Not true.' He reached down to open a hamper she hadn't noticed between him and the door on the far side of the carriage. He took his time removing a remarkable luncheon, spreading it out on her lap and the seat between them. It seemed he was in no great rush.

He explained, 'I expect I had better feed you first.'

Afraid to ask what came second, Caroline put together a lovely meal on the china plate he handed her. Wedgwood, if she didn't miss her guess. What luxury to have fine china while on a picnic in a carriage.

'I've never heard of a picnic in a carriage. We might have stopped in Richmond Gardens, you know.' She bestowed a cautious look at him. With the curtains drawn across the windows, she hadn't the faintest idea which way they traveled. Somehow she felt they were not retracing the route back to London. The sun was to their left, which meant they were going south, not east as they ought to be.

'Couldn't.' He proceeded to slowly consume a sandwich while Caroline wanted to scream with annoyance. How *could* the man sit there so calmly while she had no notion of where they were now or where they were going or what he intended to do with her when they got there! Wherever *there* was.

'Why?' she at long last demanded, a trace of her pique showing in her voice.

'Because,' he said with reasonable patience, 'we cannot make time if we are stopped.'

'How foolish of me to ask,' she said bitterly. She was now convinced Hugh was right. Rutledge intended something abominable with her. The worst of it was that she wasn't certain she cared or not. What a terrible girl she was, to be sure.

It was difficult to quietly sit in her corner, choking down bite after bite of food. She had been hungry earlier. Now her appetite disappeared with the knowledge that something dashed smoky was going on and it involved her.

'It was kind of you to see to Adrian,' she made herself say in a little while, more to persuade him to talk than out of true gratitude, not that she wasn't grateful. She was. She knew what a relief it would be to her parents.

'Both of your brothers are seen to, and your cousin is happily restored to her husband. Do you have any other relatives that need tending? I should like to know now, because I will not be in the least inclined to pay them heed afterward, you know. At least,' he amended politely, 'not for some time. I intend to be fully occupied. With you.'

Terror struck deep into her heart. She had a distinct notion that what he intended was a great deal beyond kissing. What was she to do? Glancing over to see he was occupied in sipping claret from a crystal goblet, she leaned forward to peer from the window, pulling the curtain aside with one trembling hand. Where were they? Nothing looked familiar. She dropped the curtain, sinking back against the squabs with an uneasy sigh.

Were she to jump from the carriage, how would she manage? She had the money with which she had intended to pay Baxhall plus an additional sum just for an emergency. Would that be sufficient to get her to safety?

'Something troubling you, my dear?'

'I'm not your 'dear,' you know,' she said in a near whisper. Her throat was dry and she desperately desired a drink, but would it be drugged? She didn't know and she was suddenly very much afraid. Hugh's words had taken a positively ghastly turn of meaning.

'Lemonade. There is some in the flask there on the left of the hamper. Let me help you.' He replaced his goblet to pour out a tumbler of lemonade for her.

'Is it bitter?' she said craftily. If he drank some of it, it would be safe.

He took a sip, then shook his head. 'Not too sweet, either.' He handed her the glass, smiling into his hand as he turned away toward the hamper once again.

'Thank you,' Caroline said with formal politeness. It covered the panic that welled up within her. If only she might persuade him to stop so she could run away. She drank the lemonade in two gulps.

The empty glass was removed from her hands, the remains of the meal she had forced down her throat whisked away. She sat staring at her lap in silence.

'Are you afraid of me? Odd, I never felt you were before. You always seemed happy to confide in me. I felt quite pleased with that trust.'

'Oh, no,' lied Caroline, thinking she might go on the stage with all this practice she was acquiring in dissembling. What a pity she had taken to confiding in the man. He could easily use that knowledge against her. Since he knew full well that she had no prospects, he could assume she would be ripe to fall into his hands as his mistress.

'Hmm.' Giles studied the averted head for a moment, then slowly, skillfully reached out to turn her about, facing him. 'Say that again.'

'N-no,' she stammered, her eyes wide with apprehension. She was lost.

Giles simply plucked her up from her cozy corner and deposited her in his lap. She didn't wish to struggle in an unseemly manner. She also suspected he could hold her with little effort, given the way he had polished off Hugh without a sign of struggle. Giles had not appeared in the least affected by the fight.

That was an important thing to remember, she decided. She would need cunning, not strength, to free herself. A traitorous voice in her head whispered that she would be happier in his arms. When he pulled her tightly against his warm, firm body, she fought against relaxing. He offered comfort, warmth, and tenderness — all this she sensed. But what else?

And then he kissed her once again. If she had felt lost before, she was well and truly gone now. Did it really matter if he took her to some remote cottage to establish her as his doxy? Part of her mind, the sensible part, screamed yes, it did very much.

But on the other hand, she considered as she molded herself to his form, reaching up to gently caress his face, thread her hand in his hair, feel the power of his shoulder, she had little choice by this point.

'That is more like it, little love.' His voice was strangely husky, deep with unnamed emotion.

'I've done it now, you know. Hopelessly compromised myself, just as Hugh insisted I would.' Caroline nestled against him, refusing to look up at him, lest he see how affected she was by his kiss.

'That's true.' Caroline could not see the glint of amusement that shone from the gray eyes that looked down on her face.

'Where are we going?' she dared ask, hoping he might satisfy her with the truth.

'My country estate. It's a nice place; I think you'll like it. I've noticed you are fond of flowers, and there are vast beds of them to be seen.'

'Oh.' Her eyes were huge with surprise. Not a cottage? A gentleman simply didn't take his mistress home, even she knew that.

'Problems?' That lazy drawl sent prickles of awareness from her head all the way down her body to her toes.

Had Caroline dared to look at him then, a goodly number of her questions would have been answered by the expression on his face. She didn't and so they weren't.

'It isn't of the least consequence.'

'Good.' He proceeded to kiss her again, managing to stretch out and bring her against him so they were very nearly lying down. His feet were on the opposite seat and Caroline reclined atop him. It was a leisurely exploration. Time ceased to matter as their carriage rumbled along the roads south on a sleepy summer day. At last she regained some sense.

Caroline was horrified. Passionately stirred, tumultuously shaken, but nonetheless horrified.

'Sirrah!' she exclaimed once she managed to claim a bit of air after a rather long time during which she thought she must be close to heaven. A good punch on his arm brought her release.

He sighed and straightened up, setting her once again on her side of the carriage. He turned his face to the far side of the wall, clearing his throat.

Her clothes restored to order, for her pelisse had somehow come undone and the low neck of her gown had dipped badly, she leaned back to watch him. She had been aware of his touch; his fingers had scorched her so she could scarce breathe. But then, she had trouble with his kisses as well.

'If you insist, we shall wait.'

'Wait for what?' demanded Caroline intrepidly.

The carriage went over some rather bumpy road at that point and she heard a shout from the driver, but what it was, she couldn't tell.

'We are nearly there.'

'Where? Your estate, I suppose.' Did he really think she believed that nonsense? They must have been driving for hours by now. Where might they really be?

'Correct. Allow me to help you restore order. It will never do for others to see you as I do now. Your ebony curls are tumbled every which way, and the pretty collar of your pelisse is inside rather than out. But I don't know what you will do about those lips.' He ran his fingers through her curls, fixed her collar, then allowed his hands to linger at her throat. He leaned over once again to drop a light kiss on the objects in question. 'I fear you look well and truly kissed, my love. Do you mind?' He plopped her Oatlands hat on her head and deftly tied the checkered ribands.

What a question to ask a woman who had been kissed by a master at seduction. Did a woman mind breathing, or eating? Caroline stared at him, unable to reply to his impossible query.

The traveling coach drew to a halt. The door opened and Caroline was most astonished. There before her was a lovely Palladian mansion, fairly new in design — not over fifty years old at the very least. It was a shining white, trimmed in celestial blue. Surrounding it were the flower gardens he had mentioned, and lovely shade trees under which one might rest to enjoy the vista. Turning slightly, she saw they were atop a hill with a view of miles and miles of magnificent green countryside.

'It is utterly beautiful,' she said in awe. He couldn't possibly intend her to live in this splendor. Could he?

At that moment the front door opened, and four youngsters tumbled out and ran down the broad steps calling, 'Caro, Caro, you are here at last!' Elizabeth, Anne, Thomas, and William danced about her with great glee.

They were followed by Mr and Mrs Beauchamp, who if they noticed their eldest daughter's state, discreetly ignored it. 'Caroline, my dear,' said her mother.

'I don't understand anything in the least.' Caroline placed a trembling hand on Rutledge's arm, beseeching him with confused eyes.

His slow grin ought to have prepared her. 'I have a special license in my inside pocket, and your family are come to our wedding, my little love. Hugh and Mary are not the only ones to get a surprise today.'

'You utter beast!' she whispered so that her dear, staid parents would not hear. 'Do you have any notion what I endured on this wretched drive?'

'I intend to spend hours and hours making it up to you, my dear.' That precious dimple she adored peeked at her briefly.

Caroline gave him a dubious glance, then whispered, 'When?'

They were married three days later, much to Giles' frustration. He was not as patient as Hugh.

Her family was much taken with her husband, and she was congratulated exhaustively by them prior to their departure.

Caroline watched their carriage leave, then turned to her new husband. 'Now?' Her green eyes danced with mischief and love.

He chuckled wickedly, just as she loved to hear, and swept her off her feet, carrying her past the butler and up the stairs. 'Now.'

We do hope that you have enjoyed reading this large print book.

Did you know that all of our titles are available for purchase?

We publish a wide range of high quality large print books including:
Romances, Mysteries, Classics
General Fiction
Non Fiction and Westerns

Special interest titles available in large print are:
The Little Oxford Dictionary
Music Book
Song Book
Hymn Book
Service Book

Also available from us courtesy of Oxford University Press:
Young Readers' Dictionary
(large print edition)
Young Readers' Thesaurus
(large print edition)

For further information or a free brochure, please contact us at:
Ulverscroft Large Print Books Ltd.,
The Green, Bradgate Road, Anstey,
Leicester, LE7 7FU, England.
Tel: (00 44) **0116 236 4325**
Fax: (00 44) **0116 234 0205**

Other titles published by
The House of Ulverscroft:

QUEEN OF THE MAY

Emily Hendrickson

Young Lady Samantha Mayne had no desire to be a proper lady. Let her cousin Emma dress in fashionable gowns and hunt a mate in the marriage mart; Samantha preferred to help with her brother's scientific experiments, and ride horses astride, not side-saddle. Then Samantha met Lord Charles Laverstock. Samantha had never imagined that there could be a man as handsome, and charming. Lord Charles also clearly could never be interested in a girl who broke every rule and scorned femininity. For Samantha, becoming a lady would be the hardest task — even if it was a labour of love.

THE GALLANT LORD IVES

Emily Hendrickson

Shy country girl Alissa Ffolkes prefers the company of her peregrine falcon and the comfort of sculpting to handsome London lords. With a failed Season behind her, Alissa remains at home, leaving her sisters Henrietta and Elizabeth to dazzle and charm the local beaux. Yet Alissa yearns for true love, and as she tends her herbs, she longs for a potion to help her impress her father's guest Christopher, Lord Ives. In Wiltshire to study Alissa's father's sheep, he has found far more. Drawn to Alissa's gentle beauty, can his love work a miracle to make Alissa bloom?

LADY SARA'S SCHEME

Emily Hendrickson

Lady Sara Harland was as sensible as she was beautiful. Since she had to have a husband, she decided to take her pick from a list of the choicest lords available. One name, however, she crossed off her list. Why even consider Myles Fenwick, the Earl of St Quinton, when other eligible lords were neither so arrogant, nor so shockingly libertine? Sara was sure she would easily ensnare a perfect mate whilst avoiding the infamous charm and insidious attractiveness of the earl. But though this level-headed young heiress had her mind made up, her heart had ideas of its own . . .